KŎRI

KŎRI

The Beacon Anthology of
KOREAN AMERICAN FICTION

Edited by
HEINZ INSU FENKL
and WALTER K. LEW

BEACON PRESS
BOSTON

Beacon Press
25 Beacon Street
Boston, Massachusetts 02108-2892
www.beacon.org

Beacon Press books
are published under the auspices of
the Unitarian Universalist Association of Congregations.

05 04 03 02 01   8 7 6 5 4 3 2 1

This book is printed on acid-free paper that meets the uncoated paper ANSI/NISO
specifications for permanence as revised in 1992.

Text design by Preston Thomas
Composition by Wilsted & Taylor Publishing Services

Library of Congress Cataloging-in-Publication Data
Kŏri : the Beacon anthology of Korean American fiction / edited by Heinz Insu Fenkl and
Walter K. Lew.
     p. cm.
   ISBN 0-8070-5916-1
   1. American fiction—Korean American authors.   2. Korean Americans—Fiction.
I. Title: Beacon anthology of Korean American fiction.   II. Fenkl, Heinz Insu, date
III. Lew, Walter K.

PS647.K67 K67 2001
813'.540808957073—dc21
                                                              00–054176

We all need a country. And I, in desperation, needed two.

—LUCY LYNN KANG SAMMIS, 1930–95

CONTENTS

A traditional Korean shamanic ritual lasts through a day and a night, and during its twelve phases, which are called *kŏri,* the shamaness invokes spirits and ancestors, allowing them voice in the world of the living. A shamaness may speak for a frail departed grandmother, taking on a diminutive quality, or she may embody the spirit of the Great General, whose fierce nature and stature seem to defy the ability of her body to contain them. A *kŏri* (the *ŏ* pronounced as in "on") is part of a multilayered ritual with a complex spectrum of often unexpected and previously unimagined expression.

Korean is a lively and clever language with a penchant for homophones, and so the word *kŏri* is, itself, like the parts of a shamanic ritual, a rich layering of meanings. Its range of homophones could refer to a path or an avenue, a hook, or distance or range. A related verb form, *kŏl-da,* evokes the ideas of suspension, provocation, or communication (specifically, to call on the telephone). As a suffix, it suggests the idea of "material for" (as in fixings), "cause for" (concern or worry), or the "subject matter" or "source" of a story or tale. For us, the title has served as an underlying resonance that provides both direction and sustenance for the collection. For the reader, we hope the word *kŏri* will function as a reminder of the thematic strands that weave together the selections in the three parts of this anthology, representing those things carried great distances, then summoned into literary form and exorcised or freed. A *kŏri* embodies the intersecting of one world with the other in ways we find parallel to the nature of Korean American prose fiction from its origins in the 1930s to the end of the twentieth century.

As writers, we do not always speak for ourselves. In fact, one could argue that we hardly ever speak for ourselves because the self is so complex and indeterminate—always just beyond the reach of our willful consciousness. Many well-known writers have gone as far as to say that they were speaking for their characters, who came to them fully formed. Toni Morrison, for one, has said that the final version of *Song of Solomon* came to her in her father's voice, which sustained her after many failed drafts.

It would be easy to dismiss these writerly claims as eccentric or metaphorical. After all, the notion of the muse and of the artist as the mouthpiece of the divine has existed in Western literature since its earliest beginnings. But sometimes such writerly claims, though they are not literal, are more than merely metaphorical. They represent a state of mind that defies description in any conventional language, a state of mind that can only be described by acting it out, by producing those signs or voices, whether they are of one's ancestors or some seemingly arbitrary being called a character.

To be a writer is to assume new personae or to speak in a spectrum of voices, some over which the writer has no conscious control. One of the fundamental ironies is that readers will see things in a work that often circumvent or transcend the writer's intentions. In the present collection, several of the authors trace writerly origins (in themselves and in their characters) to an urgent need to express stories told to them by other people. The narrator of Patti Kim's novel obsessively recites a litany of scenes and stories bequeathed by her father lest they be lost. One of Gary

Pak's missions is to reveal the sorrow and injustice buried in the depths of Hawai'i's history and landscape. Looking back at her first novel, *Comfort Woman,* Nora Okja Keller is amazed by how different the narrators' voices are from her own, while for Ty Pak the writing of socially relevant stories in the often horrific intersection of Korean and American geopolitics has become a lifelong calling.

Korean culture has a long tradition of speaking for—or as—others that has become both a curse and an ideal for Korean American writers. As a nation that is still one of the most conservative Confucian patriarchies in the world, it maintains the old structure of the literati as the moral voice of society, resonating with earlier times when court councillors attempted to remain morally correct even at the expense of disagreeing with the king, losing their lives, and exposing their family or clan to cruel punishments. In the face of patriarchy, one of the unspoken roles of the Korean woman was to act as the intermediary between disempowered men (sons, husbands, fathers) and higher male authority. And although often condemned by Confucian ideologues, indigenous Korean Shamanism, in both its ecstatic, woman-centered form and its more gnostic masculine form, involves the invocation of ancestral voices and the grievances of wronged spirits. the modern era, particularly following Japanese colonization (1910–45) and continuing through the partitioning of the nation under the aegis of the Soviets and the Americans, and the subsequent military dictatorships in both North and South, Korean writers have had to take ultimate responsibility for their literary works, even if it meant facing imprisonment, torture, or threat of execution.

Such traditions can be a heavy burden to carry over the arc of the Pacific to American soil and through the generations, but you will find them embedded in all of the works in this collection, even in those that attempt to escape them. Even resistance to cultural legacy conveys it through the negative space of inversion. To negate a thing, you must describe it; or, in shamanic terms, to exorcise a spirit, you must first invoke it. And so in this anthology, though you are reading writers who composed their works in English and who describe scenes far removed from its geography and people, you will find the specters of Korean tradition conveyed in tropes of displaced blood, culture, language, land, gender, and nation, sometimes most poignantly when there is the threat of loss and alienation.

The Korean language is layered with a history of appropriating and coexisting with Chinese, Mongolian, Japanese, and English. Its written form is also a sort of Cabalistic performance of the connection among the body, sound, and text, partly because the scholars who designed the phonetic alphabet in the mid-1400s made it an explicit point to show, graphically in the shape of the letters, how the human vocal apparatus formed the sounds of those letters. The importance of a standardized vernacular written in a flexible, easily learned native orthography was recognized by both Korean nationalists and Japanese colonialists; that is one of the reasons why, during the darkest period of the colonial era, the Japanese banned the use of Korean and why they viewed the Korean Language Society as one of the most profound organizations of resistance. When a language already full of irony and subversive multilingual wordplay lingers in the background of writing in English, the Korean American narratives take on a palimpsest-like quality, resonating with a literary history, even if that history seems to be obscured by the linguistic shift. Even Korean American writers who do not speak Korean draw, in their works, upon that background resonance that lurks like an unavoidable indication of cultural memory, that residue of blood, language, custom, and historical trauma.

What, then, are the conditions of the American or diasporic present that so intensify the individual's need to establish a literary form and vision that either revives or extinguishes traces from an ancestral realm? Epochal shifts in Korea like colonization, division of the country into communist North and capitalist South,

war, rapid industrialization, and movements for democraticiza-
tion have been powerful forces within the development of Korean
American literary consciousness. Certain historical circumstances
in America have also cried out for expression by literary artists:
the excruciating hardships of plantation work in Hawai'i in the
early decades of the twentieth century; the changes in class, status, and familial role experienced by immigrants while trying to
survive on the margins of the U.S. economy; the long period of
Korean Americans' relative isolation and disempowerment enforced by the Exclusion Act of 1924 until the immigration law
ammendments of 1965; the subsequent arrival of new South Korean immigrants who created tens of thousands of small businesses and several Koreatowns; growing interracial tensions in urban centers and the legacy of violence and political conflict that
eventually exploded in the destruction of painstakingly built
livelihoods in the 1992 L.A. Riots.

In the literary world, writers have either resisted, accommo-
dated, or taken advantage of the expectation that they produce
images of Korean Americans that epitomize either irreparable
foreignness or assimilation into a contented American life—both
of which are forms of racial humiliation. Examples of resistance
include Sukhee Ryu's sardonic treatment of the "American
dream" in "Severance," Theresa Hak Kyung Cha's fragmentation
of official state narratives in certain chapters of *DICTEE,* and
Younghill Kang's contestations with his prominent editor Max-
well Perkins over the plot of *East Goes West.*

Writers like Younghill Kang, Richard Kim, and Ty Pak, emigrated at a late enough age to vividly recall the events of which
they later wrote, such as the brutal suppression of the March First
Independence Movement in 1919, the Japanese Imperial Army's
forced labor camps near the end of World War II, the bloodbath
and betrayals of the Korean War (1950–53), and the liminal existence of mixed-race children in U.S. Army camp towns. Others,
even though they also spent most of their childhoods in Korea,

often set their stories in America—or in the anxious new zones that emerge between cultures, economies, and landscapes.

Still other writers originally had little direct contact with Korea, and not all of these belong to the present younger generation. Kim Ronyoung, for instance, was born in Los Angeles in 1926; because Kim's mother was intensely involved in the overseas independence movements and had her children attend a local Korean-language school where they learned nationalist history, Kim's childhood was deeply imbued with feelings for Korea. Others, however, have grown up largely among non–Korean Americans, and have had to rely on their parents' stories, visits to Korea, translations of Korean literature, and English-language scholarship in their search for symbols and experiences that could help sustain their reimagining and understanding of the relation between disparate worlds—of which almost nothing in mainstream American culture provides a sufficient or sympathetic image. The appalling history that symbolizes so much of the saga of the twentieth century; the family secrets; the unique aesthetics found in music, dance, poetry, and painting; the exhilarating landscape; and the ceaseless exuberance and vigorous resentments of Korean society have, in fact, proven so powerful that there has been no limit to the dedication with which Korean American writers have sought to create a new sense of self and world. Even in works that do not make Korean or Korean American issues their dominant focus, there are luminous touchstones and traces: certain puns and allusions in Gary Pak's work; the integration of Korean shamanism, Roman Catholic transubstantiation, and French symbolist poetics in Theresa Hak Kyung Cha's *DICTEE;* or the righteous cook, descendant of plantation workers, and "disinherited daughter of the mayor of Honolulu" who emerges from a phone booth as "Ta Jan the Korean" in Willyce Kim's novel *Dancer Dawkins and the California Kid.*

While in this introduction we have emphasized social, historical, and biographical aspects, the underlying consciousness of the works we have selected is clearly fictional, even when the surface of the narratives might seem to be autobiographical. In this sense, we are thinking of fiction in the original sense of the word as something that is constructed—and thus uniquely fitted to its topic and task—and not necessarily something that is the opposite of fact. In each work the use of language, point of view, or the structure of metaphor reveals an underlying concern for conveying meaning in the most trenchant way possible, whether the narrative is told in plain language or whether, because of extreme disjunctions, the work seems not to be a narrative at all.

For the reader unfamiliar with Korean or Korean American contexts, this collection is meant to be read in a three-part sequence. In Part 1 we have presented works that can be understood with little additional contextualization, in which the settings and allusions will be more or less comprehensible to general readers and yet introduce many of the themes and issues that pervade much of Korean American fiction. Part 2 takes a chronological leap backward to the works of formative early Korean American writers— Younghill Kang, Richard Kim, and Kim Ronyoung—who are part of a repeatedly returned-to legacy. In Part 3 we make a categorical jump to works whose context and fictional techniques may be more fully appreciated after the first two parts of this anthology. At the same time they represent the rich, multiply inscribed reality of contemporary Korean American culture.

—The Editors, October 2000

Part ONE

PATTI KIM

Born in Korea in 1970, Patti Kim immigrated to the United States when she was four. Kim has a B. A. in English (1992) and an M. F. A. (1996) from the University of Maryland; she won the 1997 Towson University Prize for Literature and was a nominee for the Stephen Crane Award for First Fiction.

A Cab Called Reliable (1997), from which we excerpt the final chapter, is a work heavily laden with the weight of autobiography, though its surface is clearly the result of much aesthetic artifice. Kim herself has said that "emotionally, the book is very much auto-biographical, but the events are not."

In fact, the events of the novel merely constitute the surface narrative, which functions rather like the chain on a charm bracelet—it provides the structure to which the more important elements attach themselves. Under the surface, the novel reads like a record of the real and imaginative longing Ahn Joo feels for her lost mother, who took Ahn Joo's younger brother and disappeared in a cab from the "Reliable" Cab Company when she was only eight years old. Living alone with her alcoholic father, enduring his depression, romances, and abuse (both explicit and implicit) for years, Ahn Joo awaits the day when her mother will return, her faith sustained by a single cryptic note. But her mother never reappears, and Ahn Joo finds voice in her increasingly complex and poignant attempts at fiction and poetry.

In the end, Kim has created a fiction about a woman whose psychology expresses itself in a narrative about her own growth as a fiction writer. It is somewhat surprising to find the novel so often marketed in the Young Adult category, but perhaps that is because the narrative begins in a naive style and becomes increasingly sophisticated, following the underlying theme of Ahn Joo's growth as a writer. In the chapter we've selected, the theme of food preparation (typical in ethnic fiction) is particularly double-edged because Ahn Joo's name sounds like "side dish" in Korean, the kind eaten as an accompaniment to liquor.

A Cab Called Reliable dramatizes what will be apparent as an odd lacuna in the work of Kim Ronyoung and suggested implicitly in the work of Susan Choi later in this collection—the complicated relationship between the Confucian father and the Americanized Korean daughter, a relationship all the more charged because of the father's loss of personal and cultural authority. The father becomes radically disempowered in a new country in which women—at least on the surface—command, and are required to display, more public power. In the way that Theresa Hak Kyung Cha draws on the shamanic tale of Princess Pari as an important subtext, Kim implicitly draws on one of Korea's central tales of female virtue, the story of Shimch'ŏng, the Blindman's Daughter.

Kim has taught at the Writer's Center in Bethesda, Maryland, and currently teaches fiction writing at the University of Maryland. She is working on her second novel.

from *A Cab Called Reliable*

You liked anchovy soup, so I stunk up my hair and the house to cook it for you. You wanted eel, I almost burned down the house smoking it for you. You liked live squid, so I fought with its tentacles to dump them in the *kimchi* for you. I cut them up, dumped them in the stinging red sauce, and they were still moving. You wanted to listen to old Korean songs, so I bought a tape of *"Barley Field," "When We Depart," "The Waiting Heart,"* and *"The Wild Chrysanthemum"* at Korean Korner for you. For weeks I heard, *"Above the sky a thousand feet high, there are some wild geese crying," "Where, along the endless road are you going away from me like a cloud? like a cloud? like a cloud?" "Lonesome with the thoughts of my old days."* I had to eat my corn flakes with crying geese and rivers that flowed with the blood of twenty lovers. You wanted to read a story about rabbits, so I borrowed *The Tales of Peter Rabbit* for you. You liked cowboy movies, so I bought John Wayne videos for you. You liked to garden, so I stole Mrs. Lee's perilla seeds for you. Your help quit on you, so I skipped two weeks' worth of classes to fry shrimp, steam cabbage, boil collard greens, and bake biscuits for you. You liked Angela's mother, so I drove to her store in Southeast D.C. to set up a dinner date for you. You thought you were losing your hearing, so I laid your head on my thigh and removed the wax out of your ears for you.

You sat on the couch. Your feet rested on top of the table. Your gray eyebrows fell over your drooping lids. On top of your heaving stomach, your hands were folded, and the remote control was balanced on your left thigh. You flipped through the channels when I told you I had grilled the croaker and that my car was up to 9,000 miles. You flipped through the channels when I asked you to show me how to change my oil. Without turning your head to look at me, you said that I had to get under the car, that I would crush my head, that I would die. Too dangerous. You told me to get it done and that it was cheap, as you handed me a twenty-dollar bill from your shorts pocket and walked to the kitchen table to eat your grilled croaker. But it was a Sunday evening. Everything was closed on Sunday evenings, and I could already hear the knocking.

"I can hear the knocking."

You broke off the tail end of the croaker and bit into it, leaving the fin between your thumb and middle finger. You chewed the bones and spit them out. "Knocking? That's something else. Not oil problem."

"Anyway, I need to know how to change my oil."

You sunk your spoon into the rice. "You write anything?"

I lied to you and told you I had written two stories.

"That's it? When you write something big? Write something big for me."

"I am not going to write something big for you. That's impossible."

"What about?"

"What about what?"

"Your stories." Your chopsticks poked the middle of the croaker. The skin slid off. You'll save the skin for last, right after you've slurped its brains out, after you've sucked its eyes out. Makes you smarter. Makes you see good.

"One's about that woman you told me about. You know, the

one who lived on Hae Un Dae Beach with her daughter. And the daughter always wore that black-and-white knit dress with the snowflake patterns?"

"What about them?"

"Well, the daughter grows up and finds a job at a bakery and leaves her mother on the beach."

"That's not true."

"I know. I'm still working on it."

You looked at me, but I stared at the thin layer of grease floating on top of your water. You wanted to call me a liar, but instead you asked, "What about other?"

"It's about your friend who had the two wives. The first one was a little crazy, so he brought in the good-looking second one who sold cosmetics?"

"What about them?"

"The crazy one ends up jumping out of their apartment window on the eleventh floor."

"Didn't happen like that. But sounds good. Second one sell better than first one. Dying at end is good."

"Just show me how to change my oil."

"The first story, that kind don't sell. You need violence. America likes violence." You spit out your bones. "Like this story. I know. Robber breaks into doctor's house with gun. 'Give me your watch, jewelry, money. Give me everything.' Doctor's not home, but doctor daughter's home. She gives him fake diamond ring, fake ruby ring, fake everything. Robber's happy and goes. Robber tries to make money, sees everything's fake and gets mad and goes back to doctor's house, kidnaps doctor's daughter, and puts tattoo snakes on all over her body. So no one marry her because of tattoos."

"People with tattoos get married."

"Not all over body. Korean man don't like tattoos."

"Then they shouldn't get tattoos."

"Man don't get tattoo. Girl gets tattoo because robber puts on her."

"And he thought she would never get married because of the tattoos?"

"Oh yeah. That's true story." The spinach in your teeth moved.

"Here, you've got spinach in your teeth." You waved your hand at the toothpick and dislodged the spinach with your tongue.

"You buy part and oil?"

"Bought part and oil." You pushed yourself away from the table. "Fry croaker next time. Not enough beans in rice. And you boil spinach too long. Too long. Nothing to chew."

I followed you outside to the driveway with my oil filter and bottles of oil. The crickets started making their noise, and you told me to turn on the porch light. I turned on the porch light. You told me to turn on the driveway light. I turned on the driveway light. The moths and gnats flew in circles above your flat top azalea shrubs like they wanted to drill holes in the air. You told me to get the lightbulb with the hook and the long extension cord on it. From basement, not back there. From basement. You hung it on the hood of my car. You told me to get, you know, car has to go up. The red metal things where the car goes up. And brown carpet in garage. Rags in shed. Bucket behind shed. Not that bucket, stupid. Flat bucket to go under car.

"There is no flat bucket behind the shed."

"What's this?"

"It's a triangular basin. It's not a bucket. Buckets are cylinders and have handles on them."

You threw the bucket under the deck, slapped your right calf, and mumbled something about hell and the mosquitos that surrounded you.

You stood in front of my car. The armholes of your tank top were stretched out showing your chest. Your plaid shorts hung underneath your round hard belly, and your socks were pulled to your knees. You waved the four fingers of your right hand to come. Come. Come. Stop. Your head jerked back, and your chin formed another fold of skin, as you burped. Tasting the croaker again, you licked your lips and swallowed. The crickets screamed from your garden. The streetlights came on, and the mosquitos gathered underneath their light. Slowly, you kneeled and pushed yourself with your slippered feet underneath my car.

Your back rested on the piece of the brown carpet that used to cover the family room, wall to wall. One inch padding underneath. Every step, our feet used to sink in, and our toes would grip the standing fibers. You used to yell, "Take off shoes! Take off shoes!" at my friends, and they would run across the carpet with embarrassment, cheeks turning pink, and leave their shoes at the front door.

The lilac bush collared the driveway light, making it look like a groomed poodle standing still in an angle of your triangular garden. In front of the light, a rock with the glowing "3309" in white paint. The left side was lined with azalea bushes like four green basketballs growing out of white pebbles. The right side was lined with pine trees that looked like four green miniature teepees. And the side that lined the edge of our front porch, more azalea bushes, but with flat tops like coffins. In the center of it all, the stump of the magnolia tree you chopped down because its leaves were clogging up our gutter. The Spanish moss you had planted surrounded the stump and began to climb the rotting bark.

You placed the basin underneath the spout and unscrewed the blue filter. The black oil poured out onto your fingers, then into the basin. You wiped your hand with an old sock.

"Where you drive your car? Oil is so black."

"Let me do it. I'll catch the oil."

"Don't touch anything. Your hands get dirty. Keep clean hands."

"I don't care if my hands get dirty."

"Keep clean hands."

"What do I need clean hands for?"

"Keep clean hands to write."

The oil dripped into the basin. Standing up and wiping your hands on the sock, you told me about Miryang. Miryang. Miryang. Miryang. I know. That was the village you grew up in and in that village was a bridge you had to cross to get to school in your bare feet even during the winter because your father bought you only one pair of shoes on New Year's Day, which you stuffed in your pocket so that the soles wouldn't wear out. And when the soles wore out, you nailed wood to the bottom of your shoes, but the wood gave you splinters, so you poured soil in your shoes; it felt just like walking in a fertilized field.

I know about the tree that stood next to the well. The tree that you climbed and napped on. The tree from which you saw the well holding the floating village virgin. The tree under which the village grandmothers peeled potatoes. You've already told me about the man with three teeth and eight and a half fingers who ran the village grocery. Who would get so drunk by early afternoon that he'd give you a bottle of *soju* rather than the bottle of vinegar your mother was waiting for at home. I've already seen the soybean woman rolling her cart along the dirt road through the village. The chestnut woman who strung her roasted nuts on strands of her own hair. The cows bumping into each other within the fence. The stink of manure in your mother's garden. The stink of sewage when it rained. The rice-grinding factory where you met your mother-in-law. You've already told me about the girl with no eyes marrying the man with no ears. About hiding from your father when school tuition day came around because he'd make you work in the field. Yes, I can hear him yelling, "What good is school? What good is school? Go work in the field." I know about how he broke your watch on your wedding day trying to strike you across the face. It was your engagement watch from Mother. You didn't know then, did you? That she would leave us. Why don't you tell me the truth? Is she my mother or isn't she? How else could she have so easily left me? Why don't you just tell me the truth? I already know about your brother reading books by candlelight underneath a quilt that caught on fire. You don't have to tell me about your sister who was knuckled by your mother so often that she had a dent on the right side of her head and lost her mind and is now steaming rice and boiling potato roots for Buddhist monks. Don't you think I remember the apples, eggs, chestnuts, persimmons you stole and hid in the hole you dug and lined with rocks next to the village manure pile? You don't have to start singing about trying to forget, trying to forget. About walking to the sea sands from day to day. About how summer has gone; fall has gone; now the cold winter in the sea. Abba, I know the women divers searching for clams have disappeared. Stop it. Stop singing about trying to forget, trying to forget by walking to the sea sands from day to day.

You closed my hood, and I drove my car down. You picked weeds out of your garden while I put everything back in its place. You waited for me. When I walked to the door, you followed me in, saying, "Joo-yah, remember when you sing *Bbo gook bbo gook bbo gook seh?*"

"Abba, I don't remember that song."

"You remember."

"I don't."

"Bbo gook bbo gook bbo gook seh . . . "

"Abba, I told you I don't remember. Stop it." You saw me roll my eyes. Your shoulders jerked back. Three folds of skin formed on your chin. You removed your gray hat and scratched your bald head. Your belly grew as you took your breath.

When I walked upstairs, I heard you say, "No matter how bad my father treat me, I never talk like that. Never walk away like that."

I did not hear the usual sounds of the evening. No commercials from the television, no faucet running, no flush of the toilet every two hours, no refrigerator door opening and closing. I did not hear you speaking to Angela's mother in Korean on the phone. *How was business today? Did you do well? How's Angela? I sent you a letter. Did you get my letter? Ahn Joo? She's writing her stories upstairs.* You didn't call me down to make you Sullok tea or peel apple-pears or listen to your stories about kite fights, crispy grasshopper legs, and midnight runs to the village nurse's window where she changed her clothes in the light. I waited for you to call me down, but I heard you climb the stairs, pass my room, and shut your door.

That night I opened my window. The passing cars on Morning Glory Way were the first sounds I noticed when we moved here. Never heard cars whiz by like that tucked away on the fifth floor of our apartment at the end of Burning Rock Court. I thought a family room with fireplace, living room, dining room, a country kitchen, basement, four bedrooms, two and a half baths were too much for us, but you said, "Future. Future. Think about future." So I thought about the future when I entered junior high and high school, and I raised my hand when I didn't understand how rectification, amplification, and oscillation worked in explaining electrical currents or why bromine was called bromine. I raised my hand when I had to go to the bathroom or if the boys in my lab group were eating all the peanuts we had to weigh. I memorized Xe for Zenon, At for Astatine, Pb for Lead; postulate number one, the points on a line can be paired with the real numbers in such a way that any two points can have zero and one; postulate number two, if B is between AC, then AB plus BC equals AC; Il a mis le café/Dans la tasse/Il a mis le lait/Dans la tasse de café. . . . I thought about the future as I stood in front of Mr. Huggins's geography class and recited Alabama, Alaska, Arizona, Arkansas, California, Colorado, Connecticut, Delaware, Florida . . . all the states in alphabetical order within two minutes. I thought about the future as I bowed and received my classmates' applause.

When future, future, future finally came, the walls of our house were too close together, the ceilings weren't high enough, the floors weren't low enough, and I needed more bedrooms.

Across the street, Mrs. Goode's dogs panted, barked, and jingled the fence. The crickets were going mad, and birds screamed at each other. Mrs. Cutler's high heels tapped quickly against the sidewalk. Mrs. Winehart's car wouldn't start. The phone next door rang. The lawn mower roared. When the wind blew, the screen of my window rattled.

I went downstairs to prepare your tea. As I waited for the water to boil, I shut my eyes tight. But the mahogany bookcase you built when I entered college, the television case for which you hand-carved the legs, the pine coffee table with the drawers that took weeks to make, the kitchen cabinets you stained, the round breakfast table you made me stand on when you cut out its top, the hardwood floors you laid in the living room, and the oyster white kitchen walls you painted stared at me, even behind my closed lids. I could let the water boil and all this wood go up in flames.

Light came from underneath your door. I put down the tray, knocked, and slowly turned the handle when I didn't hear your usual, "Uh." On my hands and knees, I slid the tray into your room.

You had already spread your quilt out on the middle of the floor. Your box of a pillow on the right side. Bare windows. Empty walls except for the photograph of Mother's blurry face tacked above the breakfast-in-bed table. I could never make out what she looked like in that picture. Her hair blew in her face, and she looked like she was shaking her head. No, No. Like she didn't want to be photographed with all those pigeons. A tape player and a digital clock on top of the same table. Underneath, a shoe-box of tapes. A pile of three red floor mats in the opposite corner. You sat under the window and fanned yourself.

"Open the window if you're hot."

"Too much noise outside."

You lifted your chin and asked, "What tea did you make?"

"You know, the usual. Sullok tea."

"I thought you make ginseng with honey."

"Why would I make ginseng?"

You reached over for the tray and pulled it to the edge of your quilt. "Because you want to say something important to me." You said it slowly. You wanted to get all the words in the right order.

With legs crossed and hands folded, you sat in the center of your quilt and waited for me to tell you. I wanted to pour your tea and join you, but I remained on your wooden floor near the door.

In Korean you asked, *"Ahn Joo-yah, what is it?"*

I wanted to tell you that I needed you to tell me about the princess-weaver and her lover, the cowherder, who met at the bank of the River of Heaven every year. How was it that they fell in love? Why did the king separate them? How is it that they meet every year?

Or that I had written a story about your first visit to your grandfather's grave. Fake pink azaleas in a tin can in front of the tombstone. That I had gotten everything down. Your pouring *soju* on the mound. Your peeling a banana and leaving it there for him to eat. Your pulling the weeds off the mound and saying a prayer about how you wanted to be good. Your finishing your prayer and getting up to go, thinking that he would never have known if you had come or gone. Your picking up the banana and eating it. And on your way out, your thinking about how your grandfather died. About how your father never took him to the hospital. If they had opened his stomach, they would have seen the disease, and he would have lived another year. I wanted to tell you that I had gotten everything down. Even the rosebushes that grew like vines on the gate. The fields of rice. The woman who carried a tub of cabbage on her head. The other one who fished for anchovies along the ditch in her rubber gloves. And that I had ended the story with you walking past the two women, leaving the graveyard, and thinking about how you didn't have enough *wons* to buy the dog soup at the end of the road.

Instead, in my best Korean I said, *"Abba, I can't stay here any longer."*

You reached over, poured the tea, and sipped it. Your gold caps sparkled from the corners of your smile. You placed your cup on the wooden saucer and rested your head on your pillow. I opened your closet, pulled out the light blue blanket with the butterfly patterns, and spread it out over you.

"Ahn Joo-yah, I don't need a blanket tonight. It's hot." Your eyes were closed. You pretended to sleep.

"Abba, I'm sorry."

"It's all right. I'm not going to die from the heat."

I folded the blanket away from you and left it at your feet.

"Ahn Joo-yah, leave the tea when you go."

"I know."

ME-K. AHN

As many as one hundred thousand Korean children have been adopted in the United States since the Korean War. At the outset, this tremendous displacement was considered a humanitarian effort to rescue orphans from Korea's postwar devastation and raise them in more prosperous material and social circumstances. Other factors that contributed to the large number include Koreans' aversion to adopting unrelated children, lack of social services for unwed mothers, and what has been called the "white baby famine": in economically advanced Western nations during the early 1970s, an increase in the number of childless couples wanting to raise children combined with a domestic shortage of infants put up for adoption. Korean agencies promptly responded: annual figures for 1972–87 reveal that Korean children were always half or more of the number adopted in the United States from other countries. South Korea's peculiar leadership in this area long after its economy had overcome the ravages of war and colonialism became an embarrassing topic in international mass media coverage of the 1988 Seoul Olympics. It was only then that the government formulated new policies aimed at slowing both the abandonment of Korean children and their adoption abroad. Scholars and activists have debated whether intercountry adoptees actually benefit from being raised in more affluent but oftentimes racist environments. Mixed-race adoptees, such as those fathered by U.S. soldiers in wartime or postwar Germany, Korea, and Vietnam, are often spurned by both sides of their ancestry, as has been hauntingly described in such works as Ty Pak's short story "A Fire" and Heinz Insu Fenkl's novel *Memories of My Ghost Brother.*

Writing by the now matured first generation of Korean adoptees itself has recently begun to receive attention. *Seeds from a Living Tree: An Anthology by Korean Adoptees,* edited by Tonya Bishoff and Jo Rankin, includes moving pieces that address heretofore deeply repressed questions and sorrows. It also includes part of Me-K. Ahn's unpublished novel *Living in Half Tones,* which excerpt depicts the narrator's apprehensive, yet insatiable inquiry into origins, family, and her own transnational history's multiple identities. Another theme in the novel is the narrator's sometimes conflicting ties to her various "mothers" and the values they represent—her lost Korean birth mother; June White, her Caucasian American caretaker at the orphanage in Korea; and Nobuko, her Japanese American adoptive mother in Minnesota. It is their care that she hungers for or pays homage to as she returns to Korea for the first time in more than two decades, trying to recognize some vital, but obscured trace of herself in other orphans' faces or in documents that she has never been allowed to see.

Writer and filmmaker Me-K. Ahn was born in Seoul some thirty-odd years ago, but she has never been told her exact birthdate. She has a B. A. in art and art history from Carleton College and has been the recipient of Loft-McKnight and Minnesota State Arts Board Fellowships, Jerome Foundation travel and study grants, and the Korea Society's Best Director Award. Her writing has been published in several anthologies and journals and her film *Undertow* (1994) and video *Living in Half Tones* (1996) have been shown at international festivals to high praise. She is currently at work on a second novel.

from *Living in Half Tones*

Imagine a girl, she is two years old.

She wears a simple red dress, chin-length hair with short, coarse bangs, her fleshy knees exposed. A blurry silhouette of her face appears, slowly comes into focus, revealing a slightly furrowed brow, only to disappear again into the darkness.

Let's name her Sun-ah.

She comes into focus again, standing in Seoul, Korea's Kimpo Airport. Waiting to be relinquished to an unknown future. An unknown fate. Her known birth country, her known language, to be surrendered somewhere over the Pacific Ocean.

Officially she was never born. You will not find a record of her birth, not even in her small hometown. A miraculous conception in Korea, an anonymous drop-off at an orphanage, a hasty but surreptitious send-off to a foreign land. She is a paper child of ghosts.

Nobody tells her what is happening as an American escort carries her onto the airplane. She recognizes no one, wonders about all the familiar faces back at the orphanage. "Odi kayo? Where are we going?" she asks over and over again. The escort can only offer sympathetic looks in exchange as the flood of tears begins. She wants to be back with all the other kids on the playground, hitting each other with plastic toys, oblivious. Finally she cries herself to sleep.

Fifteen hours of flight, 10,000 miles of disorientation. Sun-ah stumbles onto an airplane walkway in Chicago's O'Hare airport, her hand tightly clenched to the escort. Shaken from a deep sleep, she is not conscious enough to be scared. Her eyes cannot focus as she is led through an endless, winding maze. Her gait sluggish, legs unable to keep in stride, she is thrust into thin arms. The woman rushing to reach the end of this maze; the end for her, the beginning for Sun-ah.

Anxious welcomers wait in nervous anticipation.

Restricted to passengers only, security posts surround the waiting area. All others must keep out. The flight from Seoul, Korea is more than two hours late. Many people gather at doors in front of a gate guarded carefully by uniformed personnel. As time passes, and with each new delay, a loud sigh emanates from the doorway. Parents-in-waiting for their soon-to-be-children. Sun-ah will be the first through these doors, the first of thousands of ghost children to float into mi-guk, the beautiful country, this United States of America.

Now Sun-ah is someplace different. Really different. Indecipherable words bombarding her ears. Strange faces looming. They all look like the escort. At first sight of her, Sun-ah had burst out crying, her ghost-like face terrifying. But here even more of those faces surround them. Burying her head, she tries to hide, to disappear back into Korea.

They continue through a series of large glass doors and down an escalator, Sun-ah peeking at all the emerging white faces. Large masses of shuffling bodies. Suddenly she is lowered onto the floor and starts crying, wrapping her arms around the escort's legs, nestling her face into the fabric of the brown skirt. Frantic, the woman fumbles around inside her purse finally pulling out a small white sign with large, black print. She holds it high, making a slow 360-degree turn, hoping, expecting.

Eventually, a young couple walks towards them, anxious, nervous. Sun-ah sees a woman with black hair and dark-brown, moon-slivered eyes and yells, "uh-ma, uh-ma." The woman pauses for a moment in her black and white polyester dress, breathless. "So small," she says glancing up and down her tiny exhausted body. Sun-ah wriggles out from the escort's arms as the black-haired woman quickly extends hers. "Uh-ma, uh-ma," she says again. "Mommy, mommy." She breaks down, looks at her husband who towers a foot above in a grey suit. Fighting back a deluge of tears, his upper lip trembles as he rubs his balding head. But the moist emotions triumph, forcing his entire body to heave. He reaches out for delicate hands and strokes them gently. His new daughter looks into his watery, light-blue eyes with confusion.

Later, Sun-ah lies in her new mother's arms, so deep in sleep she floats lightly inside the Ford Mercury, while her new father speeds up the interstate. Mom complains, telling him to slow down, but all he can think about is getting them home. Occasionally, Sun-ah wakes up, says something in Korean. Mom offers a bottle, but worries that it will not be enough for the long, eight-hour drive.

When they arrive home, Mom runs into the small apartment, puts Sun-ah into a new stainless-steel high chair. Then she quickly scoops some warming rice into a plastic bowl, placing it in front of her new daughter. And just as she rushes to get a little spoon, Sun-ah begins eating the rice with her fingers—serious in concentration, never looking up. Mom stands back, watching in amazement.

Sun-ah pauses for a moment, glancing up from the empty bowl. "Mool, mool. Water, water," she says flatly. Mom walks over, and, misunderstanding, picks up the bowl, takes it away. Sun-ah grabs the bowl back forcefully with both hands, scowling. Mom peers into the bowl, staring with moistened eyes. A few morsels of left-over rice quickly disappear. And at that moment she vows that her daughter will never go hungry again.

*

Rose Michiko Middlestadt.

My third given name. American. Japanese. German. My mother Nobuko cannot pronounce "Rose" and my father Arthur cannot pronounce "Michiko."

I stand here at Seattle International Airport, Nobuko behind me. It is August 1990. Our first time in Seattle. The one stop between Minneapolis and Seoul—between me and the land of ghosts.

"R-r-oh-zu, R-r-oh-zu," Nobuko calls out to me with a heavy Japanese accent. She is pointing to white kanji characters on a dark-blue awning with her thick, stubby forefinger.

"Udon," she continues in disbelief. "That says udon."

"What?" I say, half-dazed.

"There," Nobuko replies, moving towards the small restaurant, not bothering to look back.

I take a deep breath and follow slowly, too tired to reconstruct half-sentences. I watch a thin body move away in blue stretch pants and a floral blouse, while short, loose curls from an aging perm dance sluggishly on top of her head. Even though her 5'2" frame is slightly stooped from fifty-five years, she still has the energy of a thirty-year-old.

I am five inches taller with long, straight hair. We look nothing alike. Although most people could swear that I am of her flesh and blood. My skin is pale, delicate, hers dark, slightly weathered. My face is almost a perfect square, my eyes small, single-lidded. Hers egg-shaped with larger almost double-lidded eyes. My voice is soft, low, hers is loud and mannish. Together we are an odd mother-daughter pair.

We reach the food runway, my head finally beginning to clear. I look down at the large stainless steel tubs and focus on the fish spam. Thinly sliced, white fish cakes lined with bright pink borders float around in the steaming, light-brown broth. A man behind the counter piles fat white noodles into a disposable container. *So that's what she was talking about.*

Japanese food. It abounded in our house. I learned to love its mildness, its sometimes tongue-stinging sharpness. Names never existed for these foods. Nobuko would try to explain, but then stop, mumble something about bad English or no translation. "Noodles," was all she would say. "Japan's noodles."

"Like a vacuum cleaner, neh?" Nobuko manages to say while inhaling the noodles.

I am embarrassed, my face flushing red with Americanness. "Just don't clog your throat," I reply.

"Good Japanese noodles make you choke," she says with a wide grin. "Can't get it back home. Those noodles you get in Chinese restaurant. They have funny taste. Don't go in the same way."

A shaky voice finally calls out from an old loudspeaker. An anonymous voice telling us to board the plane. I slowly rise from the maroon padded seats of the waiting area, follow the low drone past the large observation windows. Nobuko walks closely behind, awkward, nervous. Weary travelers rush by. A vague sense of fear pulses through my body, barely decipherable thoughts invading my already crowded mind. I concentrate on every step, on each corresponding breath, walking towards a world that will soon consume me. An abstract world of blurry proportions. A world that holds a vision of my first mother's eyes.

On the Boeing 747, I can only think of sleep. The prospect of being trapped in a small enclosed space for over thirteen hours with only the Pacific 30,000 feet below sends my stomach tumbling. I want to escape into a shelter of sleep.

I lean against the fabric of the seat, pushing back as far as it can go, fumbling with my seatbelt. As I reach over to grab a small pillow with a white gauze-like paper covering, a black and white photograph falls out of a pocket. Worn on the edges, a yellowish film has formed on its glossy surface. Underneath the cloudiness stands June White. My second mother? The director of the orphanage, the White Angel Baby Home, where I once lived. The picture was supposedly taken at a gathering where we first met. I have no recollection of this meeting, but June still lives in the small town of Taejon, South Korea. Twenty years after my departure.

As I sit back wide-eyed on the cramped airline seat, I start to think about our meeting. June will recognize me after all these years and run towards me, excited, arms outstretched, reconnecting me to Korea, making me feel special, as if she knows exactly what is going through my mind on this first visit back. Her enthusiasm and emotional reaction will disarm me of any inhibitions and I will feel wholly bonded to her, my "second mother." I had dreamed that when we arrived in Korea, I would feel as if I had returned home. That I would experience a spiritual connection as American wheels made contact with Korean soil.

But when the plane begins its descent and the scattered landscape of Korea takes shape, I am breathless. The realization of the return is slow, intense. Like trudging up a steep mountain towards the thin new air offered at its peak. Nobuko, whose head bobs up and down in short, quick movements, keeps saying, "You shouldn't expect too much. Don't get your hopes high, you'll just get disappointed." Sadness, worry and concern all collect on her face at the same time.

I shake my head. I have grown tired of advice. "Mom, I've told you. I know that I shouldn't expect anything," I say trying to hide any uncertainty. "I have no idea what is going to happen. How could I be disappointed?"

An endless body of water suddenly appears, and, like a tiny pebble, Sun-ah falls into the wide expanse, displacing it with a myriad of ever-widening ripples. Once hitting the surface, she is on her way. Headed towards an unknown edge, from one life to another, from dusk to day.

Clutching June's photo, I walk through the crowded receiving line in the expansive lobby of the airport. Nobuko follows. I don't want to look back. I just want to find June. I had been told, "Just look for a lady with light reddish hair. She'll be taller there and wears glasses." I thought it would be obvious. Korea being one of the most homogeneous countries in the world; but many Caucasians rush about, mainly bound for military posts. As I walk past the last person in line, I twist around slowly, looking back through all the Korean faces. Maybe June had slipped through my anxious confusion. My eyes flit around so fast I can't stop and focus on any one image. Everything a blur.

The line degenerates into a mass of people, hugging, shaking hands, smiling at one another. Many reunions all at once. A feeling of envy creeps up, twisting me inside out. I rarely hug anybody. Especially close friends, from whom I keep my distance both emotionally and physically. Touching these people is too scary. It might mean something, reveal something. Paradoxically, it is people I hardly know whom I find myself embracing. Hugging them is fine. It doesn't mean anything. The physical closeness feels safe, comforting. It satisfies the desire for touch. At a distance.

I pass in and out of the crowd quickly while Nobuko waits by a pillar with our luggage. Still no June. Many Caucasian faces pass by, but most look military. I stand for a while and scan the lobby. A taller woman wearing a dark-blue, cotton A-line skirt and a vertically striped matching shirt appears from behind a large group of bodies complete with name tags and identical luggage. A tour group maybe.

Suddenly a man in a white shirt and grey pants approaches, his stern eyes fixed on my face. A verbal assault in Korean. My hands go up, my shoulders shrug. I can't even tell him that I don't know how to speak Korean. He wrinkles his eyebrows, but doesn't stop. I veer right then left, trying to see past him. Why won't he get out of my way? The tall woman disappears among the throngs of bodies with black hair. He gives no indication of stopping, so I maneuver around him, not bothering to look up. His eyes slapped on my back.

I clench my hands, walk towards the tourist group. The striped shirt appears again. I stand back for a while and watch. Eye contact would help, but the woman turns the other way. My heart sinks. It must be June, I think. But I need a closer look. I approach her slowly, guiding my eyes up and down her body. Just say something to her, I keep telling myself. Just ask her if she's June. The woman doesn't give a second look. I will feel stupid if it isn't her. But then she has already passed me. I rub my nose and feel sweat seeping through my forehead. When I notice myself walking around in circles, I stop, look around for Nobuko who responds with concerned, weary eyes. The thirteen-hour plane ride has taken its toll. I turn around quickly and walk towards the stripes again.

"Ah, are you June?" I ask. My voice thin, barely audible.

"What?" the woman asks.

I clear my throat, try again. "Are you June White?"

"Yes," she says flatly. The expression on her face not changing. Her hands still tightly wrapped around her white vinyl purse.

"I'm Rose," I say, trying to smile. My hand extends, but quickly pulls back when June begins to talk.

"We saw you walk into the line and tried to signal you, but you didn't see us," she tells us, pointing towards the entrance of the lobby. She looks nervously at her assistant Mrs. Kim who has made the long trip from Taejon with her. She says something to her in Korean and looks at me again.

I shift back and forth from foot to foot looking at Mrs. Kim in her casual, plain attire. A white cotton-polyester t-shirt with brown polyester pants that you barely notice on her short, stout body. An aging perm in her graying, disheveled hair. Nobuko would have said that first she needed to cut off the old ends, get a new perm, then cut it again after two weeks to get the best effect of the new curls. Then she would have advised her to get rid of the gray. "Get the darkest of browns," she would say. "Not black because it looks too blue."

June, on the other hand, is tall, puffy, her skin a rough, pasty-white. The kind of woman with huge pockets of cellulite on the backs of her legs along with plenty of broken blood vessels. Her light brown hair is permanent-curly-short with a strawberry-colored sheen, and she moves about with a breathy heaviness, her tiny lips slightly open to suck in as much air as possible. Her movement purposeful, unapologetic. You'd expect her voice to be deep, textured, maybe a little bit gruff. But it's medium-pitched, with a softer kind of shrillness.

Mrs. Kim looks at me then whispers to June. I feel like somebody's little secret, sinking in my own fabricated reality, searching for something to say. Nobuko taps my shoulder breaking the awkward silence. Nervous energy flying around her eyes.

"Mom, this is June," I force out.

"Oh, yes, yes . . . I kind of recognize you," she says while grabbing June's hands which immediately collapse into lifeless members. Nobuko squeezing everything out of them. I look at June's face, examine her eyes. She catches my glance, shifts back towards Nobuko, then stares at the beige tile floor.

Nobuko makes small talk. Psychobabble that makes your head spin. My mind reels, my eyes water. I want to disappear and start all over again. Maybe this isn't really June. She is too business-like. I am on an assembly line, another adoptee returning to Korea in search of scattered, missing pieces. I have arrived and then I will leave, just as all others who had chosen to make this trip into their mysterious past.

"I think we should get going now. It's a long ride back," June says as she turns to leave.

Tropical trees line the large parking lot full of Daewoos, Hyundais. Miniature models of those exported to the U.S. In the distance, strange hollow sounds fenced in by mountain ranges bounce back and forth in a cacophonous roar. Car horns blaring, trucks shrieking down the freeway, heavy construction equipment bruising the landscape. It is a bright, sunny day in Seoul; the air so thick it sticks to my skin. I inhale deeply, follow my breath, try to absorb everything.

The airport disappears behind the layered hills of the rich, green landscape. I look outside the window of the compact car, hypnotized by new surroundings. The late afternoon sun descends, coating everything with a thin haze.

As we leave Seoul for Taejon, the roads become narrow, single-lane runways of death. The worst car ride ever. We weave in and out of mountains with minimal light to guide us. Cars pass each other without reservation, even on the most dangerous curves, forcing June to anticipate them screeching blindly around a bend, out of control. Quickly swerving to the right, trying to squeeze through the narrow shoulder. Somehow carrying us through the darkness of this curious, new land.

My stomach rebels as we curve in and out, starting and stopping, but sleep still overcomes. Even *this* cannot keep me from sleeping. Eventually, the whir of the tires calms me, transports me into another world.

Sun-ah's face appears from the middle of the darkness. Slowly her body taking shape. Walking down a dirt path lined with tall ginkgo trees. Rather, someone is pulling at her arm, someone whose face never appears. Only the back of a dark figure visible. The path is long, winding. The evening cold, the wind sufficiently strong. Sun-ah's face flushed with its briskness. She wonders about this unfamiliar path, the firmness of this arm's tug. The pace a little too quick.

They come upon another dark, taller figure looming among the ginkgoes. Figure one speaks to figure two, their voices low. At first. The sound steadily increases into a threatening kind of noise. Figure one still holds firmly onto Sun-ah. A little too firmly now. She starts to whimper, knowing enough to be scared. The voices continue loudly crashing, colliding. Sun-ah screams, trying to pull away. The yelling too loud inside her small head. Then the struggle begins. A struggle to end one conflict, a fight to begin yet another. Figure two walks away with Sun-ah. Figure one walks the other way.

They continue along their paths, walking endlessly, until the line of thought is interrupted. Someone is following. At first, an innocuous shadow, then a threatening presence. They walk faster. The shadow walks faster. Sun-ah does not want to look back. The footsteps are gaining. Sun-ah looks back quickly, she can't help herself now, and sees that it is a stocky man. They make eye contact briefly and it becomes clear that he does not want to hurt her. But it is also clear that he will keep following.

She keeps looking back in that knowing, curious way at this trailing stranger. His glance somewhat surreptitious, evasive, or should we say guilty. He tries to look without looking even though he knows she knows.

There is a house in the distance. A small rundown shack. They walk towards it without pause, enter through the broken door. Sun-ah sits alone quietly in a darkened room when the noise begins. Large, booming voices full of unbridled anger. She knows that she is somehow a part of the conversation, the anonymous people somewhat familiar.

She continues to sit quietly, wondering what has become of the stocky man.

As the crickets sing their mournful tunes, anxiety and fear cluster inside at the same time. A body that is outside of itself. Legs which move themselves. A mind that is not in command.

I am on auto pilot.

As if another person inside controls my mind, separating it from my body. I look from a stranger's eyes.

I walk up the dark stairwell of the orphanage and wonder whether these feelings will ever subside. If I will remember something about my early life here. And if that memory will ground me in any way. Perhaps a scent in the air, a creak in the doorway, a brick in the building, the warmth of the heated *ondol* floors. But even in the darkness I can tell that remembering will be difficult.

We pass by several miniature, plastic shoes neatly placed outside the entrance of the second floor.

A tiny, crumbling Korean shoe in Minnesota.

The one treasured item that traveled with me to the States. Only one shoe. The other mysteriously disappearing, along with my early past.

Korean children in the orphanage.

Their faces sending a shiver through my body, making my heart flutter deliriously. I stop momentarily, try to shake off the coldness.

GARY PAK

It is estimated that nearly a half-million Koreans have moved to the United States since immigration laws were changed in 1965. Many of *Kŏri*'s younger authors came from Korea while still children during this wave of immigration. The first substantial Korean immigration, however, was the more than seven thousand men and few hundred women who came to Hawai'i to work on sugar plantations between 1903 and 1906. Originally brought in by white plantation owners to lessen the threat of strikes by well-organized Japanese laborers, these Koreans had strong anti-Japanese sentiment, which only grew as their homeland lost its independence. The saga of one such individual's involvement in both nationalist movements against imperialist Japan and the struggle of Hawai'i's multiethnic proletariat against corporate power is told in Gary Pak's novel *A Ricepaper Airplane* (1998), which he began writing in 1982. At about the same time, Pak started to compose the pieces eventually collected in *The Watcher of Waipuna and Other Stories* (1992), the opening, invocational story of which we have included here. None of the short stories makes explicit reference to Korean concerns or presents a Korean main character, but underlying both pioneering books is Pak's conviction that Hawai'i's repressed histories must be retold with sensitivity to the tribulations and dilemmas of working-class and marginalized individuals, such as the plantation workers, victims of racist violence, homosexuals (*mahu*), the deranged, or the disenfranchised descendants of the Hawai'ian priesthood (*kahuna*). Pak also demands that history be used to illuminate present-day injustices at every level: economic, cultural, and spiritual.

In "The Valley of the Dead Air," the only way members of the local community can move beyond historical stagnation (the *hauna* stench) and its continued exploitation by outsiders (the state and capitalist con artists) is through honest self-reflection on Hawai'i's history and one's personal complicity in the neglect and wrongs suffered by the land's original keepers and cultivators, symbolized in the late *kahuna* Jacob Hookano. Although the story is set within the framework of Hawai'ian spirits and their cyclical relation to the land, Pak demonstrates a very Korean sense of the need to exorcize distraught spirits before moving on the next task at hand.

Born in Honolulu in 1952, Gary Pak has a B. A. in psychology from Boston University and an M. A. and Ph.D. in English from the University of Hawai'i at Manoa. He currently lives in Kane'ohe on the island of Oahu while teaching at Kapi'olani Community College. Pak has won numerous awards and fellowships, including a 1993 Association for Asian American Studies Book Award for *The Watcher of Waipuna and Other Stories* and a 1999 Hawai'i Book Publishers Association Award of Merit for *A Ricepaper Airplane.*

The Valley of the Dead Air

The day after Jacob Hookano died, that old hermit who had lived at the very end of Waiola Valley, a bad air from the ocean came in and lingered over the land. The residents of the valley thought that a Kona wind had brought in that rotten smell from the mangroves and mud flats of the coastal area, and they waited impatiently for another wind to take the smell away.

As Leimomi Vargas said succinctly, "Jus' like old Jacob wen fut and dah fut jus' stayin' around."

And stay around it did, for weeks. There seemed no end. The residents prayed for that new wind to blow the obstinate smell away, but no wind came and the air became stagnant and more foul as if the valley were next to an ancient cesspool that had suddenly ruptured after centuries of accumulations. The malodor permeated the wood of the houses, it tainted the fresh clothes hung to dry, and it entered the pores of everyone, making young and old smell bad even after a good scrubbing. The love lives of the residents became nonexistent.

"We gotta do somet'ing 'bout dis hauna," Joseph Correa complained. The retired sewers worker from the City and County sat on a chair under the eaves of an old abandoned store that fronted the main road.

"Yeah, but what?" said Bobby Ignacio. He turned his gaunt, expressionless face towards Correa, then returned to his meditation of birds eating the ripened fruits of a lichee tree across the road.

"You know, Bobby," Correa said in a voice shaded ominously, "I betchu dah gov'ment is behind all dis. Look how long dis hauna stay heah. Long time already. If was jus' one nat'ral t'ing, dah wind already blow 'em away."

Ignacio, a truck farmer up the road in the valley, spat disconsolately into the wild grass growing on the side of the store.

"But I tell you dis, Bobby. I betchu one day dah gov'ment goin' come down heah and dey goin' brag how dey can take dis hauna away. And den they *goin'* take 'em away. But I betchu little while aftah dat, dey goin' come back and try ask us for do dem one favor. You watch." Correa nodded his head. "No miss."

The farmer shrugged his narrow shoulders. "But you know what everybody saying?"

"Who everybody?"

"Everybody."

"So what everybody saying?"

"Dey saying old Jacob dah one doing all dis."

The old retiree nervously stretched out his tired legs, his head twitched a few times, then he looked out languidly towards the mango trees across the road.

"I nevah had no problems with old Jacob," Correa said weakly. "I was always good to him. I nevah talk stink 'bout him or anything li' dat."

The smell persisted, and somehow it infected the rich, famous soil of the valley. The earth began to emit a terrible odor of rotten fish. While plowing one corner of his sweet potato field, Tats Sugimura uncovered a hole full of fish scales and fish bones. He didn't think anything of it until his wife complained to him later how fishy everything smelled. The bad smell of the valley had numbed his nose so Tats couldn't smell anything worth shit now. His wife, on the other hand, had a super-sensitive nose and she often would sniff the air in her kitchen and know exactly what the Rodriguez family was cooking a quarter of a mile down the road.

"Tats, you wen dump some rotten fish around here or what?" she said. Sugimura shook his head. He wasn't the talking type, even with his wife. "Den whas dat stink smell?"

He thought of telling her about the fish scales and bones, then he thought that perhaps a bunch of stray cats had had a feast in that corner of his field. The fish were probably tilapia or catfish the cats had caught in the nearby stream. But he was tired from working all day under the hot sun and in the stifling humid air and he didn't have the energy to describe to his wife what he had seen. The fish scales and fish bones were unimportant, and he shrugged his thin, wiry shoulders and said nothing.

But something bad was in the soil. When Tats and the other sweet potato farmers began harvesting their produce a few days later, they found abnormally small sweet potatoes, some having the peculiar shape of a penis.

"How dah hell we goin' sell dis kine produce?" complained Earl Fritzhugh, a part-Hawaiian sweet potato farmer. "Dey goin' laugh at us. So small. And look at dis one. Look like one prick!"

"Somet'ing strange goin' on in dis valley," said Darryl Mineda, another farmer. "Get dah story goin' around dat old Jacob doin' all dis to get back."

"Get back at who?" Fritzhugh asked irately.

"At us."

Fritzhugh looked at Mineda incredulously. "At us?" Why dat old Hawaiian like get back at us fo'? He wen live by himself. Nobody wen bother him.

Mineda shook his head. "Somebody tol' me all dah land in dis valley used to be his family's land, long time ago. Den dah Cox family wen come in and take dah land away from his family. Somet'ing 'bout Jacob's family not paying dah land tax or water tax or somet'ing li' dat, and dah haole wen pay instead."

"But what got to do with us? I not responsible. Dah haole wen do it. Not me."

Mineda shrugged his shoulders.

"Eh, I was good to dah old man," Fritzhugh said. "I nevah bother him. When he used to go up and down dis road, he nevah said not'ing to me, so I never say not'ing to him." He paused. "But I wonder who goin' get his land now he ma-ke. He no mo' children, eh?"

Mineda shrugged his shoulders again. "Maybe das why," Mineda said.

"Maybe das why what?"

"Maybe das why he got all salty. Nobody pay attention to him. Nobody talk story with him. Nobody go bother him."

"So what you goin' do? Dah buggah dead already."

"What . . . you no believe in dah spirits?"

"Eh, no fut around."

"No. I asking you one simple question. You believe in dah kine Hawaiian spirits or what?"

"Yeah, I believe in dat kine," Fritzhugh said, looking warily across his sweet potato field, then back to Mineda's furrowed face. "But so what? Why . . . you think he wen curse dah valley or what?"

Mineda looked at this feet. He was silent for a while. "Crazy," he said finally. "All of dis. And how we going sell our produce to dah markets?"

A white car with the state emblem on the doors came by the store one day. Correa sat up and stared into the car curiously. Then he nodded his head. "You see, Bobby, you see," he said. "What I tol' you. Dah gov'ment goin' come down heah and try get somet'ing from us. I tol' you all along, dis hauna was from dah gov'ment. What I tol' you?"

Ignacio leaned forward, squinting his eyes to read the emblem. "Department of Agriculture," he muttered. He slouched back into his seat.

"What I tol' you, eh, Bobby? Look, dah Japanee going come out and he goin' try smooth talk us. You watch."

"Fritzhugh wen call dem fo' come down and try figure out whas wrong with dah dirt."

"Look dah buggah, nice clean cah, air conditionah and everyt'ing," Correa said sardonically, pretending he had not heard what his friend had said.

The man got out of the car and went up to the two men.

"Yes, sir," Correa said officiously. "What can I do fo' you today?"

The man crimped his nose at the fetid air. "You know where I can find Earl Fritzhugh?"

"Yeah-yeah. He live up dah valley. Whas dis fo'?" Correa asked.

"He called me about some problems you farmers having over here. Something about the soil."

"Not dah soil," Correa said. "Dah air. You cannot smell how hauna dah air is?"

The man nodded his head. "Yes . . . yes, the air kind of stink. Smell like rotten fish."

"Smell like somebody wen unload one big pile shit in dah middle of dah valley."

The man from the state grinned.

"So why you come," Correa asked pointedly, "and not one guy from dah Department of Air?"

The man from the state looked at Correa with dying interest. "You can tell me where Earl Fritzhugh lives?" he asked Ignacio.

"Yeah, brah," Ignacio said, pointing up the valley road. "You go up this road, maybe one mile into the valley. You goin' pass one big grove bamboo on the right side. The farm right after that going be the Fritzhugh farm. No can miss 'em."

The man thanked him, then got back into the car and left.

"You better call up Fritzhugh and tell him dah Japanee comin' up question him," Correa said.

Ignacio waved the flies away from his face, then spat into the grass.

There was nothing wrong with the soil, the state worker told them a few days after he had come up and taken samples to the downtown laboratory. Nothing was wrong. The farmers left that meeting with remorse. Then what was wrong with the crops?

A day later heavy rains came, and for three days the whole valley was inundated with torrents and flash floods. The residents welcomed the storm, for they believed that the rains would wash the soil of the inscrutable poison and cleanse the air of the bad smell. But came the fourth day and a bright sun and when the residents smelled the air again, the odor was still there, now more pronounced than ever and denser. It was as if the storm had nurtured the smell like water nourishes plants.

"You did anyt'ing to old Jacob?" people were now asking each other. And the answer was always, "No . . . but did you?" And when the informal polling was completed, it was determined that everybody in the valley had left old Jacob alone. But they all cast accusing looks at one another, as if everyone else but themselves were responsible for the curse that old Jacob seemed to have thrown over the once peaceful and productive valley.

One morning a haole salesman came to the doorsteps of one of the houses.

"Heard you folks here were having problems with fires," he said in a jovial voice, a Mid-Western accent.

"No," Tats Sugimura's wife said sourly. "Not fires. The smell. You cannot smell dah stink smell?"

The haole laughed. "Well, you know what they say," he said.

"No, what dey say?" Harriet said.

"They say that if you can't see it, then you can surely smell it." He laughed again. Harriet was about to ask who had said that when the salesman segued quickly into a sales pitch about a new fire prevention system his company was now offering in the area. And, for a limited time, he concluded, they would install the entire system without charge.

"We not interested," Harriet Sugimura said. "Go away. Go talk to somebody else."

"But you don't understand," the salesman said. "Along with this fire prevention system comes our new, revolutionary, home-odors maintenance system. And for a limited time, we will give it to you free if you purchase our fire prevention system. Here . . . smell this."

The salesman took out a small aerosol can and sprayed it inside the Sugimuras' house from the front door. Instantly, the spray cleared the air of the ugly smell that Harriet had almost gotten used to and the whole living room smelled fresh like roses.

"Your system can do this?" she gasped with delight.

"Yes, and more. Why, because our system is computer-controlled, you don't have to lift a finger. Everything will be done automatically."

Harriet's face beamed with promise. It had been so long since she smelled the scent of flowers. "So how much is it?"

"Retail, it sells for eight-hundred and fifty dollars. But for this limited offer, we will sell it to you for two-hundred and fifty dollars."

"Two-hundred-fifty!"

"Well, if you know of a friend or neighbor or family who would want this system too, I can give it to you for two-twenty-five."

"Hmm. Wait, let me call my neighbor."

Soon, the entire valley was buzzing on the telephone lines talking about that new machine that would wipe out the bad smell in the homes. If the valley was going to stay bad smelling, that didn't mean the homes had to have that smell, too. So almost every other household bought one of those systems, and the salesman, being a nice guy, even reduced the price by another twenty-five dollars, prepayment, stating emphatically that the company was now making only a twenty-dollar profit from each unit sold. The residents waited impatiently for that big brown truck that the haole promised would bring the fire-prevention-home-odor-maintenance system, and they waited past the promised three days delivery period, but the truck never came.

The smell worsened to the point that every other person in the valley was getting a constant headache.

"Somet'ing has to be done about the smell," Ignacio said. "If we cannot do anyt'ing about it, den we gotta take dis to the state."

"Nah, how you can do dat?" Correa said. "Dah state already wen say dey cannot do not'ing about it."

"But something gotta be done," Ignacio said.

"Something gotta be done," Harriet Sugimura said to her husband, sheepishly, a few days after her husband, for the first time in seven years, had lost his temper when she told him how she had spent their tax refunds.

"If this smell continue on, I'm getting the hell out of this valley," Pat Fritzhugh said to her husband.

"Me, too," Fritzhugh replied.

"You know what the problem is?" Leimomi Vargas said to her neighbor, Elizabeth Kauhale. "The problem is nobody honest wit' everybody else. I betchu somebody wen get the old man real angry. Really angry. And das why he wen curse the valley wit' dis stink fut smell before he ma-ke."

"I think you right, Lei," Elizabeth said sadly. "We gotta be honest wit' each other. Das dah only way."

"Then maybe the old man going take back the curse," Lei said.

"Maybe we should go get one kahuna bless dah friggin', stinkin' place," Elizabeth said.

"You nevah know the old man was one kahuna?"

"I know, but he dead."

"Still yet."

"But I t'ink you right. We gotta get to the bottom of this. Find all the persons responsible for him cursing the valley. Then make them offer somet'ing to the old man's spirit. Or somet'ing like that. Whachu t'ink?"

So from that conversation, the two women went door to door, struggling with the others to be honest. For starts, Lei told about the time when she was a small girl and she went up to the old man's place and stole an egg from one of his hens. And Elizabeth said one time she saw her brother throw a rock at the old man as he was climbing the road to his hermitage, and because her brother was now living on the Big Island, she would take responsibility for his wrong action. Then, slowly, the others began to unfold their stories of wrongdoings against the old man, even Joseph Correa, who admitted that he wronged old Jacob when they were young men growing up in the valley and wooing the same girl and he had told her parents that Jacob didn't have a prick and that he was a mahu. About the only person who hadn't sinned against Jacob was Tats Sugimura, who lived the next lot down from Jacob's. In fact, he had been kind to Jacob, giving him sweet potatoes and letting him use his water at the far end of the field (where Tats had found the fish scales and bones, though Tats couldn't figure out that that was where Jacob used to clean his fish).

So they organized representatives from each household of the valley to go up the road and pay their homage to Jacob's vindictive soul. They went to his place one late Saturday afternoon when the sun was beginning to set behind the mountains, parking their cars and trucks at the end of the dirt road where the road turned into a trail that led into Jacob's forbidden plot of land. They brought taro, sweet potatoes, corn, watermelons, yams, several 'awa roots, a dozen cans of meat, a basket of freshly laid eggs, a tub of fish and another tub of crawling crabs, loads of ti leaves, bunches of green bananas, and a fifth of good bourbon so that Jacob could wash all of the offerings down. They silently climbed the narrow path that the valley road turned into, winding up through dense brush and trees towards old Jacob's place. Lei was the only one in the contingent who had been up to Jacob's place before, but that was years and years ago and all she had seen were the dilapidated chicken coops, and everyone's senses were suspended in fear, not knowing what they might expect or see at the end of the trail.

Finally, they reached a flat clearing where they saw a sweeping view of the precipitous mountain range. They searched anxiously for his house until finally Elizabeth Kauhale found it hanging a few feet above the ground, with vines attaching it to a giant kukui tree. It was made out of scrap wood and looked like a big crate with a small opening on the side where a tattered rope ladder hung down. The box house began to swing and there was heard hollow laughter coming from within. The entourage retreated a few steps, their faces blanched with the expectation that Jacob's ghost might leap out after them. The laughing stopped, and they quickly dropped their offerings in an untidy heap under Jacob's pendular house, not daring to glance up the rope ladder. Then, hurriedly, they filed down the trail.

When they reached the bottom, they stopped, looked back, and made sure everyone who had gone up was back down. After they finished counting heads, they ambled off to their cars, murmuring among themselves how they hoped things would come out all right and the smell would leave the valley. Then, suddenly, there came loud, crackling laughter from deep in the valley that made the plants and trees shake. Everyone crammed into whosesoever's car was nearest. They raced down the road and did not stop until, breathless and terrified and worried for their very lives, they were down at the old abandoned store, and here they sat speechless until Leimomi Vargas shouted at the top of her lungs, "I think dis is all silly—us guys getting our pants scared off our 'okoles!"

Embarrassed smiles came upon everyone's face and there was heard some nervous laughter. Someone suggested that they celebrate in the memory of old Jacob, and, without further ado, they voted unanimously to go back to their homes and get what they had to eat and bring it all back down to the abandoned store where they would party for the rest of the night. So the people who were in the wrong cars got out and into the cars they had originally gone up the road with, and they all went back home and took boxes of chicken or beef or squid or whatever they had out of the freezers and thawed them under warm running water; the Ignacios brought down a pig Bobby had slaughtered that morning; the Fritzhughs brought a big barrel of fish their oldest son had caught that day; and Tats Sugimura trucked down a load of his miniature, mutant sweet potatoes; and the others went into backyards and lopped off hands of bananas and picked ears of corn and mangoes and carried off watermelons from the fields; and they brought all that food and all the beer and whiskey they had in their homes down to the store. Earl Fritzhugh and his two sons chopped up a large kiawe tree and made a roaring fire in the empty lot next to the store, and everyone pitched in and cooked the copious amounts of food in that sweet-smelling, charcoal inferno. Bobby Ignacio and friends—Earl Fritzhugh, Fritzhugh's youngest son, Sonny Pico's two boys and his daughter, Tats Sugimura's brother, and Joseph Correa—brought down their ukes and guitars and a washtub bass and provided the entertainment that lasted exactly three nights and two days. And when the festivities finally ended—the smoke from the kiawe fire was still smoldering strongly—everyone at the old store began hugging each other and then meandered off to their homes.

But before they fell into deep sleep, Earl Fritzhugh and his wife made love for the first time since the smell began putrefying the air of the valley. And so did Tats and Harriet Sugimura. And there were at least a dozen or so illegitimate liaisons committed that festive time—for one, Elizabeth Kauhale saw her teenage son go in the bush with Bobby Ignacio's willowy daughter—which was probably the reason why weeks ahead there would be more festivities when three of those liaisons would be legitimized, and why months later, on the same day, there would be added three new members to the community.

And before he slept, old Joseph Correa dragged his feet to the old cemetery next to the clapboard Catholic church, and there he laid a bunch of wild orchids on the grave of his beloved wife, Martha, and he sat down on the soft, wet ground, though it was a struggle for his brittle old legs to do so, and he sang that song that was a favorite of his wife—"Pua Lilia"—because his wife's middle name was Lilia, and he had often sung that song to her when she was alive and he had sung that song to her when she was dying. And after that song, he gazed up the valley and apologized once again to his former friend, Jacob Hookano, for saying those damaging things about him in the past. "But she was worth fighting for," he said with a choke in his voice. "And you can see, my friend," he added with a touch of jealousy, "that you with her right now."

When the people of the valley finally woke up the next morning, or the next afternoon—or whenever—the first thing they noticed was the smell. The fresh clean smell of the ocean. It was the smell of salt, and the warm winds that carried it over the valley swept up to the highest ridges of the mountains, and there the warm air married with the cold dampness and thick clouds formed, and soon, with the shift in the trades, rain began to fall over the silent, peaceful valley.

CHANG-RAE LEE

Chang-rae Lee was born in Seoul in 1965 and emigrated in 1968. He grew up in Westchester County, New York, and attended Phillips Exeter Academy before majoring in English at Yale University. He has an M. F. A. from the University of Oregon, where he also taught for several years. Lee is the most widely read of contemporary Korean American writers; his first novel, *Native Speaker* (1995), served as the start of a new wave of Korean American visibility in the mainstream after the long, nearly silent period following Richard Kim's *The Innocent.*

Like many other ethnic writers Lee finds himself in an ironic position—that of embodying his ethnicity even while willfully asserting himself as a writer uninterested in being read as "an ethnic writer." The situation is amplified for Lee because his best-known work deals explicitly with the complex issue of identity seen from both the inner world of the character and the outward context of the world he inhabits. For the character Henry Park in *Native Speaker,* the central metaphor of linguistic competence resonates like a double-edged blade: the mission (for which he is chosen for his ability to pass as an authentic Korean American) causes him to examine his own identity even while he is gathering damning evidence designed to derail the political campaign of a Korean American city councilman. As the campaign unravels, and the candidate leaves in failure to return to Korea, Henry himself is left in a poignant state short of catharsis as "the language monster," a helper in his Caucasian wife's remedial language class.

Native Speaker, though structured as a low-key political thriller, is actually more of a psychological detective story about the unresolvable issues of assimilated identity; the narrative alternates between what reads like a personal memoir (evoked by the tragic loss of Henry's father and his son) and a purposely vague espionage tale that permits the conjunction of two outwardly incompatible forms. Our excerpt is an example of the former narrative, Henry's reminiscence about his father.

When asked about his response to the expectations of his Asian American readers, Lee once said, "My loyalty is to my characters," reminding the interviewer that "a good story is a journey of the mind, not a record of fact." And yet, despite the involuntary nature of his role as a representative of Korean or Asian Americanness, in the highly self-conscious act of applying linguistic competence as a metaphor, he brings up the issue of authenticity with its range of ambivalence and both inner and outer contradiction—not only for his character, Henry, but implicitly for himself as the author, whose mind has created that character. In *Native Speaker,* Lee's stylistic touches serve to amplify those very themes of language and identity.

Native Speaker won the PEN/Hemingway Award for First Fiction, the American Book Award, and the Barnes & Noble Discover Great New Writers Award; it was also listed among *Time* Magazine's Best Books of 1995. His second novel, *A Gesture Life* (1999), was also widely praised. Lee is currently director of the creative writing program at Hunter College in New York City.

from *Native Speaker*

My father would not have believed in the possibility of sub-rosa vocations. He would have scoffed at the notion. He knew nothing of the mystical and neurotic. It wasn't part of his makeup. He would have thought Hoagland was typically American, crazy, self-indulgent, too rich in time and money. For him, the world— and by that I must mean this very land, his chosen nation—oper- ated on a determined set of procedures, certain rules of engage- ment. These were the inalienable rights of the immigrant.

I was to inherit them, the legacy unfurling before me this way: you worked from before sunrise to the dead of night. You were never unkind in your dealings, but then you were not generous. Your family was your life, though you rarely saw them. You kept close handsome sums of cash in small denominations. You were steadily cornering the market in self-pride. You drove a Chevy and then a Caddy and then a Benz. You never missed a mortgage payment or a day of church. You prayed furiously until you wept. You considered the only unseen forces to be those of capitalism and the love of Jesus Christ.

My low master. He died a year and a half after Mitt did. Mas- sive global stroke. It was the third one that finally killed him. Lelia and I were going up on the weekends to help—it was practically the only thing we were doing together. We had retained a nurse to be there during the week.

He died during the night. In the morning I went to wake him and his jaw was locked open, his teeth bared, cursing the end to its face. He was still gripping the knob of the brass bedpost, which he had bent at the joint all the way down to four o'clock. He was going to jerk the whole house over his head. Gritty mule. I thought he was never going to die. Even after the first stroke, when he had trouble walking and urinating and brushing his teeth, I would see him as a kind of aging soldier of this life, a squat, stocky-torsoed warrior, bitter, never self-pitying, fearful, stubborn, world-fucking heroic.

He hated when I helped him, especially in the bathroom. I remember how we used to shower together when I was young, how he would scrub my head so hard I thought he wanted my scalp, how he would rub his wide thumb against the skin of my forearms until the dirt would magically appear in tiny black rolls, how he would growl and hoot beneath the streaming water, how the dark hair between his legs would get soapy and white and make his genitals look like a soiled and drunken Santa Claus.

Now, when he needed cleaning after the strokes, he would let Lelia bathe him, let her shampoo the coarse hair of his dense unmagical head, wash his blue prick, but only if I were around. He said (my jaundiced translation of his Korean) that he didn't want me becoming *an anxious boy,* as if he knew all of my panic buttons, that craphound, inveterate sucker-puncher, that damned machine.

The second stroke, just a week before the last one, took away his ability to move or speak. He sat up in bed with those worn black eyes and had to listen to me talk. I don't think he ever heard so much from my mouth. I talked straight through the night, and he silently took my confessions, maledictions, as though he were some font of blessing at which I might leave a final belated tithe. I spoke at him, this propped-up father figure, half-intending an

emotional torture. I ticked through the whole long register of my
disaffections, hit all the ready categories. In truth, Lelia's own
eventual list was probably just karmic justice for what I made
him endure those final nights, which was my berating him for
the way he had conducted his life with my mother, and then his
housekeeper, and his businesses and beliefs, to speak once and for
all the less than holy versions of who he was.

I thought he would be an easy mark, being stiff, paralyzed, but
of course the agony was mine. He was unmovable. I thought, too,
that he was mocking me with his mouth, which lay slack, agape.
Nothing I said seemed to penetrate him. But then what was my
speech? He had raised me in a foreign land, put me through college, witnessed my marriage for my long-buried mother, even left
me enough money that I could do the same for my children without the expense of his kind of struggle; his duties, uncomplex,
were by all accounts complete. And the single-minded determi-
nation that had propelled him through twenty-five years of green-
grocering in a famous ghetto of America would serve him a few
last days, and through any of my meager execrations.

I thought his life was all about money. He drew much energy and
pride from his ability to make it almost at will. He was some kind
of human annuity. He had no real cleverness or secrets for good
business; he simply refused to fail, leaving absolutely nothing to
luck or chance or someone else. Of course, in his personal lore he
would have said that he started with $200 in his pocket and a wife
and baby and just a few words of English. Knowing what every
native loves to hear, he would have offered the classic immigrant
story, casting himself as the heroic newcomer, self-sufficient, re-
sourceful.

The truth, though, is that my father got his first infusion of
capital from a *ggeh,* a Korean "money club" in which members
contributed to a pool that was given out on a rotating basis. Each
week you gave the specified amount; and then one week in the
cycle, all the money was yours.

His first *ggeh* was formed from a couple dozen storekeepers who knew each other through a fledgling Korean-American business association. In those early days he would take me to their meetings down in the city, a third-floor office in midtown, 32nd Street between Fifth and Broadway, where the first few Korean businesses opened in Manhattan in the mid 1960s. On the block then were just one grocery, two small restaurants, a custom tailor, and a bar. At the meetings the men would be smoking, talking loudly, almost shouting their opinions. There were arguments but only a few, mostly it was just all the hope and excitement. I remember my father as the funny one, he'd make them all laugh with an old Korean joke or his impressions of Americans who came into his store, doing their stiff nasal tone, their petty annoyances and complaints.

In the summers we'd all get together, these men and their families, drive up to Westchester to some park in Mount Kisco or Rye. In the high heat the men would set up cones and play a match of soccer, and even then I couldn't believe how hard they tried and how competitive they were, my father especially, who wasn't so skilled as ferocious, especially on defense. He'd tackle his good friend Mr. Oh so hard that I thought a fight might start, but then Mr. Oh was gentle, and quick on his feet, and he'd pull up my father and just keep working to the goal.

Sometimes they would group up and play a team of Hispanic men who were also picnicking with their families. Once, they even played some black men, though my father pointed out to us in the car home that they were *African* blacks. Somehow there were rarely white people in the park, never groups of their families, just young couples, if anything. After some iced barley tea and a quick snack my father and his friends would set up a volleyball net and start all over again. The mothers and us younger ones would sit and watch, the older kids playing their own games, and when the athletics were done the mothers would set up the food and grill the ribs and the meat, and we'd eat and run and play until dark. And only when my father dumped the water from the cooler was it the final sign that we would go home.

I know over the years my father and his friends got together less and less. Certainly, after my mother died, he didn't seem to want to go to the gatherings anymore. But it wasn't just him. They all got busier and wealthier and lived farther and farther apart. Like us, their families moved to big houses with big yards to tend on weekends, they owned fancy cars that needed washing and waxing. They joined their own neighborhood pool and tennis clubs and were making drinking friends with Americans. Some of them, too, were already dead, like Mr. Oh, who had a heart attack after being held up at his store in Hell's Kitchen. And in the end my father no longer belonged to any *ggeh,* he complained about all the disgraceful troubles that were now cropping up, people not paying on time or leaving too soon after their turn getting the money. In America, he said, it's even hard to stay Korean.

I wonder if my father, if given the chance, would have wished to go back to the time before he made all that money, when he had just one store and we rented a tiny apartment in Queens. He worked hard and had worries but he had a joy then that he never seemed to regain once the money started coming in. He might turn on the radio and dance cheek to cheek with my mother. He worked on his car himself, a used green Impala with carburetor trouble. They had lots of Korean friends that they met at church and then even in the street, and when they talked in public there was a shared sense of how lucky they were, to be in America but still have countrymen near.

I know he never felt fully comfortable in his fine house in Ardsley. Though he was sometimes forward and forceful with some of his neighbors, he mostly operated as if the town were just barely tolerating our presence. The only time he'd come out in public was because of me. He would steal late and unnoticed into the gym where I was playing kiddie basketball and stand by the far side of the bleachers with a rolled-up newspaper in his hand, tapping it nervously against his thigh as he watched the action, craning to see me shoot the ball but never shouting or urging like the other fathers and mothers did.

My mother, too, was even worse, and she would gladly ruin a birthday cake rather than bearing the tiniest of shames in asking her next-door neighbor and friend for the needed egg she'd run out of, the child's pinch of baking powder.

I remember thinking of her, *What's she afraid of,* what could be so bad that we had to be that careful of what people thought of us, as if we ought to mince delicately about in pained feet through our immaculate neighborhood, we silent partners of the bordering WASPs and Jews, never rubbing them except with a smile, as if everything with us were always all right, in our great sham of propriety, as if nothing could touch us or wreak anger or sadness upon us. That we believed in anything American, in impressing Americans, in making money, polishing apples in the dead of night, perfectly pressed pants, perfect credit, being perfect, shooting black people, watching our stores and offices burn down to the ground.

Then, inevitably, if I asked hard questions of myself, of the one who should know, what might I come up with?

What belief did I ever hold in my father, whose daily life I so often ridiculed and looked upon with such abject shame? The summer before I started high school he made me go with him to one of the new stores on Sunday afternoons to help restock the shelves and the bins. I hated going. My friends—suddenly including some girls—were always playing tennis or going to the pool club then. I never gave the reason why I always declined, and they eventually stopped asking. Later I found out from one of them, my first girlfriend, that they simply thought I was religious. When I was working for him I wore a white apron over my slacks and dress shirt and tie. The store was on Madison Avenue in the Eighties and my father made all the employees dress up for the blue-haired matrons, and the fancy dogs, and the sensible young mothers pushing antique velvet-draped prams, and their most quiet of infants, and the banker fathers brooding about annoyed and aloof and humorless.

My father, thinking that it might be good for business, urged me to show them how well I spoke English, to make a display of it, to casually recite "some Shakespeare words."

I, his princely Hal. Instead, and only in part to spite him, I grunted my best Korean to the other men. I saw that if I just kept speaking the language of our work the customers didn't seem to see me. I wasn't there. They didn't look at me. I was a comely shadow who didn't threaten them. I could even catch a rich old woman whose tight strand of pearls pinched in the sags of her neck whispering to her friend right behind me, "Oriental Jews."

I never retaliated the way I felt I could or said anything smart, like, "Does madam need help?" I kept on stacking the hothouse tomatoes and Bosc pears. That same woman came in the store every day; once, I saw her take a small bite of an apple and then put it back with its copper-mouthed wound facing down. I started over to her not knowing what I might say when my father intercepted me and said smiling in Korean, as if he were complimenting me, "She's a steady customer." He nudged me back to my station. I had to wait until she left to replace the ruined apple with a fresh one.

Mostly, though, I threw all my frustration into building those perfect, truncated pyramids of fruit. The other two workers seemed to have even more bottled up inside them, their worries of money and family. They marched through the work of the store as if they wanted to deplete themselves of every last bit of energy. Every means and source of struggle. They peeled and sorted and bunched and sprayed and cleaned and stacked and shelved and swept; my father put them to anything for which they didn't have to speak. They both had college degrees and knew no one in the country and spoke little English. The men, whom I knew as Mr. Yoon and Mr. Kim, were both recent immigrants in their thirties with wives and young children. They worked twelve-hour days

six days a week for $200 cash and meals and all the fruit and vege-
tables we couldn't or wouldn't sell; it was the typical arrange-
ment. My father like all successful immigrants before him gently
and not so gently exploited his own.

"This is way I learn business, this is way they learn business."

And although I knew he gave them a $100 bonus every now
and then I never let on that I felt he was anything but cruel to his
workers. I still imagine Mr. Kim's and Mr. Yoon's children, lonely
for their fathers, gratefully eating whatever was brought home
to them, our overripe and almost rotten mangoes, our papayas,
kiwis, pineapples, these exotic tastes of their wondrous new country, this joyful fruit now too soft and too sweet for those who knew
better, us near natives, us earlier Americans.

For some reason unclear to me I made endless fun of the prices
of my father's goods, how everything ended in .95 or .98 or .99.

"Look at all the pennies you need!" I'd cry when the store was
empty, holding up the rolls beneath the cash register. "It's so
ridiculous."

He'd cry back, "What you know? It's good for selling!"

"Who told you that?"

He was wiping down the glass fronts of the refrigerators of
soda and beer and milk. "Nobody told me that. I know automatic.
Like everybody else."

"So then why is this jar of artichoke hearts three ninety-eight
instead of three ninety-nine?"

"You don't know?" he said, feigning graveness.

"No, Dad, tell me."

"Stupid boy," he answered, clutching at his chest. His over-
worked merchant heart. "It's feeling."

I remember when my father would come home from his vegetable stores late at night, and my mother would say the same three
things to him as she fixed his meal of steamed barley rice and beef
flank soup: *Spouse,* she would say, *you must be hungry. You come home
so late. I hope we made enough money today.*

She never asked about the stores themselves, about what vege-

tables were selling, how the employees were working out, nothing ever about the painstaking, plodding nature of the work. I
thought it was because she simply didn't care to know the partic-
ulars, but when I began to ask him one night about the business
(I must have been six or seven), my mother immediately called
me back into the bedroom and closed the door.

"Why are you asking him about the stores?" she interrogated
me in Korean, her tongue plaintive, edgy, as though she were in
some pain.

"I was just asking," I said.

"Don't ask him. He's very tired. He doesn't like talking about
it."

"Why not?" I said, this time louder.

"Shh!" she said, grabbing my wrists. "Don't shame him! Your
father is very proud. You don't know this, but he graduated from
the best college in Korea, the very top, and he doesn't need to talk
about selling fruits and vegetables. It's below him. He only does
it for you, Byong-ho, he does everything for you. Now go and
keep him company."

I walked back to the living room and found my father asleep on
the sofa, his round mouth pursed and tightly shut, his breath fil-
tering softly through his nose. A single fly, its armored back an
oily, metallic green, was dancing a circle on his chin. What he'd
brought home from work.

Once, he came home with deep bruises about his face, his nose
and mouth bloody, his rough workshirt torn at the shoulder. He
smelled rancid as usual from working with vegetables, but more
so that night, as if he'd fallen into the compost heap. He came in
and went straight up to the bedroom and shut and locked the
door. My mother ran to it, pounding on the wood and sobbing for
him to let her in so she could help him. He wouldn't answer. She
kept hitting the door, asking him what had happened, almost
kissing the panels, the side jamb. I was too frightened to go to
her. After a while she tired and crumpled there and wept until he
finally turned the lock and let her in. I went to my room where I

could hear him talk through the wall. His voice was quiet and steady. Some black men had robbed the store and taken him to the basement and bound him and beaten him up. They took turns whipping him with the magazine of a pistol. They would have probably shot him in the head right there but his partners came for the night shift and the robbers fled.

I would learn in subsequent years that he had been trained as an industrial engineer, and had actually completed a master's degree. I never learned the exact reason he chose to come to America. He once mentioned something about the "big network" in Korean business, how someone from the rural regions of the country could only get so far in Seoul. Then, too, did I wonder whether he'd assumed he could be an American engineer who spoke little English, but of course he didn't.

My father liked to think I was a civil servant. Sometimes he asked Lelia what a municipal employee did on trips to Providence or Ann Arbor or Richmond. Size comparisons, Lelia might joke, but then she always referred him directly to me. But he never approached me, he never asked me point-blank what I did, he'd just inquire if I were earning enough for my family and then silently nod. He couldn't care for the importance of *career*. That notion was too costly for a man like him.

He genuinely liked Lelia. This surprised me. He was nice to her. When we met him at one of his stores he always had a sundry basket of treats for her, trifles from his shelves, bars of dark chocolate, exotic tropical fruits, tissue-wrapped biscotti. He would show her around every time as if it were the first, introduce her to the day manager and workers, most of whom were Korean, tell them proudly in English that she was his daughter. Whenever he could, he always tried to stand right next to her, and then marvel at how tall and straight she was, *like a fine young horse,* he'd say in Korean, admiringly. He'd hug her and ask me to take pictures. Laugh and kid with her generously.

He never said it, but I knew he liked the fact that Lelia was white. When I first told him that we were engaged I thought he would vehemently protest, again go over the scores of reasons why I should marry one of our own (as he had rambled on in my adolescence), but he only nodded and said he respected her and wished me luck. I think he had come to view our union logically, practically, and perhaps he thought he saw through my intentions, the assumption being that Lelia and her family would help me make my way in the land.

"Maybe you not so dumb after all," he said to me after the wedding ceremony.

Lelia, an old-man lover if there was one, always said he was sweet.

Sweet.

"He's just a more brutal version of you," she told me that last week we were taking care of him.

I didn't argue with her. My father was obviously not modern, in the psychological sense. He was still mostly unencumbered by those needling questions of existence and self-consciousness. Irony was always lost on him. He was the definition of a thick skin. For most of my youth I wasn't sure that he had the capacity to love. He showed great respect to my mother to the day she died—I was ten—and practiced for her the deepest sense of duty and honor, but I never witnessed from him a devotion I could call love. He never kissed her hand or bent down before her. He never said the word, in any language. Maybe none of this matters. But then I don't think he ever wept for her, either, even at the last moment of her life. He came out of the hospital room from which he had barred me and said that she had passed and I should go in and look at her one last time. I don't now remember what I saw in her room, maybe I never actually looked at her, though I can still see so clearly the image of my father standing there in the hall when I came back out, his hands clasped at his groin in a military pose, his neck taut and thick, working, trying hard to swallow the nothing balling up in his throat.

His life didn't seem to change. He seemed instantly recovered.

The only noticeable thing was that he would come home much earlier than usual, maybe four in the afternoon instead of the usual eight or nine. He said he didn't want me coming home from school to an empty house, though he didn't actually spend any more time with me. He just went down to his workshop in the basement or to the garage to work on his car. For dinner we went either to a Chinese place or the Indian one in the next town, and sometimes he drove to the city so we could eat Korean. He settled us into a routine this way, a schedule. I thought all he wanted was to have nothing unusual sully his days, that what he disliked or feared most was uncertainty.

I wondered, too, whether he was suffering inside, whether he sometimes cried, as I did, for reasons unknown. I remember how I sat with him in those restaurants, both of us eating without savor, unjoyous, and my wanting to show him that I could be as steely as he, my chin as rigid and unquivering as any of his displays, that I would tolerate no mysteries either, no shadowy wounds or scars of the heart.

from *The Fruit 'N Food*

LEONARD CHANG

The days passed at the store, and Tom seemed to feel worse. Now, while going over those events, Tom understands more, that the lack of sleep and the stress of the grocery, of June, were converging on him, pushing him. All he knew at that time, though, was that something was wrong. He remembers that one day when he lost control, when everything was so confused and blurred. It really began that afternoon while he sat outside the store watching the fruit, and he heard a slight buzzing in his ear, and his head pounded from a caffeine headache. He was drinking too much coffee since he had barely slept at all the night before, when he had simply watched TV the entire night, lying on his mattress, his head turned towards the glowing screen, vaguely following but not really watching reruns, sitcoms, late night talk shows, and an odd yoga show at five in the morning. He had been suspended in an agonizing state of exhaustion without relief, sleepiness without sleep, and after the sun had begun rising and shining into his room, he had blinked repeatedly, unbelieving, thinking, No, not already, it couldn't be. Ever since that shoplifting incident a few days ago, he had been sleeping less and less, until last night when he had had only a few minutes, it seemed, of rest.

The early 1990s were a particularly harrowing time for Korean American urban communities around the country, especially in the aftermath of the 1992 L. A. Riots, in which Korean businesses composed more than half of the forty-five hundred that were damaged or destroyed. It is tempting to draw a straight line of cause and effect between incidents such as shopkeeper Soon Ja Du's fatal shooting of fourteen-year-old Latasha Harlins in March 1991 and the targeting of Korean American stores in poor Black neighborhoods for actions ranging from picketing and boycotts to firebombing. But the precarious existence of small-scale Korean American merchants in ghettos around the nation and the disastrous consequences of racial stereotyping have been a vexing concern among the directly involved Black and Korean communities since the 1970s. As Leonard Chang's first novel, *The Fruit 'N Food* (1996), implies, the very framing of problems as a Black-Korean conflict is to a large extent a misconception encouraged by inflammatory images in the mass media—for example, rude vigilante Koreans versus lazy, amoral African Americans—that divert attention away from broader problems in American society.

Against this background of racism and media-generated mystifications, Leonard Chang dared to assert a calm, minutely psychologized description of the daily toil, stress, and aspirations of Korean American greengrocers working almost around the clock in a hostile social setting. The Fruit 'N Food is the name of a small store in Queens, New York, operated by Mr. and Mrs. Rhee, where the novel's main character, Thomas Pak, drifts into the latest in a string of unskilled retail jobs, vaguely aware of its "inexplicable link to his past." He also halfheartedly enters into a sexual relationship with the Rhees' daughter June—a teenager who departs from the role of model student and filial daughter. One of Tom's responsibilities at the store, which has been burglarized several times in the past, is to look out for shoplifters. Several incidents, one involving a young white thief's beating of Mrs. Rhee, and Tom's physical and mental exhaustion from the unrelenting pressure of running the store, lead to his threatening a pair of Black customers with a pistol, in the excerpts that follows. The next day a Black nationalist picket line forms, and once the protest receives crucial magnification in the mass media, it escalates into a neighborhood-wide eruption of violence, looting, and arson in which Tom, coming to the defense of an elderly Black man who is a friend of the Rhees, is shot and blinded during a fight with Asian gang members.

To a great extent, the Fruit 'N Food and what befalls it are modeled on widely reported situations that developed at Korean-run stores in cities like Brooklyn and L. A. a few years before the novel was written. A crucial difference is that, unlike most Korean store workers, Thomas Pak does not identify in the least with Korean culture or community; he is an alienated loner only dimly aware of the pattern of his life. Ethnicity and its politicized tests by fire are what Pak tiredly stumbles through to arrive at a state of both spiritual and physical blindness, which, in turn, facilitates an inward collapse away from the annoying entanglements of history. At the same time, *The Fruit 'N Food* presents an early form of a style more fully developed in Leonard Chang's subsequent novel *Dispatches from the Cold,* a remarkably restrained yet richly accurate detailing of

mundane labor—and the futile ways in which working-class ind als try to elude or stave off their occupations' numbing of the

Leonard Chang was born in New York City, grew up in M Long Island, and graduated in philosophy with honors from H University, after which he earned an M. F. A. in creative writing University of California at Irvine in 1994. In addition to *The F Food* and *Dispatches from the Cold* (1998), which won a *Sa cisco Bay Guardian* Goldie Award for Literature, he is the au *Over the Shoulder* (2001). Chang teaches in the graduate program of Antioch University in Los Angeles, while living r the year in the San Francisco Bay Area.

His throat felt scratchy from breathing through his mouth all day, and it seemed, in the late afternoon sun which was too warm, too bright, forcing him into the shade, it seemed to him that if he didn't get some sleep soon he'd have to see a doctor, get some medication, or *something* or he wouldn't make it another week. Or maybe he had slept last night but had dreamed he'd been awake, and now he wasn't sure what was real or imagined, nothing was what it appeared anymore. No, he hadn't been asleep. Otherwise he wouldn't have been a zombie today, not fully aware of anyone or anything around him, moving and working from rote and paying attention only to the clock on the wall, watching the second hand move slowly over the numbers, the minute hand inching along every time he turned away, and the hour hand dragging at a tortuous pace, 11, 12, 1, 2, 3, 4, 5. . . . Only a couple more hours to go, he thought. He could do this. He could make it.

His vision was playing tricks in the low sun. Objects wavered under his gaze—telephone poles, street signs, parked cars—and he had to blink a few times, violently, for everything to keep still. He shook his head again, the pain in his temples sharpening his focus, and he took a few deep breaths.

Yesterday he had kept talking to June about that kid who had tried to steal the beer. She came over again and he was so glad to see her, so glad to have some company that he tried to make her stay longer even though she had to return home. Why did the kid want a bottle of beer, Tom kept asking her. Was he an alcoholic? For fun? To sell for some small change? June kept saying, I don't know Tom. You really need to get some rest. Let me get you some warm milk or something. Tom thought about the look on the kid's face when Tom had told him about the police, the startled look of fear and anger, as if surprised that these gooks had the nerve to call the police. That little shit, Tom said to June. But what if he had had a gun or knife? Take it easy Tom, was all June had replied.

Who was that? A man walking towards him. A customer? A big Latino man, tight T-shirt, a beard growing in. Why was he looking at Tom like that? What the hell was he staring at. Oh, he was looking at the fruit prices. He approached the store, walking past Tom. Seemed okay. Calm down. No reason to get anxious. Just take it easy. So jittery. Close your eyes and relax. Cars driving by, swishing, the sounds of tires on the road, sounding like waves—

Running. Tom sat up quickly and saw two kids running down the street, their sneakers slapping the sidewalk, a bright yellow tennis ball passing back and forth between them. The blond-headed one had a stickball bat. The one with a Mets baseball cap was laughing. They continued up the street while Tom watched them weave around pedestrians, race across the street. Tom was sweating, his breathing shallow. A painful heaviness in his chest.

The sky was beginning to darken, so he turned on the outside lights, though he really didn't have to yet. Mrs. Rhee came out and said they can switch places if he wanted to. He wanted to.

A commotion down the street. Yelling, arguing. The owner of the laundromat was throwing someone out of his store. The customer, a young man, cursed at him and said he was going to sue. The laundromat owner laughed and said something harsh. They separated, the owner still laughing. Tom watched the young man continue to curse as he walked across the street.

Maybe the whole city's uneasy, Tom thought as he walked inside. Maybe Mr. Harris had been right and everyone felt tense, unhappy, on edge, and maybe like that man on the corner of Amber and Banks had said a while ago on his soapbox, holding the New Testament in one hand and a bullhorn in the other, "Judgement is coming. The end is coming. We must repent."

Tom looked at the clock and saw that he still had two hours left, at least, so he poured himself a cup of coffee, and tried to relax since the store was relatively empty except for a customer looking at the hair and skin goods—a middle-aged man with a goatee and wire glasses putting a bottle of shampoo in his basket—and Tom added five spoonfuls of sugar because he was sick of the taste of coffee but he needed the caffeine otherwise he might not make it until eight. He better take it easy since rush hour was any minute now. The man walked to the counter so Tom put the coffee down and rang the man up who asked how he was, and Tom said he was fine but there was a slight waver in his voice which made the man cock his head but he didn't say anything, so Tom remained quiet. The man took his change and his bag and when Tom tried to get the receipt he found that the register had not printed it, or maybe it had but it was jammed, but the man nodded to Tom and left. He was balding in back. He didn't want a receipt?

Tom tried ringing up zero sales to get the receipt working but nothing came out except a choked whirring sound and he called Mrs. Rhee who saw him examining the register and she said, "It happen before. Mr. Rhee can fix. Just write out if they want receipt."

He replied that it was fine and she looked at him strangely but then returned outside, and Tom began writing out blank receipts on the white pad of paper to prepare for anyone who wanted one by printing carefully the store name on top, the date, the cost of item, and his signature on bottom. He became creative and used different colored pens, even mixing colors in the name of the store so that "Fruit" was one color and "Food" was another. His stomach churned with sour coffee.

Then a few customers came in and he rang them up making sure they got a receipt if they wanted one. He said he was sorry but the register wasn't working correctly, should he give them a hand-written receipt? Were they sure they did not want a receipt? Okay, that was fine, but if they decided they needed one they shouldn't hesitate to ask. Yes, he was fine, why did they ask?

While putting away the cash he wondered if he'd see June again this week, since summer school was taking up her time. June. He wasn't sure if he liked her or if he was just so lonely that he liked having her around, but one thing was certain: the Rhees couldn't know that their daughter was spending time with him, otherwise he could lose this job. What was he doing? She was too young, anyway, but every time he thought about her and that night they came back from the bar and she'd taken him in her mouth he became excited and though they hadn't done anything since then, he could feel the strange attraction whenever he saw her. This was crazy. Maybe he should just start stashing away money and try to get the hell out of here as soon as he could because something was happening even though he didn't know what but he didn't like how he was feeling—

More customers. Here came the rush. Six, no seven for now. No more please. No. Eight. Not yet. Too many people to watch, got to check each one carefully. Make sure that—Marlboro? A carton? Would that be hard or soft pack? Here you go. The register isn't working properly would you like a hand-written receipt? No? Okay, that's fine. Good evening will this be all? The register isn't working properly would you like a hand-written receipt? No? Have a nice night.

The customer left and Tom tallied the cash in his hands, dropping some change on the floor. Damn. He crouched down and tried picking it up, having trouble lifting the change off the floor since his nails weren't long enough and he kept pushing the coins away instead of grabbing hold of the edges, and he remembered having the same trouble at that bar with all the Asians there and he had been drunk and trying to pick up change from the bar but everything had been too slippery, or he had been too drunk, but it had been the same thing, and right now while stooping under the counter and collecting the fallen change he remembered that feeling he had had in the bar, that drunk, confused feeling with his head swimming and June had held his arm and had guided him all around the bar, to her many friends it seemed, and he had tried to act natural but had hated being there, Let me go, he had thought to her, Let me leave, but she hadn't until they had both been sick of it, and then they had stumbled back to his apartment where—

"*Aigoo!* I see you! I see you!" Mrs. Rhee yelled from the door and Tom dropped the change and his face flushed and a rush of fire burned his chest as he stood up and saw her, but she wasn't looking at him, and he tried to steady himself, his slamming heart. She was looking at a black couple at the snack food rack.

"I see you take food! I see you!"

The two customers who wore similar thin leather jackets and jeans looked at each other then at Mrs. Rhee, who hurried to them, and the man with a design cut into the side of his hair said something to the woman, then looked curiously at Mrs. Rhee.

Mrs. Rhee yelled, "Put back! Put back!" waving her finger and pointing to the woman while the other customers looked on, but the woman, shrugging her shoulders and shaking her head, said, "Hold up. We ain't took nothing."

"I see you take food!" She pointed to the cloth handbag under the woman's arms.

"What you talkin' lies for? What you lyin' for?" The woman was getting angry, her chin jutting forward, her hands on her hips.

The whole scene was blurry, so dreamlike, that the voices didn't sound real and the faces distorted and enlarged and contracted as Tom tried to focus on them, and he watched Mrs. Rhee grab for the bag, lunging forward, hand like a claw, but the woman pulled it away and the man stepped between them, the woman screaming, "Don' you be touchin' my things, bitch!" and the man saying to Mrs. Rhee, "Hold up. Take it easy." But Mrs. Rhee did not seem to hear them—all she wanted was the bag— and she yelled, "You put in bag! I see you!" and pushed past the man and lunged again for the bag, but this time the woman pushed Mrs. Rhee away into the shelves, cans of soup crashing onto the floor and amidst the clatter Mrs. Rhee cried out in pain and she called out distinctly, clearly, without a trace of an accent, as if fear and pain forced her to be perfectly understood, as if this moment both she and Tom had known each other forever and one word connected their lives—she called out distinctly and clearly his name.

Tom was partially shaken out of this dream, and he realized that she had been pushed to the ground and he didn't think, didn't plan, and he saw himself reaching for the gun, pulling it out quickly, clumsily, knocking over a box of coupons and the bags, and he heard Mrs. Rhee yell, "Thomas! Push alarm! Call police!" but he was already past the counter and running towards them because he could only think of a robbery and he did not want to be hurt and held up and beaten or shot so he had to stop anything and anyone who tried to rob them, and he waved the gun and heard someone yell, "He's got a gun!" and someone shouted and people jumped to the ground and he ran straight for the couple aiming the gun at them and the man looked confused, seeing the people drop around him until he saw Tom running to him and his eyes widened and he backed away but Tom moved forward and aimed the gun at the woman and yelled, "Give it back give it back and don't ever touch her again do you hear me don't ever touch her again!"

The gun was shaking in his hand and he couldn't seem to aim it straight but he held it with both hands now and the store was silent except for the black man holding both his hands towards Tom saying in a slow, quiet voice, "Don't do nothing stupid," and he made slow-down motions with his palms, stroking the air, telling Tom to calm down take it easy chill out, and the woman was not moving at all, a statue staring at the shaking gun, but the man had Tom's attention and Tom watched his hands and thought how they reminded him of waves at the ocean like when he had been at Jones Beach as a kid and the waves were calming, soothing, like this man's hands, and the sounds of the ocean and the voices and the lifeguard's shrill whistle and the man's voice soothed him, like the ocean and Tom began to breathe again, he guessed he had been holding his breath, and everything was coming back into focus and his own hands steadied and he realized where he was—he was not at the beach—and he took a deep breath and the man seemed to relax more and this made Tom feel better and he began to take his finger off the trigger slowly and he lowered the gun, carefully, slowly, and he left it at his side.

The man grabbed the woman and she said, "That crazy sucka

could've wasted—" but the man hissed at her and whispered in her ear and pulled her along. She was still watching the gun at Tom's side. Mrs. Rhee was now watching him, not them. She did not stop them. Other customers hurried out.

"Maybe you go home now, okay?" Mrs. Rhee said. "Maybe you rest?"

Tom nodded, and put the gun into his pants. He walked out of the store and Mrs. Rhee said, "You give gun?" but he didn't really hear her and all he could think about was going to sleep, and he walked home in a daze.

For the first time since he had arrived here in Kasdan, Queens, Tom would go to his apartment, lie down on his mattress still in his clothes, close his eyes, and feel himself sinking away instantly, falling into a deep, quiet sleep.

HEINZ INSU FENKL

Heinz Insu Fenkl, who was born in Inchon, Korea, in 1960, lived most of his first twelve years in a camp town outside the American military base there called ASCOM. The rest of his childhood was spent in Germany and in various parts of the United States, following the duty stations of his father, who was a sergeant in the United States Army.

Fenkl's autobiographical novel, *Memories of My Ghost Brother* (1996), a 1997 PEN/Hemingway finalist, documents an unpopular time in Korea's historical consciousness, the transition period between postwar reconstruction (the late fifties to mid-sixties) and the "economic miracle" of the eighties. He explores the coming of age of Insu, an Amerasian in Korea, torn between his mother's world—haunted by literal and figurative ghosts of the past—and his father's transplanted America. Insu grows up in a camp town in a district in the city of Inchon, in which the United States Army and the Korean locals mutually exploit one another. Fenkl addresses the themes of Korean and American racism, the lives of prostitutes, pimps, and black marketeers, and the impossible, often unsurvivable condition of in-betweenness that Amerasian children endure.

In this excerpt, Fenkl draws on one of the implicit threads that run through his novel: the complex implications of the narrator's relationship with his father, who simultaneously represents both a savior and a new colonizer. Although the story is set entirely in Korea, the father-son relationship resonates with other colonial narratives such as Rudyard Kipling's *Kim* and the unavoidable specter of the war in Vietnam. Fenkl's father was a multiply-displaced individual himself, having been born a German in Czechoslovakia, then forcibly moved into Germany after Hitler's annexation of the Sudetenland; he was a Hitler Youth and a student in the Adolf Hitler Schule, Germany's elite military prep school. The circumstances of his eventual identity as an American soldier and the underlying implications of the Aryan race ideology in his past all lurk like shadows in this narrative, which carries special dramatic irony because it plays against the backdrop of different wars.

The novel's locus of narration is an unusual one in recent Asian American fiction, and it is perhaps most parallel to the works of Younghill Kang and Richard Kim in being focused on Korea or on the in-between culture of psychological and geographical transition. Fenkl's writing is fueled by his sense of loss over his departure from Korea and his desire to document an unrecorded history. He originally completed the book in 1984, the same year he was awarded a Fulbright Fellowship to study language and literature in Korea, but the shock of seeing the transformations in the country compelled him to rewrite the book over the next several years. He now considers *Memories of My Ghost Brother* the first part of a lifetime project of interrelated works.

Fenkl has an academic background in folklore, shamanism, and anthropology; he is also a translator of Korean folk tales and fiction. He has taught a range of courses in ethnic literature and writing at Sarah Lawrence, Vassar, and Bard Colleges. He currently directs the Creative Writing Program and the Interstitial Studies Institute at the State University of New York in New Paltz, where he is completing *Skull Water*—the sequel to *Memories of My Ghost Brother.*

from *Memories of My Ghost Brother*

Dear Father,

 This week I read The Count of Monte Cristo. It is by Alexander Dumas. He also wrote The Man in the Iron Mask. But I like this one much better. I think Mr. Dumas is now my favorite writer. How are you? I hope you have killed many enemies. I hope you do not get wounded. Next I am going to read The War of the Worlds by Mr. H. G. Wells.

 Your son,

 Heinz

I wrote to my father at least once a month while he was in Vietnam because my mother told me that the letters made him very proud and happy. The letters I got back from Vietnam were brief and feather-light, scrawled in a practically illegible Germanic script on single sheets of translucent blue Air Mail paper. The letters never said anything about the war, but they encouraged my studies, asked after my grades, told me to be good. They were always signed, "Your Father, Heinz," as if to remind me that he was my father and not some yellow-haired stranger. It was because of the letters I had written him that, on my eleventh birthday, in the dead of winter, my father took me to the Stars and Stripes bookstore in ASCOM.

I remember squinting to make out the small Quonset hut that stood by itself, no other buildings around it to break the cold wind. I remember walking over the tarmac under the PX hill, how I could feel my thighs beginning to go numb as the wind rose and dusted us with a fine and painful mist of ice crystals. I remember us stepping down a couple of cement steps between frozen snow drifts scoured a brilliant white by the wind, and my father pulling open the wire-reinforced glass door, bracing it against the wind until I stepped inside, into the sudden blast of dry heat from the clicking diesel stove; the door slams shut behind us, startling the Korean man who sits drowsing at the cash register, and we quickly remove our gloves and our hats, unzipping our green flight jackets to let the heat in.

"Bery cold to buy book," says the Korean man.

"Taksan cold," says my father. "Like a witch's tit."

I know this bookstore, so I quickly move away from the door and stand in front of the diesel stove, holding the flaps of my jacket open as if they were fabric wings. When the numbness leaves me I shiver a few times as the warmth enters my body. I go over to comic books to wait until my father picks up his usual Time, Newsweek, *and* The Army Times.

But today he is looking in a section where we have never been before—the expensive section with the leather-bound Bibles in boxes and cloth-bound books like the ones in the school library. When my father buys books they are paperback—fifty cents apiece if not cheaper—but this one is several dollars, the price of ten books. It is Kim, *by Rudyard Kipling—blue cloth binding; a gold-embossed man running with a torch; the signatures, each distinct, precisely stacked, sewn and cut between the covers; the smell of paper and glue.*

I remember the size of my father's hand as he grasped the book by the spine and opened it to make the inscription. I remember the size of my smaller, darker hand as I received the book and opened it to look at the inscription, barely legible to me:

For my son on his eleventh birthday.

    From your father,

    Heinz

He never knew that I wouldn't read it until the fourth anniversary of his death, and by then the original would be long lost, but the inscription burned so deep into my memory that when I opened the new paper-bound copy I could see the words projected onto the title page.

My father died believing I had read the book; believing I had made some decision about its contents, his message to me; believing I had forgotten or not cared enough to mention the remarkable coincidences, the ironic resonances. Perhaps when he quoted Kipling to me when I was in high school he was telling me he had gotten over my silence. Perhaps he, himself, had forgotten. But now I remember him in his Russian-style hat, wearing his sheepskin jacket, smoking a cigar, grinning. The wrinkles around his eyes—cut deep from squinting into the Vietnam sun, from peering into the observation glasses at the 38th parallel, at the DMZ between Koreas—they fan out like the delta of a river, and he is smiling so hard, laughing his surprisingly loud and barky laugh, that tears stream from the corners of his cold blue eyes and are squeezed into those channels.

When he saw me for the first time after my birth, when Emo held me out to him as he stepped down from the green U.S. Army bus, he had held me like a piece of wood, a rifle stock at present arms. He had held his son and turned bright red from the shame of having a mixed-blood child—or was it simply that he did not know how to hold an infant? He handed me back to Emo and walked home in a foul mood. Later he erupted at my mother for daring to let him be seen in public with a child presented to him by a Korean.

Again I remember the size of his hand, that bright white palm twice the size of my face. I had dropped a clump of rice on the floor and picked it up to smear it against the lip of the lacquer table in the customary way, to be cleaned up later, and he had slapped me so hard I had fallen sideways onto the floor. "How dare you waste your food! Do you know how long I work for that rice? Eat it!" Somehow I put the soiled and sticky rice glob into my mouth and chew it, chew it until I need hardly swallow. The side of my face is bright red, later to bruise, and my mother's voice leaps up against him. "He only baby! He not know. Rice dirty! Kaesaeki-ya!" They argue and argue, but I can neither see nor hear them with my vision blurred and my ears ringing with the repercussion of his slap.

*

The day of my father's return from his first tour of duty in Vietnam, Mahmi and I waited at the U.S. military airport at Kimpo for seven hours. We had arrived early in the morning. We had taken an Arirang taxi from Pupyong to Kimpo airbase, expecting to wait only an hour or two for his out-processing after he came off the flight, but the plane was late and our wait became a daylong vigil. I did not know what my mother was thinking, whether she was imagining the flight shot out of the sky, or whether she doubted the Korea House translator's reading of my father's letter and imagined we had come on the wrong day. If we were not there to meet him, there was no way my father would be able to find us unless he wrote to her again from his new post in Korea. As the day drew on and the pleasant warmth of morning became the blinding heat of noon, and then as the shadows lengthened where we waited outside, in the shade of a deuce-and-a-half truck, I tried to remember my father's face. He had only been gone for a year, but without a picture I could only imagine him in the vaguest way. The short yellow hair, the square face, the plumped skin, the slightly downturned eyes, the sharp beak nose.

I remembered my father as an MP in the First Cavalry Division. On his shoulder he wore the shield-shaped golden patch with the diagonal black stripe and the horsehead silhouette. He would dab my cheeks with shaving cream while I crept around him and splashed the dirty water in the wash basin. When I learned to talk, I said *"Aboji myondo"* each time he shaved, and he tried to teach me the English: "Daddy, shave." I could never make the strange words, but I learned games quickly. I would imitate his shaving by using a dull knife, or play cowboy, making him snort and rear up to make the horse noise while I clung to his back. I would stop him, patting his short, yellow bristles, and motion for him to graze on the dry leaves I had strewn on the floor. I learned how to unlace his low-quarter shoes so I could use one lace as reins and the other as a whip. We would play until the sweat poured from his body, filling the room with his strange ani-

mal smell. I remembered the smell of yellow Dial soap, the gritty
texture of Colgate tooth powder, the cold sting of Mennen Skin
Bracer, the warm and wet lather of Old Spice shaving soap
brushed on my face with the two-tone bristles of a shaving brush.
I remembered the odd musk of the foot powder he rubbed between his toes and dumped into his green wool socks and into his
black combat boots, the sweet mildewy smell of the damp leather,
the pleasant bite of Black Kiwi shoe polish. I could remember all
these things, but I could not picture his face. I could see his gap-
toothed smile when he removed his false teeth. I could see the
blue and green flash of his eyes, the plumpness of the back of his
hand when he grasped a pen to write, but I could not remember
his face. I had only pieces of my father.

"Mahmi," I said. "Do you think Daeri's face has changed?"

"His skin might be a bit burnt," she said. "Maybe he's lost a
little flesh because of his hard life in Vietnam, but why would he
look any different?"

"I don't know. What if I don't recognize him?"

"You'll recognize him."

"Do you think he'll remember me?"

"Of course! He's been thinking only of you for that whole year.
You're his son." Though she tried to keep pale, Mahmi's skin was
burnt quite dark by the summer sun. In her beehive hair and her
white polyester *wanpisu,* she was darker than me. Her skin was
dark even for a Korean, and sometimes people said she had the
skin of a *sangnom,* a commoner. "Do you remember the last time
you saw him?" she asked.

"It was with the beggars," I said. "He gave them money and he
said I shouldn't make fun."

"That's right." Mahmi looked suddenly worried, and I knew
she was thinking of the wounded veterans with pieces of their
bodies missing.

"Why didn't he tell me he was going?" I said. Then I saw my
father in the distance through the waves of heat rippling over the

tarmac, and he looked smaller than I remembered. Other yellow-haired soldiers had come out before him, and I had been afraid to confuse one of them for him, but there was no mistaking when my father emerged from the terminal building—the fresh-cropped crew cut that made his hair bristle straight up like a brush, the fleshy square shape of his face. He was leaner and darker, burnt by the tropical sun and wasted by bouts of malaria. He was wearing his short-sleeved summer khakis, with his bars of decorations and the coiled blue Infantry braid around one shoulder, but he walked differently—methodically, with a step more cautious than I remembered, a step more suited for someone in camouflage fatigues. His ice-blue eyes had a distant look to them—or had they sunk subtly back in their sockets?

Mahmi did not immediately run to him as I had expected. She gave me a quick glance, and I charged forward, sprinting until I grew suddenly self-conscious just in front of my father and came to an awkward stop to look sheepishly up at him. He stepped up to me and lifted me into his hug. He patted and rubbed the top of my head as he let me down on my mother's approach. When she reached him he kissed her. That was the first and only time I saw them kiss.

We rode back to Pupyong in another Arirang taxi. I sat in the front seat with the window open so I didn't hear what they talked about in the back. We drove off the good pavement of the airbase and out into the winding dirt road through the several villages that skirted the other army posts along the bus route to ASCOM. I sat sweating in the vinyl seat, watching the meter click up nickel by nickel as we rattled on in the heat.

In the evening I bathed after my father, standing in a wash basin full of soapy water as he scrubbed me with a rough washcloth and poured cold water over me to rinse me clean. Emo cooked a steak which Mahmi had gotten the day before and kept under a block of ice. My father was happy but uneasy. Even when he pierced the top of his Falstaff beer with the can opener, making that cold *crack-hissss* sound that used to make him smile, he seemed preoccupied by something.

I do not remember what he talked about that first night. I do not remember if the dinner was pleasant or if he had brought lavish gifts for everyone. I remember being shocked at the contrast between his burnt forearms and the paper-white flesh of his armpits. I remember thinking the damp curls of hair in his underarms were the color of the hairs around an ox's nostrils. I remember how his feet filled the entire wash basin and how the room became pungent with the familiar odor of his sweat. In his duffel bag he had brought back all the cigarettes he had not smoked or traded from his C-rations, the packets of acrid coffee, the packets full of toilet paper, salt, sugar, pepper, and cream, the metal can openers, the white plastic spoons—things that we would use every day in the house. He had brought my mother a red Vietnamese costume called an *ao dai;* he had brought fresh green wool socks for Hyongbu, grease pencils and yellow wooden pencils for Yongsu and Haesuni, and a leather wallet from my grandmother for me to hang around my neck. He asked me about school and I told him that I enjoyed it. I left out all the important things.

"What you do in Vietnam, Daddy?"

We were at the edge of the parade field at Yongsan 8th Army Headquarters, just under the flagpole, and my father had put me astride the howitzer to take a quick picture. They fired deafening blanks out of the howitzer each day when the flag came down, and everything stopped to listen to the bugler play the sad taps music. The dark green barrel was hot under my thigh.

"You're sitting on top of Zam-Zammah!" said my father.

"Zam-Zammah!" I shouted.

"Thy father was a pastry cook!"

The shutter of my father's borrowed camera clicked and I quickly swung my leg over and leaped down. "What's a pastry cook?"

"Oh, that's someone who makes doughnuts and cakes. Like *ttok*."

"You not a *ttok* man, Daddy. What you do in Vietnam? You kill lotsa' number ten VC?"

"I was a red bull on a green field," he said quietly, still talking some sort of riddle I didn't understand.

"How come you not say?"

"I was on an Advisory Team near a place called Nha Trang," he said. "I helped people called Montagnards fight the Vietcong. You'd like the Montagnards, Booby. They're like Indians."

"They got Indians in Vietnam? Make fire with sticks? Wow!" I took my father's sunburnt hand, and he led me across the street, past the Main Library, to the Snack Bar. I heard a raspy metallic sound and looked back over my shoulder at the parade field, suddenly expecting to see people ice skating the way they did when the field was flooded in winter. It was nothing, just a sound like the sound of a blade on ice, but it made me shiver.

My father was quiet. He had seemed happier since he returned from Vietnam, but he was also distant, as if a part of him had not made it back. I had seen my share of limp, black body bags and rigid aluminum coffins on AFKN television, and I imagined he had left something like that—some feeling that hurt like the sight of those containers—back in the highlands outside Nha Trang.

My father treated me to an early turkey dinner at the special buffet that afternoon. He wanted me to have the dark and white meat, but I found the sliced turkey loaf neater and less like a dead animal—more palatable under the lumpy gravy and the dark red cranberry sauce. I had never learned how to handle a full set of western silverware, and today was my lesson on how to eat European-style, keeping the fork in my left hand, the knife always in the right. My father corrected me and told me anecdotes while I sawed at the turkey with the dull knife and struggled to use the fork in its upside-down position without letting the food slip off.

"I used to go swimming out on Nha Trang beach," he said. "The water was so blue it was like looking up at the sky, and for lunch I used to eat a green dragon fruit."

"Green dragon? Like dinosaur?"

"Like a cactus—you know, like you see in the cowboy movies. Green dragon fruit tastes really good."

"Can I have one, Daddy?"

"You come to 'Nam with me sometime, Booby." He tapped on his false front teeth. "One time I lost my partial plate when I went to the *benjo*. I dropped it in there and it was night, so I couldn't find it later even with a flashlight. In the morning I went out without my partial, and the Montagnards thought it was funny. I said, 'See, me Montagnard, too.' The chiefs got a real kick out of it. They file down their front teeth and they all smoke cigars, even the little kids your age."

I made a face to show him I didn't like cigars.

"Don't spill that. Pull your elbows in. That's right, and sit straight."

After I corrected my posture, my father took some change out of his pocket and put it on the table. "How about some chocolate cake?" he said. "Then we catch the bus home."

"Okay!"

The cake, I learned, was not to be eaten with a knife and fork, but simply cut apart with the fork itself. The crumbs could be compressed down and squeezed between the tines if you wanted to get them without touching them with your fingers. My father pronounced that I had made good progress, and we went down to the bus station where he bought his usual copy of *The Stars and Stripes*. On the bus we sat near the back, with the window open so he could smoke one of his pungent cigars even though the Korean women sitting around us grimaced and complained. He ignored them, but he knew what they were saying, and he actually enjoyed annoying them. He told me more about Vietnam as the bus droned on and I settled against his side, half drowsing.

"We used to go on patrol," he said. "We'd hump our gear up into the highlands and watch the big planes spraying the defoliants. Long clouds of it would come down. Agent Orange. It was beautiful. In a few days everything would be dead. Not a blade of grass for Charlie to hide under. And we used to take bangalore torpedoes—they're long tubes packed with plastic explosives—we used them to blow up bunkers and patches of barbed wire. We'd go out to the Montagnards and stick the bangalores down into the roots of their big trees and blow a few of them. When the trees fell over the Montagnard kids and women would run into the crater or to the roots that stuck out at the bottom of the trunk and catch all the stunned rats. That was a delicacy for them—a special food. They really liked us *taksan* for getting them those rats."

I fell asleep to the sound of my father's voice telling me something about a monkey and a shotgun. The pictures he took that day never came out.

My father stayed in Korea for eleven months after his return. Forty-eight weekends, and he came home on half of them. With the few three-day passes and holidays, he was home for less than fifty days before he left again. My mother and I visited him only once up in Camp Casey where he was stationed near Wijongbu, and he wasn't at all happy to see us. He told my mother later that having his men see his Korean wife undermined his authority. We never visited again.

While my father was on leave for my birthday in January of 1968, the U.S.S. Pueblo, *an electronic spy ship, was captured off the coast of North Korea, and all over the country, the military went on alert. My father went back up to his unit early after hearing the news on his transistor radio. Later that month, during the Vietnamese New Year's celebration of Têt, the NVA and the Vietcong simultaneously attacked over a hundred towns, cities, and military installations all over Vietnam. It was the bloodiest offensive of the war. The outpost where my father had served near Nha Trang was overrun, and many of his friends were among the Killed-in-Action. The mood among the GIs in Korea became thick and black, full of hate for Asian people and tense with the fear that the North Koreans might invade. The GIs were afraid to stay in Korea, but even more afraid that they might be shipped to Cam Ranh Bay to join some counteroffensive against the North Vietnamese. Houseboys and prostitutes were beaten more frequently; there were more fights in the clubs. The Korean army stayed on alert and continued to mobilize more men to send to Vietnam. There was constant news about the White Horse Division, the Tiger Division, and the Blue Dragon Brigade.*

I don't think my father ever considered our house his home that year. We were just the family that kept him occupied when he wasn't working. Korea and Vietnam were both countries divided along their middle by a Demilitarized Zone, with Communists in the north and pro-American governments in the south. Both countries had Buddhists and Catholics and Animists, they farmed wet rice, they plowed fields with oxen, they were populated by people with yellow skin. When he took me to the Snack Bar that day to teach me how to use a knife and fork, he had said something about "The Great Game" when he sent me to buy my own slice of cake. "Heinz," he said to me, "what old man is going to teach you the important things while I'm off in The Great Game?" What was "The Great Game," I had thought back then. Was my father, like my mother, playing two slot machines, but one was Korea and the other Vietnam?

I think now that what he wanted was retribution. And that is why he volunteered for Vietnam again and left before the summer of 1968. And because I had not read the blue book he had given me, I wouldn't know what he meant by "The Great Game" or "Zam-Zammah" or bulls on green fields for another twenty years.

Black hourglass against a field of red. Seventh Division—Bayonet. An Indian head in a feathered headdress superimposed on a white star. A field of black. Second Infantry Division. A black horsehead silhouette, like a chess knight, above a diagonal black slash across a shield of gold. The First Cavalry Division. In his German accent, he called it "The First Calf." These were the totemic symbols of my father, his military insignia. The four cardinal points in green, which the Germans in World

War II had called "The Devil's Cross." Fourth Mechanized Infantry Division. A white sword pointing upright between two yellow batwing doors against a field of blood. The Vietnam campaign. Golden chevrons, a white long rifle against a blue bar, oak-leaf clusters, a cross of iron for excellent marksmanship. Symbols of power. Totems of the clan that kills people whose skin is the color of mine. Indelible.

Part TWO

YOUNGHILL KANG

The first Korean American novelist, Younghill Kang (1899–1972) emigrated from Korea after his harrowing experiences during the nationalist March First demonstrations of 1919 (*Samil undong*) and subsequent attempts to elude Japanese police while traveling through Manchuria and Russia. He matriculated in the fall of 1920 at Dalhousie University in Halifax, Nova Scotia, then transferred two years later to Boston University, where he was awarded a bachelor of science degree, having originally intended to return to Korea as a modern man of science. Kang went on instead to earn a master of education degree in the teaching of English at Harvard in 1927. By then he was also preparing translations and articles on East Asian literatures and cultures and writing his serious prose in English rather than in Korean or Japanese. In 1928 he married Frances Keely (1903–70), a Wellesley College student majoring in classics who became Kang's lifelong literary collaborator.

Soon after began the period of Kang's greatest public recognition: from 1929, when his often acerbic articles and book reviews began to appear in influential periodicals such as the *New Republic* and *The Nation,* to late 1941, when he was called upon to assist with U.S. war department projects shortly after the attack on Pearl

Harbor. During these twelve years, the list of Kang's achievements includes publication of his first and most popular book, *The Grass Roof* (1931), an autobiographical novel about his youth in Korea that quickly established him as an international expert on East Asian culture and society; editing or writing more than a hundred articles for publications ranging from the *Encyclopaedia Britannica,* where he was an editor of the fourteenth edition (1929), to Korean student newsletters in which he furthered the cause of Korean independence from Japanese rule; publishing *The Happy Grove* (1933), an illustrated children's version of *The Grass Roof;* and being the first Asian awarded a Guggenheim Fellowship, which enabled him to write early drafts of his third book, *East Goes West, The Making of an Oriental Yankee* (1937) while traveling extensively in Europe. Aside from maturing as a writer, and besides working in the Oriental Art department of New York's Metropolitan Museum of Art, Kang lectured throughout much of this period in New York University's English department, where he founded the comparative literature program and taught innovative courses on East Asian literature and philosophy and Western conceptions of the "Orient."

In 1939, at the height of his reputation in the United States, Kang became a cause célèbre of leading intellectual figures who organized three unsuccessful campaigns to pass private congressional bills that would make him a U.S. citizen (as a Korean, Kang was barred from naturalization until passage of the Immigration and Nationality Act of 1952). During World War II, Kang progressed through a series of military posts, including head of Japanese language training for outbound soldiers and principal economic analyst for the Board of Economic Warfare, while writing anti-Japanese propaganda, a situation that allowed him to fulfill both Korean and American patriotic missions.

One year after Japan's defeat, Kang returned to Korea as a high-ranking civilian employee of the American occupation army (U.S. Armed Forces in Korea). Toward the end of his sixteen-month tour of duty, Kang became highly critical of the U.S. Military Government's constant mishandling of Koreans' aspirations for political independence, the brutality of the U.S.-backed Korean National Police, and what he considered the fascism and corruption of Syngman Rhee, who became the first president of the new Republic of Korea in August 1948. Indeed, until his death in 1972 in Florida, where his oldest son resided, Kang continued to openly rail against both Rhee and American policy in Asia, including the dropping of the atomic bomb and the Vietnam War. Although his political views were moderate, Kang was branded within the United States Army as "an author . . . possess[ing] leftist tendencies," which, in a time of McCarthyist witch-hunts and dogged interference from President Rhee's henchmen, had dire consequences for his career. By the time that Kang was lamenting in 1954 that his hopes for the harmonious reconciliation of East and West through "great cross-fertilizations of science and art" had all perished, he was making ends meet by laboring on truck farms on Long Island, his sons barely able to withstand the summer heat as they tried to work beside him. Aside from scattered assignments, Kang's career as an author of major works had come to an end.

The following two selections highlight two opposite yet inseparable aspects of Kang's cosmopolitanism during the still-hopeful 1930s: rapturous yearning for a realm of harmonious feeling and beauty that both gathers and rises above all cultural, ideological, and national divisions and a nearly farcical sense of the same desire's humiliation by social realities—of how, in fact, the very notions of harmony, feeling, beauty, and transcendence are inevitably tied to particular cultures, and locales.

from *The Grass Roof*

O Soul of America!

> Ah! Up then from the ground sprang I
> And hailed the earth with such a cry
> As is not heard save from a man
> Who has been dead, and lives again.
>
> *Renascence:* EDNA ST. VINCENT MILLAY

Now nothing can be seen on the four sides, but blue—blue—blue water, the great connecting sheet that is ocean, covering the surface of the earth . . . now I am in the province of the no-nation, these great salty currents, flowing from pole to pole, from continent to continent . . . the Japanese cannot get me here . . . I ride on a British boat, but around me are peoples of many lands. . . .

I have already caught humorous glimpses of my fellow-passengers. I am to know them better later on, for Mr. Luther is travelling first-class and I am free of the whole ship. There are serious Chinese diplomats coming over to Washington, inscrutable on the outside, simple and worried within. There is a doleful Chinese girl-student from Shanghai, spectacled and homely-looking, who can stimulate you by such keen individualistic thought that you would be likely to fall in love with her, if it was too dark to see her, but not in day-time, or even by dim candlelight.

There are Japanese business men, going to get more "dope" about American efficiency and up-to-dateness; they appear with bows and with gentle smiles for the Westerners and Japanese papers under their arms, telling of the latest "riots" in Korea, of quaint celebrations in honor of their emperor, and American breakfast foods in the advertisements. There is the discontented Japanese student, in thrall to the West, never wanting to return home, hating even his native religion, his soul like a melancholy butterfly that begins to find flowers few and far between.

There is a friendly Russian from Siberia with an outgoing nature toward all except Americans about whom he is already beginning to be sarcastic. Yet since he cannot stay in the region of the stormy political restlessness, he has no better place to come for a new home than to that same despised America. There is the German, with business property in China, concealing the fact that he is a German because of intolerance of other nations for his fatherland during the war; when the orchestra plays, he cries over strange Western music I do not understand. There is the French actress, who they say is the concubine of the noted Frenchman she is travelling with; it seems to shock the British and the Americans, and not the Europeans. But the Americans interest me most. There is the young Back-Bay girl from Boston given a trip to China because she was disappointed in love. It had happy end, for she met a suitable young fellow in Shanghai and is now engaged to him; her nicey-nicey little aunt without wrinkles in the society clothes is thoroughly satisfied and continually expresses herself as being surprised to find that all Chinese are not laundrymen or chop-suey waiters, but seem to speak and act with "culture." There is a retired politician from a large American city who got rich on the willing contributions of his bootleggers, and being defeated as governor candidate, now takes a vacation trip around the world. He talks with his friend Mr. Babbitt, and they agree that America is the greatest nation of the world because of Henry Ford, Edison, Wanamaker and the Woolworth Building. They laugh at China because she has no five and ten cent stores in which to buy chewing gum, but sells very good neckties for fifteen cents which you cannot buy in a Fifth Avenue store for less than five dollars. There is the Exchange Professor, who is glad to tell you everything about everything and is willing to open his trunk to show you all the data for the book he is going to write on Art, preaching China is the greatest nation of the world—except that he cannot find his keys. There is the young fellow who graduated from a small denominational college in America and went to the Orient in Y.M.C.A. work to satisfy his wanderlust, and now sails back on furlough having found he dislikes travel, not knowing what to do with himself and feeling too intelligent to be a missionary and too dumb to be a college professor, and untrained for anything else. Still he doesn't want to say much because of the conservative missionary travelling with him, who belongs to the same board. This is the missionary who tries to persuade everybody to come into the parlor for service Sunday morning,—and I begin to see why he goes to the Orient for an audience. At other times he argues with a doctor from Peking Research Institute that one hundred per cent Yankees don't come from donkeys and monkeys.

There is one more figure whose meaning I cannot understand . . . it is a young American artist—in company with an older European man. Both have gone into voluntary exile to the winehouses of Shanghai, one because his blood kinship in America seems without spiritual loyalties, who feels all races in war over his soul. He clings to the other man, who sums up all cultures of the West, yet sees no future for any but the rot, and can find only a wee bit of fragrance lingering about the great works of the past. They make soliloquy with each other about the soul of America, and they glance at me in surprise when they see my interested face.

O soul of America, I too, wonder about you. . . .

My keenest longing, now, is to be alone, not to speak. In a corner of the deck, wanting no fellowship, I stretch my hands, breathing the salt air, grasping darkness and the open space. After the excitement and activity of the last ten years involving so much change, I crave now almost a surcease, rocked like this on the waves of an infinite possibility, hope, bliss. . . . This is the bliss of a great dream come true through my own act. And there are many more dreams within me, greater and greater, also going to come true soon through my own act. It is like a revelation into the kingdom of eternity, this night of stars and clear wind in a world apart from the other worlds.

Above and around me on every side move sea-gulls, following the motion of the waves, leading on from mystery to mystery. It occurs to me that I am like a soul who has just cast off one life and is not yet born in another; these are the spirits of all the beautiful poets whom the muse has captured, attending me in my voyage to understand an alien beauty. But can beauty be alien? Then it seems to me that the poet alone has no home nor national boundary, but is like a man in a ship. His nearest kin is the muse up in clouds, and his patriotism goes to the ethereal kingdom.

How cold the sea breeze shivers my body now! I feel exiled from all humanity. Crystal Pool, who they say died in prison. . . . Mr. Brilliant Crane who, I am told by Mr. Luther, has become a millionaire by milking goats outside of Seoul. . . . Mr. Eastern Harmony who lately succeeded in having a fine child . . . how shadowy actual forms and faces are beside the visions I see in that other *kingdom*. . . . Yet tender recollections still have power to bind me. And even as my heart dissolves in yesterday's lingering memories, a figure comes between me and the mist-white horizon. It is a girl in Western dress, recalling to me another voyage, gone yet not forgotten. I like the way she lifts her head, and drinks the sea-breeze, as though she loved it like the haunting night-birds. She seems isolated like myself, a woman with no nationality. Is she of West or East? Is she a Chinese or a Japanese? Is she European or American? Now she alone touches the chord to which my heart dances, because of how she stands and looks into the night. Her eyes too are on the far off stars. And from the milky way they move to look at me. . . . Is it possible that the Princess Immortality is in the same boat going with me to America?

from *East Goes West:*
The Making of an Oriental Yankee

At last I rose and with fast strides walked the streets. And perhaps
people thought I was drunk or a crazy man. For I murmured to
myself and from time to time wiped my eyes. The great variety of
life eddied about me, and was my great Greek chorus, though it
was composed of neither old men nor captive women nor sea
nymphs nor classical maidens, but of all kinds of men on the
globe. How grateful I was to New York, my magnet of worlds, my
spiritual port, my rich harbor! How the stone pavements and
dusty stalactite buildings surrounded with rugged grandeur the
treasure of a still withdrawn room, that room where Van studied
medicine, where Trip sat, charmed, amidst papers, helpless and as
if alone!

I meant to take Trip to Chinatown for dinner, to give her some
novelty. I invited Van, too. But Van had a date with her medical
tomes, and she thrust us both out with relief. I felt both solemn
and light-headed to be again with Trip. I started to get a taxi, for
I remembered the words of George, "When with a girl, *always*
take a taxi." But Trip wouldn't let me and said, "We patronize
els." But when we got off at Mott Street, it was raining, so in a
great bustle and hurry, I hailed a taxi after all. Since it was a new

address I wanted to try, supposed to be more grand and suited to Americans, and I didn't know where it was myself, I gave the address to the taximan. And he drove just around the corner and stopped, it was only a few feet. I felt in my pocket to pay the man and I had no change. The smallest I had was a two-dollar bill. Idiotically, I pressed it into his hand and ran after Trip, to get her in from the rain.

We went upstairs to a large ornate Chinese restaurant, but nobody else was here now. A band off in one corner was playing jazz very mournfully. Trip sat down shyly and dubiously, as far from the music as she could get. But the whole place was lovely to me, lovely the murmuring rain outside, lovely the enforced intimacy of this Chinatown solitude. I noticed how, though, that the merriment which had come in Van's apartment with Van before we left, had died out of Trip's face. A passive and somber expression had taken its place. She made little effort to talk. She seemed to be wondering quietly to herself, just what she was doing in here with an Oriental, Chungpa Han. Or she seemed to be bored. I asked her if she would dance. George said you had to dance. And we went around the small deserted circle of the dancing floor once or twice quite gravely to the dismal sounds.

Obviously the place was not suited for giving a young lady a good time in the vein of George. The quietness and melancholy of this place were more suited to spiritual revelations. So I told her about Boshnack Brothers, and Miss Stein, and how unhappy I was there.

"I find that Americans can be very unhappy," I said.

"You have found that?" her chin lifted with interest. "I think that's so."

"Like Poe," I suggested.

"Oh, but that was romantic misery," said Trip. "There was some satisfaction in that. Yes, everybody seems rather unhappy and lost, in America, just now. You've felt that? But no, it isn't like Poe. It's more Chaplinesque."

"Chaplinesque?"

"Charlie Chaplin, you know. No dignity."

"Oh, yes! the fellow of laughs. Don't you like to laugh?"

"I resent being funny. I haven't much humor, I guess."

"Oh, but I'm sure you have. I like to laugh. More than to cry."

But my mind was suddenly on a paper I had written on Poe. It would be better to leave some costly jade behind, as if forgotten. Then she would have to communicate with me again. But I had no costly jade. I had only a paper on Poe.

"I want to send you a paper I wrote on Poe," I said.

"All right."

"And then I want to ask your advice?"

"My advice?" Trip laughed.

"Should I get out of Boshnack Brothers?"

"I shouldn't think you would be happy with them ever. A sensitive Oriental in America must surely find *that* hell. You were happier as a student, weren't you?"

"That, too, was a tiresome life. But I will get out of Boshnack's if you say so."

"Otherwise, when are you to write your best seller?" exclaimed Trip, dismissing the economics of my problem airily.

"When you are ready to help me."

But she immediately said she would rather write about America, and realism was the thing. And I forebore to mention that a tenuous life on paper was neither American nor realistic, for I sensed that consistency bothered Trip no more than economics.

Having prolonged our Chinese dishes, and tea, as long as possible, we went out. It had stopped raining.

We came to some posters not far from the restaurant, in brilliant colors, orange, yellow, black, cerise, and strong green. Trip stopped to look, I to read the Chinese. I told her it was news.

"And is it colorful? I should expect it to be," said she.

"My, it's very exciting. Tong war."

"What! Going on here now?"

"But you needn't be frightened. There are more police around than usual, and there are always a lot." I suggested that we walk around some and see what was going on, though Trip wasn't so keen. So we walked those curved and intricate lanes, all with their flaming posters lit by dim street lights, for always at night Chinatown seems inky—it is no Broadway. I drew her with me into a small shop, and I bought some Chinese tea and some preserved fruits for her, the kind she had liked at our dinner. I wanted to buy her more things to sample, but she said hastily, no, we couldn't carry any more.

"Then I'll get some Chinese wine. . . . "

"What is that like?"

"You will see. It is very strong, you know, like gin or whisky. I'll try here. Pardon me. Just walk along slowly by yourself. If you went down, they would not sell."

She seemed about to clutch my sleeve, then thought better of it. "Oh, we'd better go home!" But I was already moving off, in the direction of the cellar. "Just walk very slowly on. I'll be back in a minute." When I came out with the bottle inside my coat, she was having an angry conversation with a man. I saw something was the matter, and stepped quickly up. "Oh, Mr. Han!" she left me to do the talking. I spoke up very indignantly, though he had just drawn back his coat and shown his plain-service badge. He was apologizing now. He said to Trip he was a detective and had to protect American girls in Chinatown.

"Actually, he asked my age and my address and if my parents knew I was here!" exclaimed Trip, laughing incredulously, as we walked off together. "Marvellous! detectives! danger! Just what you always expect from Chinatown, and never get. I never saw a detective before in my life. But I wish you'd taken me into that dive with you, Mr. Han. The steps you went down were pitch-black, and *very* sinister." And I could tell she was merry and delighted with life once more, and the detective had done me a good turn, making Chinatown so interesting.

We took a taxi and got back to the apartment. Trip began to laugh as soon as we got in downstairs. "I hear Trip's giggle," I heard Van say gaily as she opened the door. And she welcomed her with open arms. There were two others in the room, another girl and a man. A babble of voices mixed together.

"Welcome sistah," said the tall pencil-slim girl with blue eyes and chestnut braids around her head, coronet style. She had a strong Southern accent. "Hey! What have you?" And Marietta, the third roommate, began grabbing things out of my arms, and examining them pertly, while Van, making a pretense of ferocity, choked Trip's laughter, and said, "Stop it—stop it—at once. Or tell what you're laughing at."

"Well, I've had a wonderful time," exclaimed Trip, throwing off her things and sinking down on one of the couches. "And Mr. Han is going to give us all a party now. Look! Chinese wine, whatever that may be!"

"Goody, goody!" cried Marietta, rubbing her hands together, and rolling her eyes. "Provisions, no end!" she winked. "And trust Trip for the wine. Good work, good work!"

"Libel, isn't it Trip?" said Van.

"Chinese tea. The very best!" exclaimed Trip, springing up to check them over. "Chinese ginger. Chinese fruits. I had them for dinner. All different kinds of mysterious things, and there is one thing—a little black ugly thing—when you break it between your teeth—you taste a marigold's smell—not at first, but slowly and gradually."

"Oh, Mr. Han, why didn't you take me along?—And what were you giggling about, please?" demanded Marietta imperiously.

"The girl always giggles!" said Van, with a mock-scowl. "It's the easiest thing in the world to make Trip giggle. Over nothing. Positively nothing. Isn't it nothing, devil?"

"No, it's something. Wait till you hear. While Mr. Han was bargaining for the wine, I got stopped on the street by a man."

"What, accosted!"

"What? For the wine!"

"No! For being in Chinatown with Mr. Han!" Trip leaned back weakly against the cushions laughing. "But you see, a tong was going on. . . . "

"What's a tong?" cried Marietta.

"I don't know. Something murderous. Mr. Han was explaining. A war in Chinatown. Policemen were all around. And on top of that, this plain-clothes man stopped me for loitering. Mr. Han had told me to walk slowly on, then slowly back again, while he was in that nefarious place where they sell Chinese gin. . . . That's when I got stopped for loitering. I became very respectable and haughty. And then the man displayed his badge. I was almost taken in. He should have got Mr. Han, who had the wine under his coat. But Mr. Han actually seemed to intimidate him. And he apologized very respectfully to *him*."

"Tut! tut!" Marietta held up a warning finger. "These loose ways! They'll come home to you in the end. Trip, you must look like a loose woman!"

"But suppose *you* had been along . . . "

"And she lost her naiyme again!" Van jumped up from the couch beside Trip, and with indescribable contortions of face and limb, she sang the song, the others joining in. Then Marietta ran for glasses. The tall gaunt ex-serviceman who was Marietta's cousin opened the bottle. Marietta handed drinks around. "Quaff, then."

Which Van did deeply—in milk. With a glass of milk in her hand, Van sang, "My name is Yon Yonson, I come from Wisconsin," taking deep draughts of milk, sighing huskily and wiping her mouth beerily with the side of her hand. (For she hated alcohol of all kinds.) She had a strong soprano voice, yet delicate and sweet, irresistibly lilting and droll. Released from the tension of hard study and grind, Van had become like some radiant natural phenomenon. The whole party rode the waves of her high animal spirits, and she seemed as exhilarated on her milk as any there. We melted into hysterics not only at her broad comedy, but at her delicate wit, turning this way and that like a bird in flight, suggesting deeper things in ridiculous foolery. Never had I seen a more bizarre American woman, or one more fitted to represent American woman's freedom (almost indeed to the point of caricature, including the tall skyscraper height that many of them reach). But no one could doubt the tender core of her womanliness, seeing her so unmasked and free like this, spontaneous as a little child. Her tenderness in particular guarded Trip, toward whom she always showed a special indulgence and protectiveness. She was not like Trip, resenting to be funny. (Van was more like me. At least I never objected very much to being funny. That didn't bother me.) I wished that George could see her. In Hollywood, I thought, she would have been a great success. For she was funnier than Charlotte Greenwood. And she hated what was too serious in thought. But she was very sensitive toward Trip and her desire for dignity.

The talk and the gaiety and laughter enchanted me. And Marietta and I drank most of the wine. I began to feel that Van was taking too much of the stage. Trip also must see me. I stood up before the old marble mantelpiece as on the lecture platform, a glass in hand—not of water but of wine—and Keats, Shelley, Browning, Tennyson, Ruskin, Carlyle, and Shakespeare rolled out in pages and sheets, all that had imprinted itself word for word on the retentive Oriental memory of one classically trained. The others now listened. They gave me the applause of clapped hands and laughter. I could not read the expression on Trip's face, which seemed to me trembling with the shake of water, water which held the nymph of youth, fountain of the eternal laughter. Finally she got out of sight. She was hiding behind Van's shoulder. Van sat at the head of the couch. Trip let her long bobbed hair fall down over her face, and I thought she held the handkerchief to her lips. I began to give them a Chinese poem in the old-fashioned singing, and I craned to catch Trip's eye. "Trip, you're choking! Hey! Something go the wrong way?" And Marietta clapped Trip on the back, meeting the hidden one's glance, her own face crimsoned with laughter.

Marietta's cousin got up to go. He showed Trip some book he had brought. I knew I had to go, too. That evening had passed into the realm of the lost evenings. Besides, I must catch my train back to Philadelphia, and greet Miss Stein with excuses on Tuesday morning. Still upon me the flush of the wine, and the joy of arriving in such a sweet world of eternal beauty and youth and delightful fellowship, I said good-by to Van and Marietta. Van was kind but casual; still, past offenses seemed wiped out, old scores forgotten. Marietta was most free and cordial. I waited for Trip. Trip, her face still pink and shaken, eyes darkly moist, tossing back her dark hair with impatient gesture, gave me good-by with a warmth somewhere in between that of Marietta's and Van's. But "Come again! Come again!" they all said. "It was a marvelous party."

The door of Paradise closed behind me. Marietta's cousin said a short good night and walked off. Still I lingered in the street below. Through the open windows, I heard Marietta's high staccato laughter, and Trip's in response as if she were shaken off her feet by mirth, held shaking and helpless, by an enormous God of laughter. I moved off, hardly knowing where, tears in my eyes, tears for the immortal kiss that had not been given or taken! Nor did I once think, in the innocence of my birth that day, ah, individualism! it is a lonesome world. Love, too, is lonesome.

By the middle of June, I had wound up my affairs in Philadelphia. And I severed all connection with Boshnacks' forever. Afterwards, as a free but somewhat poor man, I went to New York to call on Trip again. True, I had not heard from her, though I had written. . . . It was just a polite letter, saying how much I enjoyed that day in New York with her. And soon after, too, I forwarded my paper on Poe. But I never received any answer. When I approached that apartment again with high mounting hope, already warmed by the thought of its informal welcome, I found it had become vacant, and neither Trip nor Van nor Marietta was anywhere to be reached. Their landlady could tell me nothing, except that they had rented there that past winter by the month. All three had vanished like the fox ladies in Chinese fairy tales, leaving no trace behind.

I wrote to Laura James. I asked her cautiously of Trip. Trip, she wrote back, had gone home. And she sent me Trip's address, which was South, amid Southern mountains. I wrote Trip again. Oh, with what care I had chosen my paper, remembering the counsels of George! With what care I had penned those pale meager words! And nothing came of that either. Trip seemed a dream, or if real, hidden now by all the obstacles of fate, time, space and the world. But I did not forget her. Nor what I had come to America to find. I set out now inspired to seek the romance of America. And spurning Boshnacks' and the mean security it had offered me, I took the immemorial gypsy's trail. I became the man who must hunt and hunt for the spiritual home.

KIM RONYOUNG

Born in Los Angeles in 1926, Kim Ronyoung (Gloria Hahn) was witness to the very beginnings of what is now the thriving Koreatown
culture. Her mother, Haeran (Helen) Kim, was a poet and activist in
the overseas Korean Independence movement and her father was
an immigrant laborer; they form the basis for the central characters
in the first part of *Clay Walls*. The novel is a quiet multigenerational
narrative of emigration and assimilation, focusing on the lives of a
mother and her second-generation daughter, changing points of
view as the narrative moves forward in time and history; it is all the
more poignant because of its quietness. Although the novel is usually read as representational of the social history of early Korean
Americans (who arrived before World War II during the Japanese
occupation) and as a story of successful assimilation in the next
generation, under its deceptively accessible surface the thematic
depth is actually far greater.

    Clay Walls begins from the point of view of Haesu, a woman of
the Korean upper class, a *yangban,* who must endure the indignity
of menial labor after her marriage and emigration. Haesu's husband, Chun, who is of lower social status than she, follows the ex-

ample of some local Chinese merchants and opens up a fruit and vegetable stand that eventually allows the couple to establish themselves with family and home. But the dream of assimilation (if there ever was one) is exposed as false or unattainable for Haesu and Chun. The family disintegrates under the social and economic pressures that affect them so differently because of their incompatible class backgrounds. Haesu and the children are eventually abandoned by Chun after he loses the family savings, leaving them bankrupt; and Haesu learns after an attempted return to Korea that it is impossible for her to live there while the Japanese still rule. Haesu is a testament to the vital economic and social role Korean women have played through Korea's history as a colonized nation.

Clay Walls is almost prophetic in its depictions of the escalating tensions between African Americans and the Koreans who have, by economic necessity, moved into their neighborhoods. Kim suggests sympathy with the African American condition subtly: the most prominent Black man in Haesu's neighborhood is named Lucerne Luke to suggest clarity and light, features exactly opposite of what Haesu would attribute to him. In fact, her daughter Faye's interactions with the African American men in the neighborhood, and Haesu's response to them, foreshadows the greengrocer controversy and is, in fact, an invisible subtext to later works.

The title of the novel refers to the walls of a traditional Korean rural house. In the context of the setting, which is Los Angeles, the image has layered multiple meanings. The walls form the division between inside and outside, domestic and public, Korean and American. They are simultaneously an image of protection and of obstruction, resonating also with the Korean tradition of keeping women secluded in the *anbang,* or the inner room, of a house. In its Californian context, the novel also compares the experiences of Koreans and other immigrants by symbolically paralleling the clay of Korean walls and the adobe of the Mexican-influenced local architecture. The clay may also be read as referring to the underlying commonality of all humans in the biblical context, and so the image of protection and obstruction can also be seen as human nature, a more critical representation of the race politics that forms one of the underlying themes in the novel.

For nearly two decades, *Clay Walls* was the only Korean American novel in print, and so has been used in Korean American and Asian American literature courses as representative of the immigration experience, particularly for Korean women. It has been especially meaningful for those second-generation Korean Americans who found it difficult to communicate directly with their parents about the problems of displacement, transition, and assimilation.

from *Clay Walls*

Haesu

"You've missed a spot," Mrs. Randolph said, pointing. "Dirty."
Haesu had been holding her breath. She let it out with a cough.

Mrs. Randolph shook her finger at the incriminating stain.
"Look," she demanded, then made scrubbing motions in the air.
"You clean."

Haesu nodded. She took in another breath and held it as she
rubbed away the offensive stain.

"Th-at's better." Mrs. Randolph nodded with approval.
"Good. Clean. Very good. Do that every week," she said, scrubbing the air again. She smiled at Haesu and left the room.

Haesu spat into the toilet and threw the rag into the bucket.
"*Sangnyun!*" she muttered to herself. "*Sangnyun, sangnyun, sangnyun!*" she sputtered aloud. She did not know the English equiva-
lent for 'low woman,' but she did know how to say, "I quit" and
later said it to Mrs. Randolph. The woman looked at her in
disbelief.

"I don't understand. We were getting on so well. I . . . " Mrs.
Randolph pointed to herself "teach you." She pointed at Haesu.
"You do good. Why you say, 'I quit'?"

"Toilet make me sick."

"That's part of the job."

"No job. No toilet. Not me. I go home." Haesu held out her hand, palm up to receive her pay.

Mrs. Randolph stiffened as she backed away from Haesu's out-stretched hands. "Oo-oh no. You're supposed to give me adequate notice. I'm not obligated to pay you anything."

They were words not in Haesu's vocabulary. Perhaps she had not made herself clear. Haesu raised her hand higher.

Mrs. Randolph tightened her lips. "So you're going to be difficult. I'm very disappointed in you, Haesu, but I'm going to be fair." She motioned Haesu to stay put and left the room.

Haesu sighed with relief and put down her hand. She knew that Mrs. Randolph's purse was on top of the dresser in the bedroom; the woman had gone to get the money. As she waited, Haesu looked around. It was a beautiful room. She had thought so when she first agreed to take the job. Later, when she ran the vacuum over the carpet, she had admired the peach-like pinks and the varying shades of blues of the flowing Persian pattern. She felt an affinity with the design. Perhaps what some historians say is true, that sometime in the distant past Hittites were in Korea. She ran her fingers over the surface of the table. The mahoghany wood still glowed warmly from her earlier care. She had not minded dusting the furniture. It was cleaning the toilet she could not stand.

Mrs. Randolph returned carrying a coin purse. She gestured for Haesu to hold out her hand, then emptied the contents of the purse into the outstretched palm. The coins barely added up to one dollar. Haesu held up two fingers of her other hand.

Mrs. Randolph gave a laugh. "No. You quit. Two dollars only if you were permanent." She shook her head; it was final.

Carefully, so as not to scratch the surface, Haesu placed the coins on the table. She picked up a dime. "Car fare," she explained.

Mrs. Randolph glared at Haesu. She began to fume. "Why you insolent yellow . . . "

Haesu knew they were words she would not want translated. She turned on her heels and walked out.

*

The dime clinked lightly as it fell to the bottom of the coin box. Haesu found a seat by the window. She would put her mind to the scenes that passed before her and forget the woman. She enjoyed her rides on streetcars, becoming familiar with the foreign land without suffering the embarrassment of having to speak its language. In three months, she had learned more about America from the seat of streetcars than from anywhere else.

The ride from Bunker Hill to Temple Street was all too brief for her. Only a few minutes separated the mansions of well-to-do Americans from the plain wood-framed houses of the ghettos. But it might as well be a hundred years, she thought. Her country's history went back thousands of years but no one in America seemed to care. To her dismay, few Americans knew where Korea was. This was 1920. The United States was supposed to be a modern country. Yet to Americans, Koreans were 'oriental,' the same as Chinese, Japanese, or Filipino.

As shops began to come into view, Haesu leaned forward to see the merchandise in the windows. In front of the Five and Ten-cent Store, children were selling lemonade. A discarded crate and hand-scrawled signs indicated they were in business. Charmed, Haesu smiled and waved at the children. When she recognized the shops near her stop, she pulled the cord to signal the conductor she wanted off.

Clara's house was several blocks away. Although the rambling Victorian was really the meeting house of the National Association of Koreans, Haesu thought of it as Clara's. It was because of Clara that Haesu and her husband, Chun, were given a room, a room usually reserved for visiting Korean dignitaries. It was because of Clara that Mr. Yim, her husband, had agreed to make an exception to the rule.

The front door was open. Rudy Vallee's tremulous voice filtered through the screendoor. Clara was practicing the foxtrot again. Haesu stepped out of her shoes and carried them into the house.

"I quit my job," she announced, loud enough to be heard over the victrola.

Clara stopped dancing and took the needle off the record. "But you've just started," she said.

Haesu set her shoes on the floor and plopped into the sofa. "It was horrible. That *sangnyun* stood over me while I worked. I had to practically wipe my face on her filthy toilet to satisfy her."

"Oh, *Onni,* how terrible," Clara said, looking as if she had swallowed something distasteful.

The expression on Clara's face made Haesu laugh. *'Onni,'* older sister. The honorific title further softened her anger. "The work wasn't hard. I could have done it," Haesu said confidently. "I have to admit the *sangnyun* has good taste. Beautiful furniture. Carpets this thick." She indicated the thickness with her forefinger and thumb. "Such lovely patterns. Like the twining tendrils on old Korean chests. Do you think we have Persian blood in us?"

Clara laughed. "I wouldn't know. You're the one who always says you're one hundred percent Korean."

"I am. But I'm talking about way back. Long, long ago. It would be fun to know." She absent-mindedly picked up one of the round velvet pillows Clara kept on the sofa and ran her hand over it, smoothing down the nap of the fabric. "What difference does it make now?" she said with a sigh. "What difference does it make who our ancestors were? I don't have a job."

"A lot of difference, *Onni.* Your ancestors were *yangbans.* No one can ever deny that. Everyone knows that children of aristocrats are not supposed to clean toilets," Clara declared.

Haesu tossed the pillow aside with such force that it bounced off the sofa onto the floor. "Then what am I doing here?"

Clara picked up the pillow and brushed it off. "How many times are you going to ask me that? You're here . . . "

"Living with you and Mr. Yim because Chun and I can't afford a place of our own," Haesu said.

"Why do you let that bother you? Mr. Yim and I don't mind. We want you here." Clara sat down next to Haesu and slipped her arm into Haesu's. "You're like a sister to me. If you were in my place, you would do the same."

Haesu looked earnestly into Clara's eyes. "I would, that's true. We had such fun in Korea, laughing at everything, worrying about nothing."

"It will be that way again. We haven't been here long enough. I've only been here a year and you've hardly had time to unpack. We'll get used to America." Clara leaped from her seat and pulled at Haesu's arm. "Put on your shoes and let's do the foxtrot. I think I'm getting it."

Laughing as she pulled away, Haesu protested, "No, no. I can't do that kind of dance."

"Yes you can. Just loosen up. You act like an old lady, Haesu. You act like you're eighty not twenty." Clara put Rudy Vallee on again and began dancing around the parlor, gliding effortlessly on the linoleum rug.

Haesu drew her feet onto the sofa out of Clara's way. She reached for the cushion and held it in her lap. Clara's enthusiasm amused her. It also puzzled her. Rudy Vallee stirred nothing in Haesu to make her want to dance.

Haesu stood at the screendoor waiting for Chun. Since Monday she had been thinking about what she would say to her husband. She knew what she would not say to him. At dinner on Monday, when Haesu had explained to Mr. Yim why she had quit her job, Clara had chimed in with, "It's so hard here. Haesu's right. We had such fun in Korea, laughing at everything, worrying about nothing."

Mr. Yim's jaw had dropped, the *kimchee* he held in his chopsticks falling onto his rice, causing a momentary lapse in his usual courtly manners. "Laughing at everything and worrying about nothing?" he had said incredulously. "Then, tell me, what are we doing here?" While Haesu and Clara had searched for an answer, Mr. Yim had sardonically added, "As I recall, no one I knew was laughing at Japanese atrocities. Everyone I knew was worrying about persecution." Haesu had shrunk with embarrassment; Mr. Yim was a Korean patriot who had suffered torture in a Japanese prison, and was now forced to live in exile to escape death. "How thoughtless of me," she had replied. "Please forgive me."

Up until two weeks ago Haesu walked with Chun to Clara's house on Thursdays. Chun had found them work as live-in domestics. But Haesu could not bear being summoned by the persistent ringing of a bell and, after two months, had quit. Chun had insisted upon staying on, choosing the security of room and board and five dollars a month. Haesu now saw him only on his days-off.

As soon as she recognized his slight build and flat-footed gait, she flung open the screendoor and walked out to meet him.

Chun did not stop for her. She had to turn around and walk alongside him, matching her steps to his. "I quit my job," she said.

"Let's talk about it later," he said, speeding up. "I have to go to the bathroom. The damn food makes me sick." He hopped up the front steps and disappeared into the house.

Later that night, when they were alone in their room, Haesu told her husband the details of her quitting.

"You'll get used to the work," he said.

"Never! I'll never get used to cleaning someone else's filth."

"It takes two minutes to clean a toilet. It won't kill you," he said as he climbed into bed.

Haesu felt the heat rise to her cheeks. "I'll never understand how you do it, how you can remain mute while someone orders you to come here, go there, do this, do that . . . like you were some trained animal. They call you a houseboy. A twenty-five year old man being called 'boy.'"

"They can call me what they want. I don't put the words in their mouths. The work is easy. Work for pay. There's no problem as long as they don't lay a hand on me. Just a job, Haesu. Work for pay."

"Cheap pay and demeaning work," she said.

Chun shrugged his shoulders. "No work, no pay. No money, no house, no food, no nothing. It's as simple as that."

"That's not good enough for me and I won't disgrace my family by resorting to menial labor," she whispered hoarsely, keeping her voice down as her anger rose. She was obliged to maintain the peace of her host's home.

"I haven't met a *yangban* yet who thought any work was good enough for him. Me? I'm just a farmer's son. Any work is good enough for me. Isn't that right?" He pulled the covers over him.

"I don't want to talk about that now. I have an idea. Are you listening? Riding home on the streetcar, I saw these little stands where people were selling things. Nothing big and fancy. Little things. Standing in the sun selling . . . things. It didn't seem like hard work. Why can't we do something like that? Are you listening?" She shook his shoulders.

Chun snorted. "You? Selling things? Out in the sun where all the Koreans can see you?"

Haesu pulled the blanket from his shoulders. "I don't care about that. All I care about is that we be our own boss. Can't you see that? No one will tell us what to do."

Chun pulled the blanket from her. "Let a man get some sleep, will you?" He covered himself then turned his back to her.

Haesu walked over to his side of the bed. She leaned over him and put her lips close to his ears. She spoke softly. "I will never work for anyone. Do you hear me, Chun? I'll never clean someone else's filth. Never! You'll never make enough money as a houseboy to support us. Do you hear me, Chun? As soon as we make enough money, we are going back to Korea. We don't belong here. Just tell me, what are we doing here?" She really had laughed at everything and worried about nothing in Korea; a daughter protected from the world by her parents, groomed in seclusion for marriage.

Chun's answer was a series of rattled breaths followed by deep snores.

In the morning, Chun showed no indication that he had heard her. She raised the subject the following week. She pursued the matter until Chun held up his hand to stop her.

"All right, all right, have it your way," he said. "We'll ask Mr. Yim. See what he thinks."

Mr. Yim was the titular head of the house. In truth, the house was more his than Clara's because he was paid by the National Association of Koreans, the NAK, to maintain the clubhouse. He was fifteen years older than Clara, older than everyone who lived under his roof. He treated them all as he would his own children.

Haesu waited impatiently as Chun explained her idea to Mr. Yim. Ordinarily, Chun's terse speech left her yearning for more. Now she hoped for greater brevity.

Mr. Yim's response was important to her. She's never felt qualified to enter into debate with him about anything. He was a *yangban* higher born than she. And he was a scholar. But his life had become one of contradictions. Ten years ago, when the Japanese confiscated his land, he refused to relinquish his ancestral home to the usurpers and set his house on fire. He left for America with only the money in his pocket and found work in Los Angeles washing dishes. When be began to receive a small stipend from the NAK for his organizational work, he arranged to have a bride sent from Korea. He was besieged with photographs from potential mothers-in-law who listed their daughters many virtues; they were after his family name. Mr. Yim chose Clara. He claimed that he chose her because of her family background and honest face, but everyone knew it was because she was an exceptional beauty. "You're a classic Korean beauty," Haesu would tell Clara, "with delicate features and skin as smooth and fair as porcelain."

Remembering Clara's unfailing response, "I'd rather have your large eyes," brought a smile to Haesu's lips.

"I see that Chun's idea appeals to you," Mr. Yim said. "What will you sell?"

Chun looked at Haesu. Her mind went blank; lemonade was for children.

"Hmm. How about fresh produce?" Mr. Yim suggested. "Men who work at the produce market often come to the cafe where I work. I could find out how you can get produce wholesale. You can quit your job as houseboy, Chun." He waved his hand in the air. "Don't worry about having food in your stomachs or a roof over your heads. Consider my home yours." He nodded. "I approve of your idea. Selling anything to someone is better than polishing his shoes."

The sky was just turning light as Chun pulled and Haesu pushed the crate of apples up Temple Street. They had invested in a wagon for their new business. Haesu had assured Chun that no risk was involved. If the business failed, she would sell the wagon to some child in the neighborhood.

At Sunset Boulevard Chun said, "This is as far as we go."

By the time they had finished stacking the apples, the sun had risen and shone obliquely on the skins. Haesu had polished each apple the night before. They now glowed a magnificent red. She selected one for its elongated shape, skillfully cut it into a floret then set it atop the pyramid of apples. She stood back to examine her handiwork. *"Ibuji?"* she said, asking Chun to confirm that it was beautiful.

He nodded. "It looks like a lotus."

His poetic reference took her by surprise. Her look made Chun blush.

"Cigarettes," he blurted and dashed across the street to a drugstore.

How strange he is, Haesu thought. They had been married several months and he was as much a stranger to her as when she first learned she was betrothed to him. Her parents had arranged it; she never wanted him. She had begged them to reconsider, reminding them that his family was socially beneath theirs. They would not listen. They would never go back on their word; they could not. Chun had asked his American missionary employer to act as matchmaker and Haesu's parents could not refuse the esteemed foreign dignitary. When Chun had to leave Korea, Haesu was sent to California to marry him, committed for life to a man she did not love.

Haesu took a lemon from the pocket of her apron and cut it open. She squeezed the juice over the cut apple to keep the white from darkening.

The lotus was a Buddhist symbol of purity, a flower that bloomed even when rooted in stagnant water. Her family were Buddhists before their conversion to Christianity. So were Chun's.

He can't forget, Haesu told herself, he still thinks of home.

She looked up as a streetcar passed. A Chinese woman sitting at a window seat was staring at her.

She'll think I'm part of the American scene, Haesu thought. She couldn't help the smile that came to her face.

Faye

It was while Momma was working at the dining table that I learned to cook rice. She yelled the instructions to me while I was in the kitchen. "Keep rinsing the rice until the water is clear. Then add water to cover the rice and it reaches the first joint of your finger."

"Which finger?" I shouted back.

"Bring it here and let me see." When I brought the pot to her, she poked her little finger into the water. "Just a bit more," she said as she wiped her hands with her apron.

"When did Halmoni teach you to cook rice?" I asked, proud that my first pot of rice was cooking on the stove.

She laughed. "No one taught me. I taught myself after I came to America. We always had cooks in Korea."

I pulled out a chair and sat down. "Did you ever play hop-scotch?"

She unraveled a length of thread from a spool and bit it off. "Of course. But the game I loved most was jumping on boards, something like a seesaw but instead of sitting down, we stood up. If I had a good partner, I could jump higher than anyone." She licked the end of the thread and pushed it through the eye of the needle. "Another thing my girlfriends and I did in the spring was to take a picnic lunch to the mountains and go looking for *kosari*." She tied a knot at the end of the thread.

"*Kosari* grows in the mountains?" I had only seen the dried edible fern after it had been soaked and made into a salad.

She nodded. "While the snow is still on the ground; young shoots that are still curled and tender," she said as she began to sew.

It was while she was telling me about washing her hair in mountain streams that we heard the rice boil over. I scrambled out of my chair and ran to the kitchen.

"Take off the lid and lower the flame!" Momma ordered.

As soon as I took off the lid, the frothy bubbles settled down into the pot. I lowered the flame. Before I could ask, Momma yelled, "Put the lid back on." I sighed with relief. Everything was under control. All I had to do was follow Momma's instructions.

At dinner, Harold and John complained that the rice was too dry. Momma looked at me and said, "It's not bad for the first try, baby." She said 'baby' the way Koreans say, *nae dari,* tenderly and filled with love. She once told me there was no English translation for *nae dari* but that 'my precious child' or 'my darling' was close. I liked Momma's way of saying 'baby' best.

I began to cook rice every night and soon discovered that the first joint of my forefinger measured the right amount of water. The boys no longer complained. While the rice steamed, I visited with Momma. I learned about the things she did when she was a young girl in Korea: about her having to walk through forests where tigers lived, about her love for roast corn in the fall and roast chestnuts in the winter. She filled my imagination with her remembrances until her memories became mine. Stories of her childhood ended when she said, "Until I was sixteen years old, I had nothing to worry about. Then I became engaged to your Papa." I never asked her to go on, afraid she would say something against Papa. I only begged her to repeat the stories she had already told me.

Thursday, when I came home from school, Mamma's chair was empty. A note on the table said, "Bring the baby carriage. Meet me at the bus stop." The message was for me. Harold had to deliver newspapers and John was out selling magazine subscriptions.

The carriage was jammed in the corner of the back porch, filled with empty bottles and bundles of newspaper, ready for the junkman. I piled everything on the floor, knowing that before Saturday I would have to put everything back into the carriage. As soon as we heard the call, "Rags, bottles, papers," and the clop of horseshoes on the asphalt pavement, Momma would tell one of us to wheel the carriage to the curb and sell everything in it.

The straw-colored wicker baby carriage, its white damask lining torn and gray with soil, was part of our household furnishings: whenever we moved we took it with us. I have seen baby pictures of me lying in the carriage when it was new. Harold suggested we junk it with the bottles and papers, but Momma said, "We can't get anything for it and it does come in handy."

I buttered a piece of bread, sprinkled it with sugar, and started for Western Avenue. Managing the floppy bread in one hand and pushing the carriage with the other, I followed the carriage on its zig-zag course. The wheels were worn and bent out of shape. They no longer rolled straight. At Western Avenue, I stuffed the last bit of bread into my mouth to have both hands free to turn the carriage at the corner.

As soon as I made the turn, the sounds of people working, walking, shopping, and driving cars became louder. Colored people were yelling to friends on the street. Most of the owners of shops lived upstairs or in back of their businesses. Cooking smells hovered over their cash registers. I looked at the gaudy window displays as I pushed the carriage, passing by the handmade signs that said, "Come In."

As I neared the poultry I held my nose, careful to avoid running the carriage into the rabbi who sat on a wooden lug box in the path of the late afternoon sun. He was reading, deaf to the din of squawking hens and the gutteral gobbles of turkeys. It was his job to purify the birds when they were slaughtered, when they would be silenced forever. Harold had told me that the rabbi made the poultry kosher.

Count Basie's music filtered into the street. Some boys were hanging out around the record shop. We shared the neighborhood with Blacks, but when they grouped together, it became their territory. I pretended to look at something on the other side of the street and walked rapidly by them.

"Hey! China girl! Ain't you a little young to be pushing a baby carriage? Come on, give us a look-see at this miracle of nature."

I knew his name. It was Lucerne Luke; he lived on our street. He was dark, muscular, and intimidating. I always knew when he was around, but I would try to avoid him.

He flicked the brim of his cap with a snap of his fingers then grabbed the edge of the carriage. "Hey, slow down there, China girl. What's your hurry? I'm not going to hurt you." He looked into the carriage then jumped back in feigned shock. "What's this? An empty baby buggy? Isn't this a shame? A tra-ge-dy." He grinned at his companions. Without changing their stance, without moving from the spot they had staked out for themselves, they smiled. "This chick needs help," Luke went on. "What d'ya say, man? We can help China girl fill the buggy with a bronze bundle of joy. A baby Buddha." He did not bother to look at me as he sauntered back to his buddies, laughing quietly.

"Man, no baby of yours is going to be bronze," one of Luke's friends said with a chuckle.

Lucerne Luke gave him a look of surprise. "Whatchu mean, man? When I mix up the colors, anything is possible." He emphasized the words 'what' and 'anything.'

They looked away from one another to laugh, a quiet chugging laugh.

I saw my chance and ran. No one was chasing me but I wanted

to get as far away from their gibes as I could. I never knew what to say to them; nothing glib or clever came to me. Anything I said to them fell flat, like a 'lead balloon' as John says. I crossed the street to the bus stop. Lucerne Luke had resumed his place among his friends. They continued to watch the scene on Western Avenue, as if waiting for something to happen that would amuse them. They were through with me.

"Whatchu mean, man?" I repeated to myself, trying to sound like Lucerne Luke. I tried several times under my breath, but it didn't sound right. Harold and John knew how to talk jive; they learned because they did not want to get picked on by the boys in the neighborhood. But Momma would not allow them to speak it in the house. Once, when Harold and John bantered in jive talk, Momma said, "Stop that! You sound like Amos and Andy." I had laughed when the boys took it as a cue to shuffle out of the house, swaggering like Lucerne Luke and his friends. Even Momma had laughed.

A bus arrived and pulled up to the curb. The door opened and released boys and girls carrying schoolbooks and men and women clutching the handles of shopping bags. Momma was not among them. As the bus roared by, I slid my gaze down the street. Lucerne Luke caught me looking and waved. I spun around and stared into the window of the drugstore, pretending to be absorbed with the display of razor blades, aspirin bottles, and bandages. I read the labels over and over again until the next bus arrived. The door at the front of the bus hissed open and Momma stepped down. She was carrying a large package.

"Wow! How many dozens of handkerchiefs did you bring?" I asked, giving her a hand.

"Ten. It's heavy," she said. We dropped the package into the carriage. "It took time to count them and then the buses were full. Did you wait long?"

"Kind of. Is Mr. Seligman going to pay you more?" I struggled with the crooked gait of the carriage.

"Two dollars and a half, just like everyone else." She helped me guide the buggy. "I'd better get Harold to oil the wheels," she said.

"You never told me you could embroider," I said.

She smiled. "You're too young, baby. You don't know anything," she teased. She looked beautiful when she smiled.

I slid my hands along the handle bar closer to hers. "I'm almost eleven."

"I know," she said.

We were walking by Lucerne Luke. He tipped his cap and bowed.

"Pay no attention to him," Momma said to me in Korean.

I helped Momma count the handkerchiefs and divide them into six piles.

"A stack for each day," she explained. "It will help me keep track of where I am." She would be counting the days that passed by the number of handkerchiefs she sewed.

The next night, Momma took time from her sewing to cook for the members of her political group. Papa had called them the Five Cave Dwellers, but Momma said their real name was Koreans for Progressive Reforms. They used to meet regularly, but after Papa left and we began moving from house to house, the meetings were often postponed.

When Papa was home, I could not understand why Momma had to meet with the men, but with Papa gone, I liked having them in the house. Uncle Yang was my favorite; he took time to tease me. The others were more serious, but I considered all of them close friends of the family. I knew them so well that I could mimic the mannerisms of each: blink my eyes like Uncle Yang, shout and wave my fist like Uncle Lee, sit all huddled up like Uncle Kim, or gaze at the ceiling and smack my lips like Uncle Min.

My mimicry amused Momma, but she told me, "Don't let them see you do that. They'll think you're disrespectful."

They usually met in the parlor, but Momma was behind in her work so they sat around the table while she sewed.

"Can't you put that down for a minute?" Uncle Lee asked impatiently.

"I'll be up all night if I don't work on them now," Momma told him.

Uncle Lee threw up his hands. "What kind of meeting is this? A secretary is supposed to be writing, not sewing," he complained.

"I'll write it down later," Momma said, pulling the needle through the cloth.

"Do you do that all day?" Uncle Yang asked. "My back would kill me if I sat like that all day."

Momma waved her hand toward a pile of unfinished squares of linen. "I have to finish these by tomorrow."

Uncle Yang reached into his pocket and pulled out a twenty dollar bill. He was blinking like crazy. "It's for the food," he said, putting the money on the table. Momma thanked him but she did not touch the money until everyone had left.

Before the next meeting, she tried to teach me to cook meat and vegetables for the men, but had to throw out what I had cooked.

"I'll just have to tell them they can't meet here anymore," she said.

"Maybe after I practice," I said, knowing I could never cook Korean food like Momma.

"No. There's no reason you should be cooking for them."

When she told the men her decision, they would not hear of it.

"Never mind the food," Uncle Kim said.

"I'll take the minutes," Uncle Min said.

"I'll stop in Chinatown and pick up something to eat," Uncle Yang offered.

"Our organization's a joke," Uncle Lee declared.

"I'm sorry," Momma said. "I just don't have the time."

Everyone became used to seeing her sit at the table sewing. Ladies from her church dropped by and sat at the table to gossip. At first, Momma stopped to make them coffee. But one night she told me, "They're taking up my time with their foolish gossip." When she continued working while the women talked and no longer served coffee, they quit coming to visit. Aunt Clara's phone calls also became less frequent. She told Momma that she was reluctant to take her from her work. She never came to visit. Ever since the operation on her face, Aunt Clara rarely went out of her house.

The K.P.R. held fewer meetings because Momma was too busy working to do anything about Korean independence. Soon, she had only the radio to listen to and Harold, John, and me to talk to; mostly to me because the boys were finding more to do away from home. I became so used to seeing Momma sitting at the table that seeing her anywhere else seemed strange.

I carried reports of what had happened to me while I was away from home to the dining table and waited for Momma to tell me what I should make of it all. I omitted only information that I thought would upset her or was of no consequence. Each day's report differed little from the one before. But Bertha promised changes.

"Why don't you come out to play after dinner?" she asked me one afternoon.

"I have my homework to do," I said.

"That doesn't stop your brothers," she said.

"They have to be in by nine," I told her.

"A lot can happen between seven and nine," she said.

"What do you mean?"

"Come on out and find out for yourself."

That night, I asked Mamma. She said, "Absolutely not! You cannot go out after dark, not in this neighborhood."

"What about the boys?" I asked.

"They're boys and have to learn to take care of themselves."

"It's not even a school night," I whined.

She motioned me to a chair. "Come and listen to the radio. You don't understand now, but someday you'll thank me."

"I'd be just outside. What could happen to me there?" I asked, plopping into a chair.

"If I didn't love you, I wouldn't bother to forbid you to do anything," she said.

"Can't you trust me?"

Momma stuck her needle into the pin cushion to lean forward and turn up the volume on the radio. "Sshh. I want to hear this."

I slid off my chair and crawled under the table. Lying on my stomach, I wondered how she could justify treating me one way and the boys another. I knew it was an argument I could not win. Even Papa and the boys would side with her. They would say I'm too young to understand. I sat up and raised my voice.

"Momma, are you glad you're a woman?"

"Of course. Where are you?" She peeked under the table. "What are you doing down there?" She went back to her work and said, "Although, if I had been a man, I certainly wouldn't be sitting here sewing."

I crawled out from under the table and sat in my chair. I folded my hands on the table and said, "See what I mean?"

At nine o'clock, we heard the back screendoor slam. "We're home!" Harold shouted.

I got out of my chair and ran back to see my brothers. I gasped when I saw John. He was holding a blood-stained shirt over part of his face. Harold put his finger to his lips to silence me. He motioned me back into the dining room.

Momma had put down her sewing and was rubbing her eyes. She folded her arms on the table to form a pillow for her head. "My back aches, Faye. Could you pound your fists over it for me?"

I started beating Momma on her shoulders and worked down to her lower back then worked my way up.

"Where's Harold and John?" she asked, her voice waving in and out as I pounded.

"They went to their room," I said, alternating striking her with the side of my fists and the edge of my opened palms.

"Oh, that feels good," she warbled.

I traveled over her back, sometimes vertically, sometimes horizontally, and sometimes in circles. At first, her back felt as hard as stone, then gradually became softer.

"Momma?"

"Umm?" she murmured.

"When is Papa coming back?" I felt her muscles tighten under my hands, but she did not answer.

RICHARD E. KIM

Born in Korea in 1932, Richard Kim emigrated to the United States after the end of the Korean War, in which he fought for the South. He was educated at Middlebury College, Johns Hopkins University, the University of Iowa, and Harvard.

Kim's public visibility after his best-selling first novel, *The Martyred* (1964), has yet to be matched by any subsequent Korean American writer. Based upon his experience and knowledge of the Korean War, *The Martyred* met with universal praise, and has been compared to the works of Albert Camus for its intense and relentless engagement with existential issues. Kim, unlike most writers of fiction, composed *The Martyred* and its sequel, *The Innocent* (1968), with the clear intention of inquiring into profound moral and philosophical themes such as the meaning of truth and the nature of good and evil, innocence and guilt.

In *Lost Names* (1970), from which we take our excerpt, Kim takes a very different approach to the theme of Koreans living under the Japanese colonial regime before the end of World War II. Whereas his two earlier novels are structured around the exploration of their themes, the linked stories in *Lost Names* are clearly literary renditions of Kim's childhood experiences; even in their depiction of troubled and grim circumstances, their tone is often wistful and nostalgic. In "Is Someone Dying?" Kim's depiction of the Japanese, who seem as much oppressed by the power of the colonial administration as the Korean students they are oversee-ing, is particularly unexpected with its implicit sympathy (or per-haps, more accurately, objectivity) toward the Japanese. In recent interviews after the reissue of *Lost Names,* Kim has been quite hon-est about his recollection of those colonial times, noting that for the typical Korean peasant, living under Japanese rule would have been little different from his hard life under a Korean regime.

Kim wrote *Lost Names* while he was teaching in the English de-partment of the University of Massachusetts, Amherst. It was praised by such prominent literary figures as Pearl S. Buck and Ed-ward Seidensticker. Of the title (which refers to the Japanese colo-nial law that required Koreans to give up their names and take Japa-nese names), Kim says, "I loved the word 'lost' and all the things that it conjures up, especially in English—*Paradise Lost.* Lost is al-most damned, almost sinful. *Lost Souls*—which was at one point my working title. I like 'lost' because it has a lot to do with my sense of my generation. . . . Kind of like I am now. I don't belong." (Kim uses "lost" in another title, *Lost Koreans in China and the Soviet Union* [1989], a book of photo essays.) Unlike many of the writers in this collection, who find it problematic that readers cannot under-stand the literary transformation of life into literature, Kim is proud of the fact that his novels and stories are often taken as factual memoirs and not fiction.

from *Lost Names: Scenes from a Korean Boyhood*

''Is Someone Dying?''

Yesterday, those who did not have blisters on their hands were given a pick and shovel and were ordered to work on the runway. Along with my classmates, I shoveled all day, digging up rubbery red clay, to a depth of four feet, barely clearing a ten- by twenty-foot sector, which was our class's quota for the day. We are building an airfield about thirty miles south of Pyongyang—or about twenty miles north of our town. The airfield, we are told, will have two runways and will serve as a refueling station for the Kamikaze planes that are being flown from Manchuria to the mainland. That the planes are to come all the way from Manchuria means—a friend of mine says, with a knowledgeable air—that either the Japanese are running out of planes in Japan proper or they are running out of pilots so fast, they can't keep planes flying in Manchuria.

In any case, so far, we have been spending most of our second year in junior high school in Pyongyang, on this so-called airfield; so-called because, although some four hundred to five hundred high school students have been working on it at all times for the last several months, the airfield has only one runway barely completed, and we have yet to see a single Kamikaze plane, or any plane, either land on the field or even fly over it.

We all live in tents, one class to a tent; after several months in use, the tents still exude a rancid odor of tar and grease melting under the broiling August sun. The tent has raised wooden platforms with an earthen path between them. The platforms serve as our sleeping quarters; that is, each of us is given a straw mat to put on the platform, and that becomes his bed. At night, it is very damp, and so are the straw mats, and, what with the smell of tar and grease and the mildewed, rotting straw mats, the air inside the tent is always stale and nauseating. We have learned to breathe with our mouths open, to avoid, at least, the sickening sensation we get when we inhale or sniff the air through our noses. When it rains, the earthen floor and the path usually get flooded and muddy, and the reddish brown clay stays wet and squishy for several days, giving off a smell that reminds you of rotting fish.

There are about sixty of us in our tent, plus our teacher, a middle-aged Japanese, a scholar of Chinese classics, of all things, who, like the rest of us, sleeps on the straw mat on the platform by the entrance to the tent, though he is separated from us by a bed sheet hung by straw ropes between his bed and the next bed. He could have slept in a tent specially constructed for teachers, but he insisted on sleeping with us, as well as working with us on the field, saying, "We are in this together, aren't we?" In spite of that, he is not popular or respected, though he is not disliked by the class. He has been lately confined to his bed, because he was stricken by a severe case of dysentery. Once a day, he is visited by a Japanese medic, who gave us permission to have someone stay in the tent at all times to look after our teacher. The medic also doles out aspirin tablets and small bags of bitter white powder, which is for diarrhea. Nearly everyone has diarrhea.

Although we suffer from dysentery and diarrhea and chronic indigestion, we can't really complain about our meals—mainly because we do get to have three meals a day. Most of us would be having two meals or, more likely, only one meal a day if we weren't working on a Japanese airfield. Each day, we take turns for "kitchen" duties and take buckets over to the field kitchen and bring back cooked barley and soy-sauce soup that always has bean sprouts or several cubes of bean curd floating in it. As it is about a ten-minute walk from our tent to the field kitchen, our meal is cold by the time we get it to our tent, and, on rainy days, transporting the meal to our tent becomes a major operation. We all have our own utensils, which we brought from home, as well as our own bedrolls.

Speaking of our homes, once a week, for a day, we are allowed either to go home or to have visitors, and most of my classmates, except those who happen to come from nearby towns or villages, learned to stay. What with the shortage of trains and buses, which are now running on charcoal, travel is not only difficult but also demoralizing. If we are late in reporting back to the airfield, we have to do extra work. Some of the well-to-do boys, when they have visitors, manage to get cakes or candies, which become as valuable as money. Although there is a canteen for students by the field kitchen, most of us are without money and try to avoid going to the canteen even if we have money, because the canteen is a favorite gathering place of the Japanese students, who can get things there by using ration coupons while we pay in cash. The Japanese students live apart from the Korean students, in their own tents at the other side of the field, with a cluster of tents for the Japanese airmen between us. We seldom meet one another, even when we are working on the field. We have been here over two months this time.

After work and after our evening meal, which is the same as our breakfast as well as our lunch, though without the soup, we have classes in our tent. "The school must go on," says our principal. So—for two hours a night, under the dim, flickering halos of kerosene lanterns, we study; that is, we keep up with the progress of the war, which is supposed to be going very well for Japan, or we read from Japanese history. Having worked all day out on the field in the hot sun, it is difficult for some of us to stay awake through the two hours of nightly classes, especially because we have to kneel and sit on our heels Japanese style on the straw mat, straining our eyes in the dim light.

"Why don't we quit the school?" we often ask ourselves. Most of us would have liked to quit the school and go home. But, getting into the school was difficult to begin with: The competition was fierce, and, for those of us who came from small towns and villages, it was doubly difficult to be admitted, and, then, once we quit the school, we would never be admitted to another high school anywhere in the country—that is, those who withdraw from the school to avoid "serving the Emperor through labor" become, automatically and by law, *personae non gratae.* In my own case, I have a special reason for not quitting; I was told that if I quit the school while the school is "requisitioned" to work on an airfield or in a munitions factory, my father would have to give a report once a week to the local police as to what I was doing and so forth, like a man out on parole.

This morning, the Japanese corporal who is in charge of our class inspects our hands and, seeing that my hands are bubbling and oozing with blisters, orders me to work, along with eight others, as a gravel-carrier. I and a classmate will, as a team, go outside the barbed-wire fence (which surrounds the entire field, including our tents) to a gravel pit worked on by the students from another high school, load the gravel into a big straw sack, run a wooden pole through the sack, and carry it, Chinese-coolie-style, to the section of the runway in which our class is digging. Everything is done by hand; we have not seen a single piece of machinery on the field, except for a dozen or so stone rollers. Even the cement that has not been used yet is transported to the field by oxcarts. When the Kamikaze planes land, they will be the only machines on the field—if they ever arrive from Manchuria.

I am weak from diarrhea, and I have a splitting headache. My hands are wrapped in an old towel, which I also use to wipe the sweat from my face. The sun is glaring hot on our bare backs, which are blistering and peeling from the heat, and our shoulders ache and chafe from the weight of the wooden pole. Our feet are also blistered, and, after a while, our thin cotton socks get glued to the burning skin of our feet, and, soon, the rubber soles of our sneakers will stick to the socks, and our feet will begin to feel as though they were walking on squishy, wet rubber.

Usually, we manage to start the day laughing and chatting about what we would like to eat and what we miss most, which always turns out to be something edible. We have breakfast at six-thirty, start working at seven-thirty, and, by nine in the morning, no one is talking very much—until lunch time comes around.

Around eleven in the morning—I must have made ten or twelve rounds carrying gravel—the Japanese corporal wants to see me. The corporal is young, barely twenty, and so thin that, when he breathes in, you can see the whole of his rib cage. He, too, is suffering from dysentery or, at least, from heavy diarrhea; he has a pallid face, yellowish and hollow around the eyes, as if he hasn't slept for days.

When I report to him, he tells me that my mother has come to see me. "Visitors are allowed only on Mondays," he says, "unless it is for something very urgent, like when someone dies." He orders another boy to take my place. He does not seem upset or angry with me, and, as though he were reciting a regulation for my benefit, he speaks matter-of-factly. "However, in case of emergency, students may be allowed to receive visitors at the discretion of the officer of the day. Permission granted. Make sure you return to duty as soon as you can. Dismissed." The corporal stands in front of me, not knowing what else to say or do, panting and gasping, his naked torso streaming with sweat. He is actually a college student in his first year who was drafted as what we call a "quickie" soldier, to be assigned to labor forces, especially to supervise students working on airfields or at munitions factories. He is as exhausted and undernourished as anyone else, going through his work mechanically. He is so frail and thin that we are not really afraid of him at all. He is not as strict or mean-tempered as most of the other Japanese soldiers supervising us; in fact, some of us suspect that he is more afraid of us than we are of him. We think—and we have a small bet going—that he is going to collapse before we do. "All he needs is a little push," says a wrestler friend of mine, "just a little push." The corporal shrugs for no apparent reason and gives me his water canteen. "When you are through, have it filled and bring it back to me."

I take his canteen, give a little wave of my hand to my classmates, and head for the main entrance to the airfield. I pass by a line of my friends who, stripped down to their waist, are carrying gravel, waddling under the heavy sacks. They all want to know where I am going and why I am not working. I tell them that my mother has come to see me. I move on. The field is swarming with hundreds of students shoveling, hoeing, removing dirt, carrying gravel . . . and yet the sizzling field is strangely quiet.

A large tent just inside the main gate is reserved for visitors. The tent has long wooden tables and benches. On Monday afternoons, when we are allowed to have visitors, the tent is packed with parents and relatives, not saying very much to each other, just looking at each other, the boys munching on cakes or fruits, some mothers crying quietly and embracing their children when the sergeant of the day comes and announces that the time is up.

The tent is roasting in the sunlight. My mother is standing in the shadow of the tent. She is wearing Japanese-style women's pants, which all women have to wear these days; they are the regulation "uniform" for women, who are not allowed to wear Korean dress outside their homes. My mother looks uncomfortable and terribly out of shape in that baggy colorless get-up.

I drag one of the wooden benches from inside the tent and place it in the shade. We sit down, side by side, not saying a word for a while. She is holding my hand in her hands. Her fingers are rough, and her fingernails are cracked. She has gotten quite thin lately. She unwraps a small bundle and hands me an apple. I take a bite from it.

"Visitors are not allowed, you know," I say to her, eyeing the Japanese sentry at the gate, "except on Mondays."

"I told them a little lie," she says, trying to smile. She is not successful. Her eyes are filled with tears, watching me munch the apple. She wipes my back with her handkerchief. "Hungry?"

I shake my head. "No."

"I brought you some clean underwear," she says, touching the bundle, "and—this." She takes out white cotton sheets folded into little squares.

"I don't need sheets."

"These are not sheets really. You said you were bothered by bedbugs and insects, so I sewed sheets together, you know, so you can just crawl into them and tie them up around your neck. Won't that help a little?"

I nod. "But how did you get in? What did you tell them? Anything wrong at home?"

"I told them your grandfather is very ill or something like that, and they let me in."

, "Which grandfather?"

"Well, both our grandfathers are fine, really. I had to tell them something. I wanted to see you, and then Father thought I should come." She dabs her reddened eyes with the handkerchief.

"Father sent you?"

She looks down for a second. "In a way," she says.

I crush the core of the apple on the dusty ground. "Something is up then," I say.

She hands me another apple. "How is the work going here?" She looks toward the field; hundreds of tiny figures on the field seem hardly to move. "Poor things," she says. "You all have to work like laborers in the sun like this!"

I laugh. "We are laborers, you know."

She shakes her head. "Have you seen any planes yet?"

I laugh again. "That'll be the day. Nothing much is getting done here, you know, and we don't have any machines, like trucks or bulldozers. It'll be a long, long time before any planes can land here."

"It will probably be too late then," she says, lowering her voice a little.

I give her a hard look. "What do you mean?"

"Well, the way the war is going . . . "

"What is the latest news? We don't learn anything new here, except that everything is going all right. Of course, we just don't believe a word of what they say anymore, anyway."

"It won't be long," she whispers, casting a quick glance back to the sentry. "It won't be long at all. That's what Father says."

"He knows something then."

She nods. "Just between us."

Her meaningful look and whispered words make me serious and contemplative, and, for no reason at all, I think of the Japanese corporal whose canteen is dangling by my feet. "No, it won't be long. Even I can tell that." I look at her to emphasize that I am not simply making an idle remark. "A little push, Mother, as we say here. Just a little push—and they will collapse like a man with only skin and bones left."

"Well, they've had that little push already," she says quietly, trying to look casual. "Not many people know about it, though."

By then, I know that my father has something directly to do with her coming to see me and that they are both trying to tell me something. "What happened?"

She takes out of the bundle three cakes of millet with dark sugar. "Germany surrendered a long time ago, almost three months ago, and we were never told about it, of course. And the Russians are attacking the Japanese in Manchuria."

I am too stunned to respond immediately. I only mutter, "In Manchuria . . . the uncle . . . "

"Father was in Manchuria to see our uncle about two weeks ago. They had a talk, so your uncle should be all right."

"The Russians . . . "

"That's not all," she says, her voice hushed. "The Americans have dropped some sort of new bomb on Japan, and the rumor is that it is very powerful, some sort of scientific weapon. One bomb can wipe out a whole city, and Father has heard that two cities have already been destroyed by these bombs. Japan can't last long fighting against that kind of a new weapon with bamboo sticks and boys like you slaving on a puny airfield like this."

"It won't be long then. It really won't be long this time."

She nods. "The Americans have landed on Okinawa, too," she says, as though she were saving that piece of information for last. "They have really landed, and it won't be long before they will land in Japan itself. You'll see."

I feel my heart beating wildly, triumphant yet afraid. "When was that!"

"Almost four months ago. How can the Japanese hide that sort of thing from us!"

In my imagination, I see hundreds and thousands of Japanese charging the Americans on the beaches of Okinawa with bamboo sticks and the American soldiers simply machine-gunning them down . . . the shovels, the picks, the straw sacks, the gravel, the barley, and the soy-sauce soup with bean sprouts, my Japanese teacher down with dysentery, the skinny corporal with hollow eyes, and the Japanese Kamikaze planes that never showed up. . . .

I look at her. "Does Father want me to come home?"

She says quickly, as though she had been waiting for me to ask that, "Do you want to?"

"Well, Mother, if it won't be long before the war is going to be over, I think I'd better come home and stay alert, you know, just in case. Father would need me around to keep my eyes open and that sort of thing."

She stares at me in silence, then, with a sniffle, tears shine in her eyes. "We should all be together, of course," she says.

"Yes, I want to come home," I say firmly. "When the Japanese are defeated, it will be chaotic everywhere, you know. For a while, anyway. It may not be easy to travel back and forth, and who knows when I can ever get home?"

Without a word, she takes a piece of paper out of her pants pocket. She hands it to me.

It is a notice of withdrawal from the school, already signed by my father.

"Things are pretty urgent then," I say. "It really won't be long then, if Father feels this way. Why didn't you let me see this in the first place?"

"We wanted you to decide. We didn't want you to feel that you were running away, you know, deserting your friends. You are in this together, and you don't want to look like a weakling, not that slaving for the Japanese is important or worthwhile. The only thing is that we really mustn't and can't tell the others. I mean, you simply mustn't tell your friends why you are quitting. Do you understand that?"

I nod. "We can't take a chance like that. It is too dangerous."

"It's too bad, but we really can't."

"All right," I say, getting up. "We'd better hurry then. I'll take this to our teacher and tell him I am going home."

"Do you want me to come along?"

"Of course not, Mother. I can handle this. I'll be right back."

She takes out four apples and the three millet cakes I have not touched. "Do you want to give these to your friends?" She wraps them up in a clean towel. "I did bring your clean underwear and the sheets, you know, just in case you didn't think you should quit now."

I take the apples and the cakes. "I'll be back in a minute."

"Will he let you go?"

"I'll just tell him off if he makes a fuss about it."

I run toward our tent. I am going home, I am thinking, I am going home; I am going to quit this rat hole and go home. It won't be long; it won't be long. . . . My running feet raise a cloud of choking red dust, and the sun beats down on my bare back, but I don't mind. I've been waiting for this moment for a long, long time. And now it has come—and I am going home.

The boy who stays with the teacher to look after him is outside the tent, doing laundry, which is one of our duties when we get our turn to stay with the teacher. I tell him to stay outside while I talk with the teacher.

The air is broiling and sickening in the dark tent.

The teacher is sitting cross-legged on his straw mat, reading a magazine, smoking a cigarette. He looks up when I come in. "Oh, it's you," he says, adjusting his thick eyeglasses. He has lost weight, too, I think, as I look at his bony fingers rubbing his nose. "What are you doing here?" he says.

I go up to him and give him the withdrawal notice.

He takes one look at it. "So—," he says, looking me up and down. He takes off his glasses and bats his eyes a few times. "So— it has come to that."

"Sir?"

"I always wondered when you would quit."

To my surprise, his tone is neutral and subdued. I am at a loss what to make of his words.

"I am not going to ask you why you are withdrawing from the school at a time like this," he says. "I am only interested in the fact—yes, the fact—that you are, indeed, quitting us."

"Sir, I don't understand you."

"You don't have to say anything," he says, bidding me sit down beside him on the mat. "Now that you are going to leave us, we must have had it. This is the end of us, isn't it?"

I am silent.

He takes a fountain pen from a leather briefcase by his mat and signs the paper. "There," he says, handing it to me. "Now, you can go home."

I don't know what to do or say. I was expecting a tirade from him, and I was determined to have it out with him if he became unpleasant.

He is silent, too, looking past me toward the open entrance, through which he can see the boys working on the field, which shimmers in the sun.

At last, I manage to say, "It is not that I am a weakling and can't take the work . . . "

He quickly interrupts me. "No need to say anything, boy, because I know the real reason for your withdrawal."

His words frighten me a little. I feel uneasy with him. With the paper in my hand, I try to find the proper moment to take leave of him—for good.

Abruptly, he says, "Have you any idea how the war is going?"

I shake my head. "No, sir." Then, quickly, "I mean, sir, everything is going fine."

"You don't have to tell me that, especially you. It is not going well, and you must know that. Don't you? You and your father must know a way to find out, don't you? And that's why I have been wondering when you would decide to go home. You know, I used to tell myself, 'Well, when that boy quits, we've had it.'"

I squirm, without a sound.

"Don't be afraid of me," he says, smiling. "Not all Japanese are evil men, you know."

"No, sir."

"But you mustn't repeat this to other Japanese."

"I know that, sir."

"We've lost the war," he says in a voice so hushed that I am awed by it. "To continue the war is sheer lunacy. You have not seen Japan or Tokyo, of course, but let me tell you that it is a vast wasteland. Last time I was back home, it was . . . ah, but why go into that? It is too late. Did you know or do you know that the Americans have already landed in Okinawa?"

I remain silent.

"The have," he says. "The landed there a long time ago."

Without realizing it, I let it slip out of me: "The Russians have invaded Manchuria. . . . "

"Where did you hear that!"

I say quickly, frightened, "It's just a rumor, sir."

"You must never, never tell that to anyone. Do you understand that? If that is true, then the end has really come. There is nothing in Manchuria to stop the Russians. You know there are no planes left there to come all the way down here and use this airfield! Lots of nonsense! The only planes left are old primitive ones, unfit for flying. But the Russians! They have waited this long! Ah—it means troubles. What dirty, double-crossing opportunists those Russians are!"

I am afraid of the nature of our conversation and am also afraid he is getting off the track. "Sir, my mother is waiting."

"She is here?"

"Yes, sir."

"Then you must go. Wait. They may give you trouble at the gate if you show just that withdrawal notice. I'll write out a pass, and you don't have to tell anyone about your withdrawal."

He takes a blank pass and fills it out for me. It says I am going home for three days because of an emergency at home.

"Thank you, sir." I am, to my surprise, really grateful.

He nods. "I suppose you don't understand why I am being kind to you, do you?"

I am touched and say, "I hope you will get better soon, sir. You've lost a lot of weight since we came out here. I do hope everything will be all right for you, sir."

I climb down from the wooden platform and stand on the earthen floor. I bow to him and turn around. I go to my straw-mat bed and collect my things. I leave the apples and cakes on the mat, with a note to my friends to help themselves to them. I wrap up my things in a bed sheet and put them in my bag. I feel the teacher's eyes on my back as I take a step toward the exit, with the bag in one hand and my bedroll in the other. I have to pass by him, and, as I do, I bow to him again, without looking at him.

"Wait a moment," he says.

I feel a big lump in my throat, afraid he may change his mind. "Sir?" I face him.

"Will you remember me?"

Taken aback, I mutter, "Of course, sir."

"Well, your father is a big man in your town, isn't he?"

Bewildered, I don't answer him.

"Oh—I know all about your father."

"Yes, sir?"

"Perhaps—well, I don't quite know how to put it to you," he says, raising his eyes to the tarpaulin ceiling of the rancid tent. The air is hot and suffocating. He lights a cigarette. "Perhaps, one of these days," he says, blowing smoke from his cigarette, "who knows?—I may come to your town."

I don't understand what he is trying to say. "Yes, sir?"

"If I ever come to your town, do you suppose your father would help me?"

I stand silent.

"When we lose the war, we Japanese will have to get out of Korea. That's quite obvious, isn't it? Well, I was just thinking, perhaps your father could help me then. Do you think he would?"

I am now beginning to grasp what is going on between us, and I say, rather boldly, "You mean, sir, like hiding you for a while?"

"What do you think?"

"You won't have to hide from us, sir."

"It may become almost impossible to travel, you know, and anything can happen."

I don't reply.

"You Koreans hate us. I know that in the marrow of my bones."

I keep silent.

"I help you now," he says, smiling, peering at me through his thick glasses, "and you help me later. That's the general idea, you know. What do you think?"

I do not say a word. I know I am not going to reply.

"Please give my regards to your father, will you? And tell him what a fine man I have always thought he is, judging from the way he has brought you up. And you may tell your father what you and I talked about a moment ago. That's quite all right."

I want to get away. I want to run out of the stinking tent, but I don't want to make him angry with me. "I'll tell him that."

"You never know. Perhaps, we'll see each other again before long."

It suddenly strikes me that he is saying this sort of thing to other boys, too. To a select few . . . just in case. And, with a jolt, I remember several other boys who were given a special pass by him to go home for a few days—and I know the boys well, because we all share one common bond, among others, of having a father who has been convicted for his "Thought Crime," or for his activities in the Independence Movement.

I've got to get out of here, I tell myself. Fast. I bow to him. "Take care of yourself, sir. I may see you again someday."

"Remember me, now," he says with a smile. "And don't forget! The war isn't over yet, you know."

I am running—away from the tent, away from him, and away from my bondage to their tottering empire. I am running toward my mother. "I'll never see you again," I keep telling myself as I run . . .

. . . but I do see him once more, back in Pyongyang, after our Liberation. . . . I see him working on the streets of Pyongyang, a member of a Japanese labor gang, shoveling and sweeping out the trolley tracks, under the watchful eyes of sullen Russian soldiers in black jackboot with burp guns and German machine pistols. . . . He does not see me, but I see him, and, for one fleeting moment, I am sorry for him, but then I think—For thirty-six years, you and yours have trampled on us and tried to destroy our souls. . . . Love and compassion that have been smothered by the memories of thirty-six years cannot be resurrected by pity that lasts only for a fleeting moment. . . .

My mother is waiting, and I nearly run into her, choking with pounding, aching emotions, trembling with a dizzy swirl of ecstasy and fear. I tell her about the Japanese teacher.

"He must be frightened," she says matter-of-factly. "What do you want to do with this?" She holds out the Japanese corporal's canteen.

I toss it onto the wooden table inside the visitors' tent. "He can get the water himself."

At the gate, I show the pass to a young Japanese private, the sentry. Cradling his rifle, he looks at my pass. He is young, too, not much older than I am. His uniform is soggy with sweat. He gives the pass back to me.

"All right, boy," he says, tossing his head, eyeing my mother. "Is someone dying or something?"

I merely nod my head. Yes—someone is dying, I want to shout to him. You and your Empire are dying . . . and I am going home. . . . I am going home, Boy! . . .

By the dusty, rutted road far from the airfield, we are waiting for a bus . . . and my mother tells me that my maternal grandparents are now at our orchard. My grandfather in Pyongyang, the Presbyterian minister, was put in jail after every Sunday church service, sometimes for a day and sometimes for a few days. A pair of Korean and Japanese Thought Police detectives always came to the Sunday service, taking notes on what my grandfather said in his sermon. Three weeks ago, says my mother, they came and took grandfather away as usual. He didn't come home for more than a week, and, when he was finally released, everyone could see that he had been beaten. He had cuts on his face and a broken rib. They kept him, my mother says, because they didn't want him to come home until they had patched him up in a hospital. His church, as well as the other Christian churches, was ordered to close down when he was taken away. My parents went to Pyongyang and brought my grandparents to our town.

"They are staying at the cottage," says my mother.

"Is Father staying out there with them, too?"

"No." She puts her hand on my shoulder, drawing me to her. "Don't be afraid," she says. "They took your father away to a detention camp." She begins to sob. "Four days ago," she says.

Part **THREE**

SUSAN CHOI

Susan Choi was born in Indiana and grew up in Texas. After receiving her B. A. at Yale, where she won the Wallace Prize for Fiction, and an M. F. A. at Cornell, she took a job as fact checker for *The New Yorker,* where she was employed until 2000. Choi has published in numerous journals, including *The Iowa Review, Epoch,* and *Documents.* Her first novel, *The Foreign Student* (1998), from which we have taken the following excerpt, is an unusual example of imaginative recovery and projection.

The plot of *The Foreign Student* follows the unlikely intertwining of two lives: that of Chang Ahn, a foreign student at the University of the South in Sewanee, Tennessee, who bears with him the profound effects of wartime trauma that this emigration and renaming (as "Chuck") cannot ameliorate; and that of Katherine Monroe, a local outsider who began an affair at age fourteen with an English professor three times her age, and who is lingering as a scarlet woman in the margins of both town and university. The novel turns on ironic parallelism—that of illegitimate war and illegitimate romance—and its thematic force is in playing out the tales of Chang's and Katherine's etiology of alienation as their paths crisscross into eventual romance.

In this excerpt, we get an unsettlingly vivid depiction of Chang's torture at the hands of his own countrymen on the island of Chejudo, a stronghold for dissidents and guerrillas during the Korean War (1950–53). Choi pulls no punches, so to speak, and her descriptions are startlingly specific and visceral as she dramatizes the burden of memory in the context of local and national history. Readers will be compelled to go biography hunting in *The Foreign Student,* but Choi has done a masterful job of constructing fiction in the best sense of the word.

Choi, along with Nora Okja Keller, was among the recipients of an NEA Award for 2000. In her award statement, she says, "I'm a born skeptic, and my first reaction to the message from the NEA on my answering machine—'We have a question about your application'—was to assume that I'd done something terrible. Now I understand that the caller was cryptic in order to enjoy, firsthand, the sound of me screaming when I found out the truth." She might have been indirectly commenting on the theme of her novel.

from *The Foreign Student*

The freighter dropped anchor off an unsettled strip of Cheju's coast and sent its refugees to shore in overloaded rowboats. Chuck had come on deck looking frantically for what he expected, the teeming disorder and climbing roofs of Pusan harbor, and instead there had only been the waste of land creeping out from the foot of the cliffs, and an unpaved road winding out of sight around the bulk of a headland, the flat sky, and the screaming gulls. Once on-shore people began making camp, digging pits and building fires, feeding them with garbage and wet kindling pulled out of the hills climbing up from the coast. A few U.S. Army–ROKA joint patrols arrived from the far side of the island with a small number of tents. After setting these up the soldiers got back into their jeeps and bumped around the field, holding their rifles ostentatiously over the sacks of rice they'd brought. They started arguments with those refugees who had set up their own tents and built fires inside them. The army-issue tents quickly filled up with piles of clothing, chickens, cripples, children. There hadn't been stakes to pin the flaps down and these lifted in the cold wind, like blown skirts. It might have been warmer in the open air, where every fire became the hub of a wheel of bodies.

The camp had sprung up out of only the contents of the ship, but he knew that the following morning, as soon as it was light, the army would arrive in greater force to solidify it. In spite of the government's efforts the guerrilla presence on Cheju had never completely disappeared. It persisted in small, isolated bands throughout 1949 and the first half of 1950, and after the war had broken out it was constantly enlarged, by people acting on the rumors that the network of caves sheltered army deserters and North Korean partisans who coordinated the guerrilla activity on the mainland, in the rear of the front line. National Police and ROKA units patrolled the island constantly, picking up young unenlisted men, older boys, surly trouser-wearing girls. All the risks he had run on the mainland were concentrated here. If he was still in the camp the next morning he would either be drafted or arrested. He saw no able-bodied men at all: only girls, women, cripples leaning on sticks, and sexless children, unattached to anyone, deeply self-absorbed and hungry, trotting on the lookout for food.

As the evening turned into night he kept picking his way in circles through the camp, wrapped in his great dark coat. Everywhere he went he was followed by eyes. His coat was expensive, conspicuous wool, and he was young, uninjured, and male, although he coughed incessantly, doubling over to spit clots of phlegm. He was running a fever, and the rich-looking cloak hid a swarm of lice. He had become infested on the boat. Walking, he pulled his arms out of the huge sleeves and his hands scrabbled inside his shirt, trying to claw the vermin off his body, but they seemed to have burrowed just beneath his skin to feed, like ticks. The itching was terrible but the constant awareness of infestation was worse. He flailed as he walked, like a lunatic. He paused briefly at one fire and was given a handful of undercooked rice. Eating it he tasted feces on his fingers. "What are you doing here?" a woman asked him. "How are you not in the army?" Gulls were wheeling overhead, inflamed by the ripe smell of garbage that was carried upward by the warm drafts from the fires, in spite of the cold air. He could see their pale, bulletlike shapes, lit up from below. "I have contagious tuberculosis," he said, hoping this would make a space of wordless loathing around him, but the eyes didn't waver.

He waited until sleep overtook the camp and then he slipped away from the field of prone bodies and walked into the woods. There he took off his coat and shirt, quaking from the cold, and banged the shirt with a rock. His panic erupted. He banged so hard he broke a sweat. He could hear his breath bursting out of him, like steam from a valve. When he was done the shirt was peppered with his own blood, smashed out of the insects, but when he put it back on, it still crawled. The lice were living in his coat, on his head, in the safe thatch of his pubic hair, under his arms. He didn't return to the camp. Instead, he stood leaning on the trunk of a large tree all night, sometimes grinding himself against it like a dog, to ease the itching, but mostly standing, letting it support him. His eyes had adjusted when he left the open slope, blazing with fires, for the dark trees. Now they grew even keener, and he could see the delicate tracery of the undergrowth, the bare interlocking canopy, the roosting shapes of birds. His breathing grew even and calm. His heart throbbed within him, firmly held, his flesh conveying the pulse to the soles of his feet, and out, into the ground. He heard the wind moving in the needles of pines, and beneath that irregular noise, the constant washing sound of the ocean.

When the sky grew pale he climbed the tree and tried to sleep, but his fear he might fall kept him awake. He sat in the tree all day, growing numb from the cold, and that night began walking. He walked for three nights, always keeping the sound of the ocean to his left so that he would not stray inland and become lost. During the day he slept in dead leaves or under low shrubs. Although he saw no one, his vigilance never relaxed. It wouldn't have surprised him to stumble upon another filthy, starving, and paranoid person curled up in the mulch that he plowed through each morning to bury himself. He ate bark, and the lice from his body. His gums bled continuously; wiggling one of his teeth as he walked, it came out. It lay on his tongue, a little claw with a spongy root.

On the third day, crashing like a drunk through the trees, he heard a church bell striking discordantly. It was late morning. The bell gave him eleven baleful notes to follow and he rushed downhill toward it, seeing the scrolled shingles of rooftops before the sound died away. He entered the village clumsy with incompetent precaution, inching along the side of a building with his arms flung out for balance as if he teetered on a ledge, but the village was motionless. The weight of illness or stupor hung over it. Children lay asleep in the street. The church building stood at the head of a dusty square, anomalously European and solid, and ornamented by a pair of stone pillars that he might have wondered sarcastically about, imagining them ferried from the mainland by a platoon of missionaries, if he hadn't been mindless from hunger. Very slowly, trying to make no noise, he opened the door and immediately met a wall of bodies. It was a food line, winding back from the altar and bending past the entrance. He pushed his way in.

The line shuffled forward by inches. He was almost asleep when he reached the priest, a smooth-faced, hesitant-looking white man, perhaps no more than twenty. Chuck realized he had no bowl and cupped his hands, losing the water the potato had been boiled in. He hurried to a wall and wolfed the food, lapped his palms, sucked his fingers dry. Now the taste of his own filth on his hands made him dizzy with food-lust. He looked like a mad hermit, the coat crusted with mud, bark, bugs, the skeletons of leaves, his fingernails black with dirt, his mouth colorless.

He lingered hungrily at the edge of the room and watched the rest of the line labor past, his fingers playing desirously against his palms. It wouldn't have been so difficult to force his way past these people and take another potato. Each human in the line was a mindless segment, seemingly impassive, except for the barely perceptible, unyielding pressure by which first a tottering old man, and then a girl of about six, were squeezed out of the line by those behind them. If the priest was aware of what had happened he did not show it. The food dwindled and disappeared, but for some time the priest continued to dip his ladle into the pot, filling cups with the gray, starchy water. The pot looked like army issue: scratched aluminum with a pair of metal handles. When the ladle scraped bottom the people who had not yet been fed lingered uncertainly, tilting empty bowls as if something might fall from the ceiling. Finally they melted away. He stayed, watching the priest through the fringe of his hair. His hair had become streaked with gray. The whites of his eyes, he would see later, staring into the priest's small, flaking mirror, were yellow, the precise shade of phlegm. The priest's head and shoulders sloped forward even when he was not bent over the soup pot. His sad movements through the bare chamber, extinguishing candles, were led by his forehead. When the room was dark except for a tin-can oil lamp he was holding, the priest lifted the pot under one arm and forced himself to face the lingerer. "Go home?" the priest asked, in Korean.

Chuck answered in English. "Tell me your name."

The priest's eyes widened with fear. He had been guiding AWOL soldiers, leftist guerrilla farmers, teenaged boys who could very well have been Soviet agents for all he knew, from the gateway of this village into the island's hidden caves for almost fifteen months, since before the beginning of the war, and he had never been questioned before. In part, he thought, because he refused to know any more than he had to about the people he met. He had become a priest who refused to take confessions. "I'm Frank Todaro," he said. "I'm a Catholic priest from Cleveland, Ohio. I'm here to help these people, that's all. I don't know anything. I'm not on any side."

"I'm not on any side."

"What do you want?"

"Take me to the place," he said. "Hide me."

That evening Todaro deloused him. He stood naked in the

washtub as Todaro carried water in and boiled it, using the same pot in which he'd boiled that day's ration of potatoes. The room they were in had a trapdoor to the cellar, where the grain and potatoes were stored. Todaro slept with a gun beside his bed which he had only fired once, taking it to the beach and shooting straight out to sea so he would not hit anyone, to be sure that he could. He added the steaming water to the washtub, thinning the black soup Chuck's body had made. Then Todaro gave him a pair of scissors and Chuck clipped his pubic hair, and scrubbed himself with kerosene until his genitals were red and the coarse stubble stood out hideously. Again he was riveted and saddened by the stuff of his flesh. After he had bathed, Todaro seated him in a chair and sheared him to the scalp. As the matted locks fell the priest said, "The hills above this village are just like your head. Swarming with creatures, and all of them perfectly hidden. There's no way to get them out apart from cutting down the trees."

"I'll be safe there?"

"There, yes. But you can't stay up there all the time or you'll starve."

They left the mission after midnight, in the dead hour. The wind stood still. The snap of a twig carried for miles like the report of a pistol. He followed Todaro, for a long time no more than a dark motion, until they entered a gorge and suddenly, where the rift in the trees allowed the moonlight to fall on them, he could see the other man again, moving with remarkable agility in his heavy skirts, his scalp glowing through his downy hair. They shrank against the rock face, into the margin of shadow, walking on the level, dry streambed. He heard the waterfall before they saw it, a thin, persistent stream dripping between long teeth of ice. Behind it the rock was eaten away in the shape of a small amphitheater; crouching in the total darkness of this shelter the curtain of ice and the open gorge beyond seemed to blaze with light. There was no natural cave here, but the mouth of a tunnel. They had to feel, crawling blindly on all fours, to find it. "Are you claustrophobic?" Todaro asked him. The opening felt about as wide as a barrel. Its walls were dry, powdery, as cold as metal to the touch.

"Tell me what it will be."

"This continues for a quarter of a mile, slightly uphill, and then joins with a natural cave. The tunnel widens very slightly sometimes, enough to crawl, but for most of it you'll need to wriggle on your stomach. It's tight."

"Okay."

"After this, as much as possible, you know nothing of me, and I know nothing of you. It's safest for us both that way. This is the only place I have ever been shown. If your friend has moved from here I don't know where he'll be."

As Todaro was turning to leave Chuck said, "Why do you do this?" expecting the answer to be, As a man of God I have a duty; All human life is a sacrament; War is a sin.

"You people don't touch my stores. Didn't I say that? My stores are off limits to you. My rice, my potatoes, my poultry. If I am ever robbed, I give this place up."

He watched Todaro slip past the gleaming teeth of ice. For some time after the other man had gone Chuck remained motionless, listening to the quick percussion of the thread of water striking down on the stones, like his butterfly pulse. Then he closed his eyes and pushed himself into the tunnel.

He had never meant to come to Cheju. The history of his actions over the course of the war consisted of lucky accidents and terrible blunders ameliorated by lucky accidents. He was still shocked by his own failure to leave Seoul, although he knew, at the back of his memory, in the place where he consciously sought to exclude humiliations and heartbreaks from thought, that he had stayed out of loyalty to Peterfield and selfish, naive excitement. He had imagined phones ringing, wires keening and sawing like a flock of locusts, pounding feet, the focused, angry, crucial work of urgent dispatches. He'd had boyish ideas of covering the war, enclosed in the American machine. He'd seen too many movies. His resolution of loyalty to himself had been a punishment. It cut hard against the grain of what he wanted, of what would give him comfort. The night that Miki brought him the message from Kim, he had tried to close his ears to the finer points of it. His first reaction, even before his stunned gratitude to learn that Kim was alive, had been disciplined scorn: joining Kim was a romantic, suicidal daydream that didn't even belong to the realm of ideas. He would go to Pusan, as he should have done in the first place. But he had decided to stay with Peterfield, and been abandoned by him, and he had decided to spurn Kim, and instead been thrust onto the island from which Kim had sent word. He was superstitious by nature, an optimistic propitiator of luck and a passive fatalist. He began to suspect he was at the mercy of a force of correction.

The cave was a great, cold lung, a space of utter darkness that throbbed, invisibly, with breathing. It was full of sleepers. When he pulled himself out of the tunnel, scraping desperately against its closeness and then suddenly falling unmoored into space, he heard a match strike. In the tunnel he had made himself a void, a nothing encased in a body, carried by the body's steady humping, writhing progress but in no other way touched by it. Simply carried. Then he felt the breath of the larger space curl down to him, and went mad with claustrophobia. Even when he reached that space, he would be buried in the ground. The yellow globe of light cast by the match struck every wall of the cave, and the three other men, awake now. The cave continued, narrowing again, into another chamber. Its natural mouth was a mile away, on the opposite side of the hill. The men raised themselves on elbows and watched him from beneath heavily lidded eyes. They were filthy, like him, but dressed in farmers' loose pajamas, and straw slippers. This cave was a haven for men who were wanted by the police or for desertion, but it was also a gateway; beyond it lay a network that encompassed the island. The physical connections between the underground chambers were few. If one was found, it

could be cut off from the others and abandoned. The man holding
the match could clearly see the quality of his coat, even through
its grimy camouflage.

"Who are you?"

"I'm looking for someone named Kim. Kim Jaesong. He was
here."

"He's not here anymore."

"He might be somewhere else?"

"I don't know." The other men were squinting at Chuck skep-
tically. The man with the match said, "Todaro brought you?"

"Yes."

"This Kim told you to look for Todaro."

"Yes."

"Well, this Kim isn't here."

"But he was."

After a moment the man said, "I think so. I never asked him
his name."

"What did he look like?"

"Like you."

"How so?"

"He dressed like you." The man raised his chin, denoting
Chuck's coat. "He wore fancy shoes. Good leather shoes, made
with nails."

"Did they look like European shoes? They would have had a
pattern in the leather, like little holes."

"They didn't have holes. They were nice shoes. Rich-looking."

"No, the holes would have been decorative. A pattern."

The man was shaking the match out. They all vanished into
darkness again. "I never looked that close."

"Please. Light another match. Was there a piece at the toe,
stitched like this?"

"Yes," the man said.

"There was?"

"Yes. Now I'm sure this was him."

"But what did he look like?"

The man shrugged dismissively. "It was him. He was like you. He talked like you."

"How long ago did he leave?"

"I don't know. In the fall. But you can stay here."

"Will you take me to the other caves?"

"You can stay here," the man said again, with finality. Knowledge propagated in relay, by inches, formed message chains, and crept everywhere. But no one knew what lay beyond his grasp.

He lasted two weeks, maybe more, maybe less. He would never be sure how long this period of preparation was, during which his body preoccupied him entirely, its needs swelling to eclipse the world, shrinking slightly to admit the world again, the return of which only brought his body fresh needs and embarrassments. In those intervals of clarity and terror he looked for Kim, but he'd begun to suspect Kim had sent him the message to lure him to safety, and that Kim had already moved on. Kim would never hide for longer than he had to. He would be organizing, and fighting. And so Chuck's vigil became as desperate and hopeless as it had been in the first months of the war, when he waited the whole occupation for Kim to appear. He slept curled in the cave, waiting, his coat coiled around him like a shroud, or he groped his way to the cave's real mouth and slipped into the woods. He sucked icicles, threw himself on rabbits which bounded lightly away. And then he was finally starving, and he became a beggar, loping coyote-style through the streets of the coastal villages, emerging only after dusk. The torn hem of his coat trailed. His ears were always pricked for the sounds of a patrol, his nose high in the air, leading him.

His senses weren't his anymore. They were exquisitely sharp now but he only carried them, like cold tools, in the same way that his body carried the cold void within it, which was nothing but emotionless awareness of itself, made by these senses which weren't his. His eyes scanned the streets for Kim, but they were a dog's eyes, indiscriminately interested in company. He lingered in kitchen doorways and stared at women until they were too frightened to refuse him food; there were no men left to protect them. As Langston had predicted, Seoul had fallen again, just days after Chuck had escaped. The Chinese and North Korean forces had advanced so far south that the only territories left from which the southern army could restock its forces were the peninsula's southernmost tip and the offshore islands. Cheju's villages were emptied of all their remaining boys, young men, older men who had no trouble walking, all of them rounded up by the American MPs and the National Police and gathered into blinking, silent crowds, straw sleeping mats or wool army-issue blankets rolled up and tied to their backs. Small children and women and the very old gathered in a crowd opposite and also stood wordlessly, a strange reflection, to watch them walk away in motley columns, without looking back. No one expected them to return. Their departure was a funeral, every man wearing or carrying his most cherished item of clothing, the thing he was willing to enter the next world attired in. Their best clothes: some owned real wool coats, aviator-style sunglasses, hats with bills or ear flaps, felt fedoras. Some had leather bags slung across their chests, fragile wire-rimmed glasses, American-made combat boots. Others wore only loose pajama-style shirts and pants, dark vests, canvas slippers, with lengths of cotton tied around their heads to warm their ears. If you were a man walking through one of these villages from which every man had been taken, then you were a ghost, or a beast. Women dropped bowls of rice on the ground and withdrew quickly, slamming their doors, as he leaped on the food. Thinking of finding Kim had been a way to mark time, but time stopped for him. He only wanted to gorge his body on hot food, slake his thirst, fall asleep overcome with the drunken sensation of having been fed. He excreted solid waste with tremendous pleasure and regret. When he was not dizzy and amnesiac from hunger he moved through the village streets deliriously, enthralled with his body's continuance, forgetting more and more often to withdraw to the woods until twilight, falling asleep curled like a lover against the warm flank of a building, his hands squeezed between his legs, dreaming of food, shit, flesh, liquid. Preparing. At last he woke howling in pain; his hand had been yanked from its ardent embrace with his body and stamped into meat. There was still the boot on his hand, still stamping its heel, his flesh shredded back to the cool blue knuckle. When a second officer stepped forward and doused the wound with gasoline he fainted. He had been arrested by the National Police on suspicion of espionage. He woke up in the back of a bouncing jeep, screamed, and was clocked in the side of the head with the butt of a rifle.

He was put on a boat and sent to Pusan, to a detention center that had been made from a converted school building. While he was conscious he argued so strenuously for his release that he was repeatedly knocked out again. When he came to he would resume the litany, listing every superior he had ever had during his employment by the United States Army, naming Police Chief Ho, his uncle Lee, his father. "My father is in Pusan," he sobbed, as his head snapped back. And then, the black mist moving aside again, he lunged forward, trying to butt the driver of the jeep. "Minister Su is a friend of my family," he gibbered, "My father is a famous professor, my uncle is Congressman Lee," rushing the words out before he was struck. He threatened his captors with jail. A used bandage was stuffed into his mouth, gooey with fluids. By the time he arrived at the school building both his eyes were swollen to slits. He wove when he walked. The ground seemed to be bucking up toward him. Inside the school building there were still maps on the walls, but scrolled up, and the windows were covered with tar paper. He was taken into a classroom that had been cut in half with a thin wood partition. At first he thought the classroom would be his cell. Later he understood that this never could have been the case, because the classroom had to be periodically withdrawn from him, so that he would live in fear of seeing it again.

On his first day he was beaten with a sawed-off length of wood left from the construction of the partition, and a baseball bat found leaning in a closet. Two soldiers beat him while an officer watched. The officer said, "Avoid his head." When he fell to his knees he was kicked in the stomach, ribs, and buttocks. He bent his face into the cage of his forearms and went sliding back and forth across the floor. A boot tip hit his scrotum and he vomited a clear splash of liquid. "You're a spy," the officer said. "No," he gasped. "First the lies come out," the officer said, as if he were a doctor calmly talking his patient through a procedure. "Stand him up."

The two soldiers stood him up and he crumpled. They stood him up again and one pushed the end of a rifle into the soft pocket of flesh beneath his jaw. Unknown reservoirs of strength opened in him and he continued to stand.

Now his body would fail him by enduring, to be damaged further, and by failing to endure, for which he would be damaged further. There was an exposed pipe bending into the room near the ceiling, covered with blisters of rust, steadily leaking dark rust-thickened water that looked like clotting blood. "Do you see that pipe?" the officer asked him. He nodded. "Point to it." His arm lifted, jerking violently. "Salute the pipe," suggested the officer. "Say, I salute you, pipe." He said it, gurgling. A fire spread from the center of his back up the ropes of his arm, and down the backs of his legs. His kneecaps popped. One of the soldiers was dismissed. The other came and punched him in the sternum with his gun. He doubled over but did not fall. "Louder," said the officer. He shouted again. He was made to stand perfectly still with his arm extended, shouting his salute to the pipe. He did not know how many times he shouted. He could not adjust his body, accommodate its pangs which quickly turned to blinding, unrememberable, voiding black pain. He fainted, waking as he struck the floor.

The officer stood over him. "Are you a spy?"

"No," he said.

He was made to stand up again, immobile, with the arm extended, shouting his salute at the pipe. He could not endure the posture for more than a few minutes at a time without collapsing. Each time he did the officer told him he could remain lying down if he admitted that he was a spy. The soldier kicked him idly. He rose again, stood, saluted, fell, was questioned, kicked idly, made to stand. At the end of the day he was taken to a cell in the basement of the school building, on an empty hallway. The cell might have once been a cement shower stall, a few feet square, with a drain in the center of the floor and a stub of pipe extending out of the wall just beyond his reach, about a foot below the ceiling, with a threaded bolt set like a bar across its mouth. His right arm was handcuffed to this. He had to stand on his toes to keep the cuff from dislocating his wrist, but in spite of this he plunged into a deep sleep, and broke his wrist with the weight of his body.

The next morning he tried again. His wrist had swollen so astonishingly that the guard who retrieved him called a doctor. "My father is here in Pusan, my uncle is a congressman, I'm not a spy," he told the doctor. His face was washing itself with tears, but these tears were like the tears the eye always produces to roll in its socket, they meant nothing to him. His purpose was to communicate his point to this doctor, who was a good man, an educated man, and must have taken some kind of oath to protect human life. The doctor said, gazing past him with mild surprise, "I think that is your father coming now," and when he whirled to look the doctor squeezed the wrist, snapping the bone into place. His voice tore out of him unbelievingly. *"Haaaaaaaaaaaah . . ."*

He was taken back to the classroom, with the wrist bound. He begged the officer to call Eighth Army headquarters, USIS, his father, the government. "What?" the officer said. "Are you talking? All I hear is blah blah blah blah!" Nothing he said was ever audible. "What?" the officer shouted, striking him across the face. He hadn't been heard. He saluted the pipe until his voice was so strained he was nauseous. He was stood beneath the pipe, and made to throw his head all the way back, so that it screamed on its hinge, and then to swallow the rust-thickened drip. When he fell backwards he was punched in the sternum with the butt of the rifle, or the baseball bat, which stood in the corner when not in use, at an impudent angle, observing him. He would be allowed to stop swallowing if he admitted that he was a spy. When he screamed his own name, the name of his father, the name of his uncle, the two soldiers kicked his scrotum and buttocks, slapped him across the face with their gloves, stood him up, and pulled his head backwards by his hair until he thought his neck would break, while the officer said, "What? I don't understand you. What language is this?" He was stood beneath the drip again and made to swallow, with his head thrown all the way back. The rusty water filled his mouth and ran in streams down his neck. He vomited again, like his gut being withdrawn through his throat. The officer strolled the perimeter of the room, dangling the baseball bat thoughtfully. "Are you a spy?" he asked. He wanted to know where the Communists were hiding on Cheju. The soldier's rifle was resting against the soft pocket of flesh under his jaw and he was made to swallow his vomit, and the rust-thickened water. The sound the pipe made as it dripped was like a kind of incontinence.

That night he was given a piece of putrefying meat to eat; the next morning, when the guard found a pool of feces quivering on the floor of his cell he said, "Make that disappear," and stood over him with his gun cocked while he pushed the waste through the grate of the drain. He was shackled by his left hand now. He learned to haul himself up by it, to gash the inside of his right forearm against the sharp end of the bolt. He made a new gash every night. The marks spread across his arm, crisscrossing sometimes, but still readable, like the lines on his palm. He did not know how else to keep track of time, and he was determined to control at least the passage of his body through time. He could not control anything else. He could not control what his body expelled, or even what it ingested. He was given cattle feed, and ridiculed as he wolfed it down. He was so hungry he ate whatever was given to him, no matter how rotten or inorganic. His body suffered from the lack of everything, and it convulsively took in material, in the same way it convulsively vomited. Five marks on his arm, then eight. Looking at them, he did not experience the duration they represented. He only felt the pain in his body and even this became a dome he lived inside of.

On the ninth day his jaws were held open, and the officer took a straight razor and made small cuts all over his tongue; then he was given a bowl of salt. He ate it, weeping. "Are you a spy?" the officer asked. He said he was. He could have said, so long ago, I am a spy. The officer unfolded a piece of paper in front of his face. There were words coursing across it. He was only watching them, not trying to read them. Words came from a world which did not exist. His face washed itself with tears that were made in the same unfeeling place where his urine was made, and his blood. It meant nothing to him. The officer gave him a pen but his hand couldn't grasp it. His swollen wrist was numb and bound, and his fingers were broken. The officer placed the pen carefully between his fingers and it fell out again. The soldiers laughed. Although they couldn't have said why, this seemed very funny. The officer had to hold his hand, with the pen in it, so that he could sign. They performed the maneuver together, painstakingly. When they had finished, the officer sat down across from him, without releasing the hand. He held it lightly, with a regard for its injuries. "Thank you," the officer said. He nodded gratefully. He was so glad to have done it at last. His hopes kindled. He was being spoken to. The officer watched him with interest and he watched back, enraptured, his breathing quick from his exertion. Then the officer asked, "Where are the caves on Cheju?" He was returned to his cell.

After this there was very little left of him. He mimicked his torturers, making himself deaf to his body's cries for help. His knowledge of his body propagated in chains, telephone lines, bridges between a limb and his love for it, coursing braids of communication wire. He sliced through lines and wires, exploded bridges, excised his mouth and his groin, amputated his limbs. He no longer knew when he urinated. Cast outside the boundary of itself, his body had ceased to obey any boundary between itself and the world. He was always damp and acrid with urine, trickling out of him the way blood trickled out of his various wounds. His terror at the mangling of his fingers had evaporated, and the memory of that terror was as unrecognizable as any of his other possessions. He watched his hand being mangled from a great distance. He had already sawed it off. He had thrown away his body as if it were ballast, not to speed his death, but to survive. It was his body that would kill him.

He stopped keeping track of the days, and his torturers grew tired of him. Truckloads of captured guerrillas and other prisoners of war from all across the peninsula were arriving at the school, naked from the waist up, roped together at the ankles. They filled the school yard, squatting on their stringy haunches in the cold, falling asleep on top of each other. They were too unwieldy with their arms bound behind them, unable to pick themselves up when they fell over, and bringing the whole column down, and so they were allowed to keep their hands and arms, holding them clasped against their chests as if in prayer. Their shaved heads and bare shoulders shingled together like the scales of a single, ailing creature. In the classroom he was made to stand on a wooden chair that was set on top of a desk, beneath the pipe, with his hands cuffed behind him. The cuffs were attached to the pipe with a short length of chain; he had to double over as his arms were pulled up. He dropped his head and swayed dangerously on the chair, his toes grabbing ineffectually. He was left alone.

He fell, finally, tumbling off the chair, and dislocating both his shoulders as the chain snapped taut. Then he hung, his toes brushing the desk, swaying slightly. This was how the officer found him. The upset chair lay on the floor. The baseball bat leaned in the corner. The officer cut him down and stretched him on the desk, knees bent, arms stuck out behind him. "Can you tell me anything?" the officer asked.

He was desperate to be useful. He didn't want to disappoint. He didn't want to be discarded. "I went to church," he whispered. His voice crawled out of him.

"Where? What church did you go to?"

"Moon," he rasped. He saw the bright moon. He remembered the way from the cave's natural mouth to the village where he had been captured more clearly than the way from the mission to the tunnel, but even this memory was flattened and distorted, like the globe of the world unpeeled and forced onto a map. Ravines were very deep and particular landmark trees very large, but he could no longer assess the distance between any two points on his route. He struggled to feel the short trip again, but he needed his body around him. "Moon," he repeated. To betray the world he'd stopped believing in it. He no longer saw it clearly to describe it. Something in him kept dragging that memory to safety and he could not save himself.

The officer sighed. "Where are the guerrillas on Cheju," he said. His voice did not inflect this as a question. He intoned it, soothingly. "Give me a name."

Chuck reached and only felt a void, the silty, lightless bottom of an ocean. Within it he brushed against things that darted from him in the instant that he sensed them. He was sweating profusely, a cold, coursing sweat he was not aware of. The officer wondered if he was in shock. "Todaro," Chuck said suddenly. He remembered that man's gentle hands on his head, shaving the lice from his scalp, and the intense relief of his skin coming clean.

The doctor was brought to him and he was untied. He could not raise himself up. The doctor lifted him into a sitting position and then embraced him, wrenching the shoulders back into their sockets with the tightness of his clasp. He collapsed in the doctor's arms and did not move until the doctor pushed him away. "Hold yourself," the doctor said. "Like this." The doctor took hold of his arms for him and folded them across his chest, and closed his fingers around his elbows, so that the weight of his arms did not hang from the joints. "Can you?" the doctor asked. He nodded mutely, cradling himself. He began to cry. "Yes," he said, in the high, thin hiccup of a child. He held himself. The doctor walked him outside and the cold spray of wind struck him, carrying its atoms of the sea. He saw the prisoners squatting, their faces downturned.

Later he would realize that they had been there for days, but at that moment they seemed to have materialized as a result of his confession. Their posture remained frozen but their eyes rotated swiftly and found him. His heart accelerated, hammering so hard his ribs bounced as they tried to contain it. He was following the wall of the yard, the steady pressure of the doctor's arm across his back. His feet spun forward, paddling the ground. Gulls burst out of the storm clouds. Even in that twilight, his vision was stunned. The prisoners' gaze rippled after him, the perfect repetition of heads with their close fur of stubble, the large, delicate ears, the quick shift again and again of the eyes. Then he saw him. A pair of outsize eyes met his, stared. He stumbled hard and the doctor shoved him forward. The other face passed out of sight. He twisted and tried to look back but there was only the ocean of bowed heads, bare napes, humped shoulders, rolling away. The doctor walked him through the gate and steered him out into the street. He sank down where he was but the doctor prodded him. "Not here. Go away. Disappear."

SUKHEE RYU

Sukhee Ryu emigated from Seoul to the United States at the age of thirteen, went to high school in New York City, and earned a B. A. in English in 1996 from Harvard University, where she was awarded a Rona Jaffe Creative Writing Prize. Ryu then worked at a Korean immigrant workers organization in Los Angeles and wrote stories based on her experience, supported by a fellowship from the Echoing Green Foundation. She also spent a year in the University of Oregon's graduate creative writing program.

Much of "Severance," however, was written while Ryu was still in college. The story's disturbingly detached tone and continually displaced story lines undermine any expectation of comforting narratives of familial love, chivalry, Korean tradition, or immigrant success in America. Like a cynical gender-reversed transformation of *Kuunmong* (*Nine-Cloud Dream*), the famous seventeenth-century Korean romance about a young scholar and his encounters with wise and beautiful women that the exiled Kim Manjung wrote to entertain his mother, the stories that Christina tells her father make a mockery of stereotypical images of personal dignity, achievement, and connubial bliss. In doing so, Ryu begins the process of narrating those shame-ridden, unspoken existences being lived out everywhere in Korean American communities, including a cold shadowing of the hidden emotions that transpire between father and daughter.

Severance

It is the last Saturday of the month. My father and I are once again at the Starlight Diner. I picked him up from the Lana-Goldstein Home for the Elderly and brought him here in my Mercedes, the only inheritance from my father I've kept for myself. My father doesn't remember the car. He thinks it belongs to my husband. When I was a child, he used to let me straddle the armrest that goes up and down with a touch of a button, but now he doesn't recognize the car.

More often than not, he doesn't even recognize the regularity of our monthly rendezvous. The table in the front by the window where we always sit. Our waitress, Chrissie, who knows him well enough to not show any sign of recognition which, more often than not, puzzles him. The menu with dinner entrees listed in the shape of a Big Dipper.

He always orders the Turkey Dinner Special saying something like, "Well, I think I'll try the special tonight," or "Hmm, the special looks interesting." He likes the special. Always has, though now, he often forgets that he does. But he has not lost the habit of pondering over the menu for a long time, asking meticulous questions about the kind of eat-and-go food they serve here:

"Gravy homemade? No MSG?" Always the same questions, as if he's never tried it before in his life, although the turkey dinner has been the only Saturday special here for the past three years.

He keeps both of his fists on the table while the waitress puts the plate in front of him. His stomach recognizes the food, but there is nothing on his mind. There is nothing on his face except the readiness to chew and swallow. As always, he goes on eating until there's nothing more than streaks of congealing gravy on the plate. When he is finished, he becomes impatient. He starts shaking his legs under the table. Another habit he has not lost. When he becomes aware of the table jolting, he turns his body sideways to pull his legs out from under the table, and crosses them as if to prevent that mindless shaking. This, too, I know well enough to anticipate. This and much more. I know his every movement, every gesture, every sound he makes. I can recognize every single strand of his still graying hair, but does he? Does he know he has hair growing on his upper back where his hands cannot reach? When he stands in front of the mirror in the men's bathroom down the hallway on the third floor of his rest home, does he find his face familiar?

Does he know why he orders turkey all the time? Because that was the only food he could stomach when hung over. He used to be a drinker before the injury, before he lost his memory. He'd lie in an alcohol-infused slumber for half a day, get up to vomit almost pure alcohol into the toilet, fall asleep, then get up again. Repeat this cycle until his stomach was completely empty, then he'd ask for food. Linda, our housekeeper, would hurry upstairs to his bedroom with a tray of soft turkey and boiled, almost disintegrating vegetables, all doused in creamy gravy. It was his comfort food. He used to say that in some strange way, turkey always tasted vaguely like some Korean dish.

But, I don't tell him any of this. Though I recognize the assured and slightly saucy abruptness in the way he crosses his leg, though I recognize the way he casually flings his arm over the back of the chair, I look at him straight in the eye and tell him that he used to be a poor, hard-working man, a security guard and parking lot attendant. This time, I am thinking of Mr. Suh, who used to park my father's car when we went to eat at the Shilla in Koreatown, our favorite Korean restaurant. I think of Mr. Suh strutting about in a navy blue, mock-police uniform, his gray hair neatly trimmed. He always patted me on the head and marveled at my quickly lengthening legs, and never forgot to brag a little about his own daughter's academic achievements, though my father always considered him a garrulous fool, an embarrassing specimen of his countrymen, and never welcomed his ingratiating amicability. Mr. Suh was hit over the head with a "blunt object"—the newspapers said—while fighting off a carjacker, and he was in a coma for three months before he came out, albeit with no recollection of his past life. He went crazy little by little after that. Several times, I saw him crouched in the far corner of the parking lot that he used to guard. His wife and daughter would come eventually and drag him away, apologizing profusely to the manager. My father said that it was very foolish of him to try to fight off a jacker single-handedly, and that he was lucky that he didn't get shot. But my father always shoved a twenty-dollar bill into Mr. Suh's hand whenever we chanced upon him in the restaurant parking lot.

I tell my father that all the Korean newspapers called him a hero. My voice is full of pride, exuberant. I even add that there was a woman in the car who might have died if it hadn't been for his courageous intervention. My father smiles weakly, unimpressed, incredulous even. My heart contracts. I think his body is rejecting the story I am telling him. Like silent ghosts, the cells in his body blink in outrage and disbelief. But he says nothing. For a while, he merely gazes at the tip of his sneaker, the lace double-looped so that he won't step on it and fall. Then he looks at me, and in his eyes there is that tender sadness I know so well. He asks me how I got on by myself when he was in a coma, how I managed to take care of myself. I offer him a quick, assuring smile, but the look in his eyes does not fade.

Of the last twenty or so years of his past, nothing remains. The rest of his past, too, is forgotten except for the occasional flashes of disconnected images, dreamlike because they are disconnected and meaningless. I weave them into my story.

Sometimes he remembers what I tell him for several days straight, sometimes even for weeks. He'll ask me different questions, about his parents, his friends, hobbies, rebuilding his memory little by little. Then the doleful look in his eyes will disappear little by little, the constructed memory overcoming his instinctual disbelief, the ghostly echo of his dead brain cells. But always, there comes a time when his face simply goes blank all of a sudden. Then we start from the beginning. *What happened to me?* he asks.

The father I once had used to ask me about my boyfriends. Though his voice would only betray half-hearted curiosity, he would not stop asking until I told him. So I would tell him. Bill, Mark, Larry—names I've gleaned here and there, bold, black etched letters I saw on a name tag of a cashier at the supermarket, the names from a book I was reading. Faceless names. I'd blurt one out. And it was always the same sugary fairy tale I told him. They are all very tall and very handsome, smart and successful, all of them so very tenderly in love with me.

He no longer asks me about such things. But in the silent moment after I pay the bill and before we get up to leave the restaurant, I think he may once again ask me about the boyfriends I've had. He may even broach the subject by asking me what I was like as a teenager; then ask me about the kind of guys I dated. I think that may be the question brewing in that silence.

He does not ask me, I know he will not ask me, but if he asks me now before I pick up my pocketbook, I will tell him. I will tell him about this man. It does not matter what his name is. Adam, Ben, Charles, David . . . it does not matter. I know the tone of his skin, the shape of his face, mouth and lips, the wrinkles on his forehead. I can describe him standing there leaning against the doorjamb, in front of my dorm room one December night, three years ago; I see him clearly, the sheen of his pomaded hair, his pale lips trembling. A day's growth of stubble on his cheeks. His clothes a hasty ensemble of the warmest clothes he could find at the last minute.

He's flown in from L. A. and come straight from the airport. I feel the shock of seeing him once again. We have not seen each other for two years, and we do not yet know that this will be the last time we will see each other. We talk of nothing in particular. Roommates, school work, his business, the weather—things that do not interest us. Then when he finally blurts out *Are you seeing anyone?* his eyes are downcast, his voice is choking. There is no question mark at the end of that sentence, just a brutal finality that answers what it is asking for. My mind goes blank. Though we've broken up, though it's been two years since I saw him last, I think he is still crazy about me.

Because I can no longer stand the suffocating heat that fills the small rectangle of my room, I want to go out. Windows closed and the heater rasping, the room is a cemetery wherein all that's once dead and quiet comes alive—breath upon breath, a residue of smells that have lain dormant till animated by the heat, a mélange of dead skin cells that must be floating around me. Each corner of the room a tomb of near-forgotten recollections now re-exerting themselves. Each piece of clothing piled upon the chair now remembering the movement within—pulling up, pulling down, flinging, dropping, smoothing, crumpling. Then, each postage-stamp-sized surface of my flesh remembering what each remembers best, my body, too, come alive and undone.

We go out. We are walking together in the park. My gloved hand is in his. The moon is on us. The night sky has that purity of dark blue illumined by the snow on the ground. Flecks of snow whirl around, glistening like rain or piss in the globe of saffron yellow under the lamplight. I'm tired, weary. Maybe that's why I don't hear them coming.

Then all of a sudden, they are upon us, a pack of hooded kids. It is as though the trees themselves have come alive by witchery, uprooted themselves to encircle us. But they wear shirts, sweat-shirts, jeans, sneakers. Guns in their hands, clumps of snow on their shoes, menace in their methodical movements. It seems to me that they have said something, but I do not understand what it is that I am told to do. Their words are as surprising as their sudden appearance, incomprehensible. I do not move, but he squats at their angry bidding, perhaps a little too promptly, like a well-trained school kid.

There are maybe a half-a-dozen kids in all. *Is this a joke?* I may have looked around for their mothers, if he had not taken a pre-mature fright and knelt down. He even voluntarily puts his hands behind his head, hostage-style. He is petrified, eyes devoid of any-thing but this, the fear. Standing five steps away from him, I see everything, but I feel no alarm. Perhaps I'm just one of the gang, incognito, or better yet, invisible. My face painted yellow under the saffron light of the lamp.

The kids move quickly with unbelievable dexterity. They take his lambskin jacket, his watch, his alligator-skin wallet so fat with bills that it pops open by itself. Then they whack him on the head as if scornful of the alacrity with which he has yielded to their intimidation. With each blow, his head jerks to the right, then springs back to the left. He's bleeding now. Maybe his nose is broken. I see his face because he turns his bleeding head side-ways to look at me. He seems to be doing it instinctually, some-thing in him telling him to turn in my direction, not because he wants to see me. I see his face, and I go cold. Before he collapses, I'm given a sliver of a moment to see that our history together is wiped out. I do not see a reflection of myself in his eyes. I am like a mirror upon which he sees his own image. I take comfort in this anonymity.

When they see me, I'm still under the lamppost, watching them taking turns kicking his curled-up body. My gloved hands still in my coat pocket. The tips of my fingers are cold, numb. I rub them against the ball of my palm. Then I see them looking at me. I realize I'm not much older than they, and suddenly, I'm visible, I feel myself unveiling. They now loom larger, corporeal, like the moisture in the air crystallizing into snowflakes to surprise your forehead, to whip your cheeks.

They come at me one by one. But each one comes to join the other till they are all in here. They are the bats in my skirt, flapping their bony wings against my thighs. Buzzing of teethy mouths. Sharp teeth clawing my skin. Discordant music of clapping escalates, the sound of a hundred fuses igniting, phzz . . . phzz . . . phzz . . . all at once. Beating of bat-wings, fluttering of young whiskers. Tiny, blinking eyes. Faster, faster, without reprieve. I hold my breath. I shut my eyes. My skirt flies up, buoyed up, yet rigid like taffeta taut over the dome of a wire cage. There's cold wind in my skirt. Cold wind rubbing against my skin as if to generate the warmth of friction. I'm seething. I bite my lips. It's hot in here suddenly. I open my mouth to welcome the snow-flecked wind. *Like this, huh?, shut your fuckin' mouth, chink.*

I'm leaning against the pissing lamppost. In the sudden absence of commotion, the snow-covered benches and the moon that peers from behind the silver clouds are eerily the same. They are all gone. I don't know why, but I am thinking of *The Lion, the Witch, and the Wardrobe.* A bedtime tale. For a moment, I think if I looked hard enough, I can find a path that leads to the wardrobe filled with soft fur into which I can disappear. I want to bury myself in mink and fall asleep. I look around for a while, but I don't find the wardrobe. Instead I find him, unconscious and bloody in the snow, several feet away from where he was before.

It is the last Saturday of the month. The evening of the annual Christmas party at the Lana-Goldstein Home for the Elderly. The residents groom themselves for their once-a-year visitors—daughters, sons, former colleagues, forgotten and remembered again, resurrected as if from the dead and alive for this one night.

Mrs. Pierce wears a hat she made over twenty years ago, and has been wearing ever since, every Christmas. It is a green, conical knit hat with a dozen small red bells that jingle cheerfully as she walks. But her face is sullen as usual, her thin lips pinched down in an expression of cold disapproval and even disgust. That is how she looks all the time. That expression is etched onto her face. I meet her on the stairs. I say hello. She passes me by without saying anything. Her bells jingle as if to greet me instead of her. She hasn't had any visitors for twenty years. But every Christmas, she's met new people who do not fail to gawk at and comment on the ingenuity of her hat. Except for me, my father hasn't had any visitors either for the past three years.

The stairs are festooned with blinking Christmas lights. I smell roast turkey, glazed ham, the vaguely fishy smell of boiled shrimps laid out in a swirl around tureens of cocktail sauce on the table downstairs. I go up to my father's room on the third floor. The door is open, but the room is empty. Green light emanates from a small Tiffany lamp, which my father bought at an auction years ago. Last year, I gave it back to him as a birthday present.

"Merry Christmas!" Turning around, I see Susan, the nurse. Two hundred pounds of flesh in a starched white uniform. I return her greeting and ask her where my father is. She doesn't know, perhaps mingling with the crowd downstairs. She lingers a moment to tell me that last week an old man, a resident, toppled over the second-floor balustrade and fell right down to the basement, through the open space in the center of the spiral staircase. His old, brittle backbone snapped like a licked chicken bone. He's hanging on for now, but his once-a-year-visiting son is shopping for a coffin.

Holding a shiny white enamel bedpan under her armpit like a book, Susan asks me, "So, did you bring your family? Do we finally get to meet your husband this Christmas?"

I lie. "Afraid not, he's with his folks in Korea. Took the kids, too. I would've gone as well, but you know, I couldn't let my father spend Christmas alone."

"That's thoughtful of you. I am sure your father appreciates it.

Well, I am disappointed that I won't get to see your husband and kids, but there's always the next time. Say, do you celebrate Christmas back in your ol' country?"

I nod. I lie. I've never been to Korea. For me it's a shape on the map, chapters from history books, newspaper articles and the stories I've heard in passing. My father has not gone back to Korea since he came to the U.S. in his twenties. His parents passed away long before I was born, and his relatives, the children and the grandchildren of the relatives who must have known him once, do not remember him now, I am sure. Susan thinks, because my father told her what I told him, that I'm a graduate of some Ivy League college, now a successful pianist with a rich husband and two bonny kids. Most important of all, she thinks of me as a filial daughter who visits her father once a month, pays his bills, and gives her a crisp hundred-dollar bill for a tip once in a while. I am the immigrant dream come true. A scintillating exemplar of hard-won success and stability of the kind that only the seamless assimilation into American life makes possible, and at the same time, exemplary, too, of the old-world tradition of filial devotion that remains sacred, uncompromised by that success. The best of both worlds, if you will.

In truth, I'm not married. Where I live, the elevated track rattles every five minutes when the Manhattan-bound train passes through. I've been a waitress for three years. It's a job that demands nothing more than my body. I become the soreness in my wrists, stiffness in my legs, the facial muscles that ache from saying the same thing all day long. Back and forth, all day long. I do not complain. It's the kind of a job where you don't need to make acquaintances if you don't choose to, and the acquaintances you do make do not last long.

I've gone from one restaurant to another. I always say I'm taking time off from college or graduate school. They know I'll soon take off again. At a Korean restaurant, the manager tells me it's a waste of time, taking a year off. Better graduate as soon as possible and get on with your life. I tell her I need to earn my tuition.

That seals her mouth. I plaster a smile on my face. I pocket my tips at the end of the day and head home.

When my father was in a coma, I sold his house in Bel Air, his yacht, art collection, properties in Napa Valley and Montana— everything except for his personal belongings, things of sentimental value. His clothes, shoes, books, the rings and necklaces he wore, things like that. The money provided for his year-long stay at a hospital, a hefty severance pay for Linda, our housekeeper, and Mr. Alvarez, our handyman, and there's more than enough left in the bank to pay for a life-long stay at the Lana-Goldstein Home for the Elderly. And a lifetime's worth of hundred-dollar tips for Susan. I give her an envelope containing a hundred-dollar bill.

I go downstairs. Three steps from the frayed carpet-edge of the first floor, I see my father, my beautiful, frail, aged father with translucent eyes and each wrinkle on his face like a careful carving, standing there in what he thinks are my husband's Ferragamo shoes and old Armani jacket with cuffs that now cover his arthritic hands. His sweater is four-ply cashmere with moth holes, and his pants, he thinks, used to be my husband's favorite summer slacks until he grew too fat for them. But the baseball cap on his head is the blue one I bought for him years ago, when I was in second grade. I used to say it made him look younger. It does make him look younger. I see him, a boy in clothes two sizes too big. He stands half-embarrassed like a seven-year-old in a handed-down Sunday best, awkward as if the clothes are too heavy for him. *Daddy, you look swell,* I say and he smiles.

It is the last Saturday of the month. My father and I are once again at the Starlight Diner. The diner gets its name from the translucent plastic stars—dozens of them—that hang from the ceiling. They are very pretty. Ruby red, cellophane yellow, turquoise— they can be mesmerizing on a cold, clear day like this, glittering like so many jewels in the brilliant orange of the setting sun. The air itself grows soft and melodious with their chiming. Though my father is big, built like a lumberjack gone flaccid in later years, he stares up at the stars with childlike curiosity in his eyes. It is nice to see an aging man wonder. But in winter, dusk is short, and the noisy dinner rush begins at an early hour. When illumined only by the harsh white electrical light, the stars become quite tawdry, clacking and shedding scales of dust onto the table underneath each time the door opens. I lose interest in them, but my father keeps looking up at them, marveling still, long after they've lost their glitter. Only the arrival of his dinner compels him to tear his gaze away from them.

Today, my father thinks he used to be a janitor. He asks me why he came to the U.S. What kind of dreams and goals he had in life. In truth, I do not know. I'd never really asked him. But I tell him something. This time, it's the story of Mr. Ahn, who used to clean my father's office. He left Korea when the student demonstrations were at their worst in the late Seventies. He just wanted to be left alone to work hard, live well. Didn't really work out that way. Worked hard, yes, but never lived well, never could afford anything better than the roach-infested two-bedroom apartment in Koreatown. It was always sad to see an old man emptying trashcans, fussing over an area of carpet under the desk which the vacuum cleaner could not reach. While waiting for my father to finish his day's work, I used to crawl under the desks to pick up garbage for Mr. Ahn.

Although Mr. Ahn was poor, he had three sons and they all went to UCLA, and then on to law schools and medical schools. Eventually, they came back like knights on white horses, plucked him from his dingy apartment in L.A., and transplanted him to the five-bedroom home of the first-born somewhere in Westchester County, New York. But Mr. Ahn always remembered to call on Christmas. He said he lived in a guest room furnished with a sofa bed and a dresser and a chair—undiscarded furniture from his son's student days. Then he stopped calling one year. I don't know if that meant that he died.

My father asks me how I met my husband, the big business-
man who loves me, provides for me, and pays for his father-in-
law's hospital bills. The working-class Korean immigrant parents' ideal son-in-law. I tell him it's a long story. But he waits
with an expectant stare. So I tell him a simple story instead.

It's about this middle-aged Korean guy. In high school, all the
girls are in love with him. So handsome with Bruce Lee features,
so mature, impeccably dressed. Has a nice car. Everyday he comes
to pick me up from school in his white Mercedes or silver-gray
Jaguar, and the girls watch him languidly like swans. I see it in
their eyes, *You're so lucky.* But he's a drinker and he's jealous.

In my nightmares, he is a huge bat hanging upside down, filling the doorway with his black bulk. I can see him from my bed,
swaying there, regarding me. I do not know how long he's been
there. Only his outline is visible in the faint moonlight that
streams in through my window. *I must get up,* I think, but I can't.
If only I could scream out . . . but in nightmares, your body turns
into stone and only your eyes are alive. Your mind is just awake
enough to be wary of this terrifying quasi-reality. I see him tottering towards me. Enfolding me in his wings, he licks my wound
and feeds me regurgitated blood. His touch becomes an army of
ants on my legs, crawling up and up. Tell me, he whispers in my
ears. His voice is the smell of his breath, the feel of his lips on my
earlobe. He wants to know what the girls at school were giggling
about. What do they know that he doesn't. He wants me to tell
him. C'mon, I just want to know, he says. The tingling spreads
from my legs, to my stomach, to my arms, to my mouth. He says,
C'mon, until I tell him. The men at the supermarket checkout
stand who tell me that they fought in the Korean War and met
many nice people there. The boy who invited me to his church.
Names upon faceless names stored up in my head—he pinches
them out of me.

Then he drags me to the basement of this cavernous house, to
the dimly lighted indoor racquetball court. Then he beats me

with a racquet. Naked, I am cold at first, but I grow warm and feverish with each blow. How I wince and twitch my body to avoid the hard ash-wood frame of the racquet. I whimper. Then he abandons the racquet and simply punches me, his legs straddling my body. I hope for nothing else other than that he would once again pick up that racquet so that I can hope for the cushioned blow of the nylon netting. How it hurts! But soon, I can separate myself from it all. I am a pillar of ashes, ashes meticulously sewn together. Then the pain burns me, setting my ashes free. Cell by cell, I drift up, to the paint-cracked surface of the high ceiling. I crawl, fumble along the surface, but I cannot find an outlet.

I give a lame ending to my story. I tell my father I dumped the boyfriend, went away to college and met my husband there, a man who understood and sympathized with my past. He looks at me quizzically. I realize I'm smiling. How can you smile? He seems to be saying. I smile even more, nearly laughing, almost crying. I tell him everything is fine now. Don't you remember? It was you who told me to go away, I tell him. You told me to dump the bastard and go far away. To college, travel around, do whatever I want, but just go somewhere I cannot be found. I was afraid and I didn't want to, but you begged me to. It was you who saved me. I ramble on. My head is full of stories. I can tell him whatever he wants to hear.

He looks at me, even more puzzled. He says, *Who are you?*

Tonight I have a lover. It's been a long time since the last time I saw him, but I have not expected to see him at all. Even in my heated room, he shivers, nervous and cold in his cotton slacks and thin leather jacket. How he missed me. After a strained talk about nothing in particular, silence engulfs us. Two years of separation are simply blinked away in that silence. How quickly the familiarity returns and takes root once again. And how eerie, too, is that familiarity that no passage of time can erase. He lingers by the doorway, I stand across the room, watching him. Two of us here, alone in this room with a bed and a desk and a dresser, in the heat reminiscent of the Los Angeles summer, everything is as it always has been.

So I want to go out, I suggest taking a walk in the park. I want to hear the snow crunch under my feet, the cold air upon my cheeks. But he lingers. *Later, not now,* he says softly. He sits on my bed, and says, *Come here,* extending his hand out as if to anchor me in. I go. His grip is firm. I'm on the bed when the phone rings.

"Wait, the phone's ringing," I say. He does not say, Let it ring. So I pick up the phone.

"Hello?" He unbuttons his shirt and stands up to unbuckle his pants. A vortex of hair around his belly button, visible through the gap in his shirtfront.

"Christina, it's Dad." I want to remind him to turn the light off before undressing.

"Hello, Daddy, is everything all right?" He looks at me as he pulls his pants down, and grins sheepishly. A row of even, cigarette-tarnished teeth. He removes his necklace, a thin strand of gold. He removes his ring, platinum with a tiny orb of sapphire embedded in it which he wears on his pinkie. How effortlessly the ring slides off! I hear the cold, toneless *ting* of the ring against the polyurethane surface of the desk.

"It snowed a lot here. Ten inches at least. They've cancelled the morning walk. Is it snowing there, too?" His erect penis peeks out through his shirtfront. His thighs align without a gap from his groin to his knee and the rest of his legs bow outward a little. It upsets me that he did not take his shirt off first. I turn away from the sight of him, standing there, naked except for his shirt and socks.

"Yes, Daddy, it snowed in New York, too, but I have my heater on. In fact, it's hot in here." So hot that I wish I were suspended in midair, away from the clinging sheets and damp pillows. The smell makes me frown in my sleep.

"Well, I know it's silly. But I can't help worrying. I can't help but think that you're out there somewhere, hungry and cold and with no place to go to and no one to take care of you. What can I do? I cannot do anything. I am so sorry you have a father like me. All day long, I've been thinking why you had to be born to a poor father and live like a sewer rat . . ."

When he's completely naked, he heads toward the door. I stare at the ceiling. Soon I hear him checking the door to make sure it is locked. Now no one can surprise us. I laugh callously into the phone.

"Daddy, Daddy. That's ridiculous! How could you think of me hungry and cold! You're just being sentimental. Do you remember what I gave you for Christmas this year? The sapphire on that ring is real, you know, it's worth a lot."

He doesn't undress me, he never does, never. He pushes my sweater up to my chin and my bra halfway up, so that my breasts are indecently exposed, taut and squeezed under the stretched elastic. He pulls my pants down to my ankles and he pulls my legs apart, as wide as he wants to, until he can hear me gasping.

"Christina, you're too good to me. I keep it locked up in the drawer for now. I'll wear it to your wedding when you get married. I'll wear that nice tuxedo you gave me, too. When you get married someday . . . you with a husband and children! It's hard to imagine. I remember when you were little. When you first went to school . . . You were so shy. You didn't even dare turn around, but tried to find me from the corners of your eyes. I remember trying to move to a spot where you could see me but there were so many parents there! They wouldn't let me move! It made me desperate. The white of your rolling eyes. If only you could see me, I thought, you'd feel better. Christina, I know it's silly but I have to know, because always, I always think of you. Do you keep yourself warm? Do you eat well? Do you have someone to take care of you?"

He doesn't pull my underwear down. He pulls it to the side, like a curtain, so that he can be a voyeur. I feel his fingernails in me. Always well trimmed. Round and filed smooth. Extending a little beyond the tips of his fingers. It's hard against my softness.

Cold against my warmth. My whole body contracts and expands at its bidding.

"Don't worry, Daddy, I can take care of myself." He says, *Lie down on your stomach and grab the bedpost.* He puts a pillow, folded in two, under my stomach. Then he rams it in to the hilt. I think I can feel the pain all the way up in my throat. But I say nothing. Nothing at all.

"Good, that's really good, Christina."

He says.

TY PAK

Ty Pak, born in 1938 during the Japanese occupation (like Younghill Kang and Richard Kim), lived through major events in modern Korean history: the liberation from Japan in 1945, the partition into North and South Korea, the Korean War, and the industrialization under the regime of Park Chung Hee. Pak came to the United States in 1965 with a degree in law from Seoul National University, but he changed his path and earned his Ph.D. in English at Bowling Green State University in 1969. Over the years, he has worked as a reporter for several papers, including the *Korea Times,* and as an English professor at the University of Hawai'i (1970–87).

According to Pak, he began writing fiction quite by accident in 1980 when he was so moved by the life story of a Korean American repairman that he was compelled, immediately and unselfconsciously, to put it to paper. He has written two short story collections, *Moon Bay* (1999) and *Guilt Payment* (1983), and a novel, *Cry Korea Cry* (1999). Pak has no qualms about drawing parallels between his fictional representations and real life, but he also invokes a more general humanitarian consideration that underlies his work. "My characters are flawed, vulnerable—some lucky and successful, some otherwise and abject failures," Pak says, "but in every case I see their dignity, beauty, pathos."

Pak has been a sort of literary commentator on the headlines resonant to the diasporic Korean community, casting into fiction and into thematic truth the complexity of experience behind journalistic accounts of such events as the L. A. Riots and the Soviet downing of KAL Flight 007. "The Water Tower" is set in Saudi Arabia and is quite unusual for the precision with which it describes the details of large-scale engineering projects and the subtly differentiated Korean and Korean American characters on the stage of international business. At the same time, we discover that, despite the political and economic workings of the global contracting business, in which Korea is a significant player, the underlying connections among the main figures remain very much in keeping with the Confucian values of honor and reverence for the continuity of family descent.

"The purpose of my fiction," Pak says, "is to validate, exalt, and sing about that giant step . . . our generation took, when we pulled up stakes and headed out this way, half around the world, into the sun, eyes half closed, in search of a new home, new country. Our arrival at these American shores alone is an accomplishment in itself."

The Water Tower

Seething with rage, John Bay stomped from the customs area. As if acting on a sure tip that he was a dope smuggler or espionage agent, the Saudi officials had subjected him to the worst indignities, breaking open his luggage, inspecting the most personal crannies of his body. The opaque glass door with the restricted-area sign on the opposite side opened to let him out. A figure stepped off the wall of waiting people, almost bumping into him.

"Wonsok!" the man said, calling his former Korean name.

It was his friend Tago Byun.

"Let me take that," Tago offered, grabbing at John's suitcase.

"No, it's light," John said, jerking it back but quickly regretting his churlishness. Tago had taken him by surprise. Somehow John had not expected to be met by the head of the Seven Star Middle East Builders at Riyadh Airport, several hours' drive from Buraydah, their current job site.

"Over ten years, hasn't it been?" Tago said, leading the way to his parked car.

"Just about," John said.

"You don't look changed a bit," Tago said. "America must treat you right."

"You look fit, too," John said perfunctorily. "Saudi Arabia must agree with you."

John shot a furtive glance at Tago, hoping the insincerity or malice of his remark had gone unnoticed. His friend's paunch was gone and so was the oiliness of face that John remembered. But it was something other than fitness. The man's stretched skin and protruding bones gave him a haggard look, though the deep tan camouflaged it.

"Yes, the world's best sanatorium, with year-round sun that burns up all germs," Tago said.

"Is it always this hot?" asked John, wiping his neck under his shirt.

The air-conditioner of the Cadillac huffed, pumping in hot air.

"This is cool by local standards," Tago said. "It gets to 150 degrees shortly after the meridian. So how was the flight?"

"Okay," John said, looking at the bleak desert scenery dancing in the heat and haze, suppressing his irritation at being reminded of the sadism of the Saudi customs. "So what's been the problem?"

"What problem?" Tago said, laughing hollowly.

John looked at Tago askance. What was that urgent telephone entreaty if it wasn't a mayday?

"Come on," John said snappishly. "You wouldn't have hauled me all the way here if there wasn't an engineering crisis of some sort. Tell me all about it and let's get it over with."

"Everything's been wrong," Tago said, after an aborted attempt at bluffing. "The supervisor has been at us, faulting everything we do. Now he's sent this ultimatum."

Under the impressive colored letterhead, Cagle and Manson, Engineering, Inc., London, the missive declared: "I have repeatedly asked for a meeting, both orally and several times in writing, which you have consistently ignored. I am not sending any more notices. Unless you appear for a conference at my office at nine

Monday morning and we work out an understanding, not only your present contract but all other pending ones with his majesty's government will be voided." It was signed George Winthrop, Engineer, MA, PhD, PE, CSE, HMU, etc., etc.

"That's tomorrow," John said.

"Yes," Tago answered dully.

"Why haven't you met him?"

"To hear the same old rubbish? He's out to wreck me, insisting on impossible conditions."

"A title-conscious Englishman, eh?"

"That's the name of the game. The Arabs are too fat and dumb to do anything themselves, so they specialize in the art of manipulating their foreign servitors by pitting one against another. They hire a Swede to draw the plans, an Englishman to supervise, and a dirt cheap Korean to do the job. Doesn't it stand to reason to make coterminous the contracts for both supervisor and contractor, because the supervisor can supervise only what the contractor performs? Not with the devious Arabs. The supervisor's contract is open-ended, and he gets paid by the day as long as the job lasts, but the contractor has a deadline. He must complete the job by that date or he pays a heavy penalty unheard of anywhere else in the world, like one per cent per day. Naturally, the engineer punk wants to prolong his paid vacation. It pays him to make the job run over."

"Why take on jobs here of all places?" John asked.

Tago took a while answering the simple question, as if addressing a profound metaphysical issue.

"Because in this recession this is the only place left in the world to pick up a few dollars. Korean goods are not selling too well on the international market. All we can do is dump our labor."

"What's the total value of the job?"

"One hundred and fifty million dollars for each of the three towers."

"What was the next lowest bid?"

"Three hundred and twenty-five."

Heat danced in waves, blurring the two-lane concrete road, hot as fire brick. John was on edge, anticipating the imminent blowout of the tires. But the greater danger lay with the Arab drivers who roared past as if the highway was meant for one-way traffic, their way.

"Look out!" John yelled in horror, bracing his hands and knees against the dashboard. A Ferrari had jumped into view from the other side of the hill and zoomed head-on towards them. Slamming on the brakes, Tago jerked the steering wheel to one side, sending the Cadillac screeching and plowing into the sand. The Arab in the Ferrari went his way merrily, not even turning his head.

"That bastard was on our side of the road," John protested, throwing his weight at the door jammed up against the sand outside.

"Ya," grunted Tago, pushing open his side door. "But the cops would never see it that way, nor the judge. A foreigner had better watch out here. Once I parked in a marked parking stall on the street. An Arab came along and banged my car, but you know what he said? He said it was all my fault and I had to pay for the damage to his car."

"You're kidding."

"I'm not. He had a point, though. I shouldn't have parked where he was going. He told me to pay $500 or he'd call the cops."

"*He* call the cops?"

"I ended up giving him $200 and drove off. You see if the cops come, they just put you in the can, no questions asked. A foreigner in trouble with an Arab is automatically guilty, until proven otherwise. You rot in their jail without food or water until your case comes to a hearing days and days afterwards, if at all."

"Where is the consul of one's country?"

"How do you get in touch with the consul if you are physically cut off from the world, locked up? Your friends and family may go to the Saudi police and only get the famous Arabian runaround.

They don't, or pretend not to, speak English, and after gesticulating and trying a dozen different languages, all you get is a blank stare and a shrug to the next desk or office."

Tago walked to the back of the car and from the trunk took out a shovel and traction mats. Apparently he was prepared for such events. Fortunately, the sand was easy to dig and after a few minutes of puffing they put the car back on the road.

From slightly higher ground, they could see the highway stretching out like an arrow, intersecting with another in the distance to form a big cross astride the expanse of shimmering white. As they neared the intersection, traffic was slowing down. Tago brought the Cadillac to a standstill at the end of a long line. The light, hung over the intersection half a mile ahead, had changed to green twice but there was no sign of forward movement.

"Is there an accident?"

"No, they're waiting for the cross traffic to stop."

"Didn't they stop when the light turned red on their side?"

"Oh, that. No Arab observes the lights. They just come to an intersection, look left and right, if they're considerate, then zoom across. So once the traffic in one direction gets going, the cross current has to stop and wait for its turn, which may take a long time. Meanwhile, the lights may change five or six times. The longest I've had to wait was 31 cycles. Let's hope this doesn't break the record."

"Why do they have the lights at all?"

"Just for looks. You see the highway planners are foreigners, and the Arabs who approve them have been abroad and seen the traffic lights. So they leave them in."

They were within the city limits of Buraydah with a population of about 70,000. The construction site was on the other side of town. The two other future job sites were located further south near Abha. The entire citizenry of Buraydah had poured out and headed for the square in front of the City Hall, where thousands already were packed around a high dais.

"Is it some kind of national holiday?" John asked, watching

the veiled faces, strange physiognomies, gaits, heavy unwashed coats and head wrappings, shouts and laughter, unintelligible babble and cackle, not minding for the moment what seemed an interminable wait.

"You may say that," Tago said. "It's a flogging day."

"Flogging!" John exclaimed. He had heard that the Arabs still administered corporal punishment like amputation of hands against thieves. But public flogging seemed ludicrous in this day and age.

"It's a Frenchman, a tourist, that is to be thrashed publicly. On his bare rump. Buraydah is the sixth largest city in Saudi Arabia but probably the most conservative. Every woman must wear a veil and there is no exception to the rule. In Riyadh, the capital, foreigners are exempt from this rule, but not in Buraydah. Foreign women must comply with the law. Either out of ignorance or in contempt, the French couple, hotel owners in France on a sightseeing tour, came riding into town, the wife sitting primly in the front seat, her face not covered."

"But why is the man to be whipped?"

"There's Arab chivalry for you. The offender is considered the man who does not keep his women under proper control. So he is punished. All the Arabs are coming to see the exposed backside of a white man. The news has gotten around. It should be quite a sight. I think the Arab sheiks hold on to their power because they have the knack for providing exactly the kind of entertainment their benighted countrymen want."

"Is the Frenchman taking it like that?"

"He's screaming his head off but what can he do? The wife is in custody until her infraction is expiated by her husband. Even if the French consul knew about it, he would probably do nothing, especially since his government is anxious to wangle Saudi contracts."

The swing gate led into a barbed-wire fence compound, built around a huge circular pit, about 500 feet in diameter and 50 feet deep, except in some sections where digging was still under way in solid rock. On this footing a cylinder 200 feet in diameter and 600 feet in height would rise to support a globe 500 feet in diameter. Only the lower half of the globe was to be for water storage, while the remaining space was divided into three floors. The first was to house the elevator, water pump, air conditioning, and other electrical and mechanical units. The second would have a 1,000-seat restaurant and bar, and the top floor, at the pole of the sphere, would be a lookout room completely of glass. What one would look out on in the middle of the desert was a mystery to John. Maybe the stars at night. Weren't the Arabs the astronomers of the Middle Ages?

"Didn't you make a soil test before digging?" John asked.

"No. The site was fixed in the specs and we had to build it there, no matter what. That was our first row with Winthrop."

"You've been busting the rock with those?" John asked, indicating the backhoes with hydraulic Horams rigged at their booms.

"Yes," Tago said. "We tried to blast with dynamite, but the Arabs have a thing about earthquakes. According to them, even a firecracker might start one. So we had to chip away, eating up all our time."

Parked by the backhoes were giant Caterpillar 977 loaders on tracks, equipped with formidable rippers in the rear, which looked curiously dwarfed by the enormity of the excavation. At the end of a Poclain crane a cable dangled above a bucket half-filled with rocks. The men were at lunch in a long equipment storage shed, slapped together out of plywood and two-by-fours. Glancing at the glassed-in cab of the crane in the sun, John ran his eye over the diners, certain that he could pick out its operator, the one with broiled meat curling off his cheeks. But they all looked sooty, dried up, hard as coal and indestructible. Teeth flashing, lips smacking and slurping, they ate their rice, kimchee, and soy sauce soup with sullen intensity. What struck him was the total absence of spoons and chopsticks, let alone forks and knives. The men dipped their fingers into bowls and jars for any solid pieces they couldn't suck up or clamp up with their lips.

Out in the sun on the sand, about ten feet from the shed, lay a four-by-eight foot sheet of metal, its zinc-plated surface gleaming iridescently. A man dashed out with a container full of eggs. With one hand he picked up an egg, dug thumb and finger on opposite sides, and broke the shell in two neat halves. The contents flopped on the sheet metal and began sizzling. In the time it took him to walk around the rectangular space, rows of white circles with yellow centers streaked the length of the sheet. The cook was now dancing around the rectangle, sprinkling salt and crushed sesame seed. From under his arm he produced a broad wooden paddle which he proceeded to use as a spatula.

"It sure saves on the heating bill," Tago said.

There is the secret of the Korean contractor's ability to bid low, John mused. They have workers who eat nothing but rice and pickled cabbage, and an occasional egg as a treat, then go into the furnace to work fifteen hours or more for pay that an average American worker would refuse for an hour.

The executive suite was at the end of an army-style quonset. The interior was exquisitely paneled and well insulated; the air-conditioning was effective, though a bit noisy, and the contrast with the outside was chilling. Tago led John to a carpeted room with a private toilet and shower. The white sheets of the twin bed seemed particularly tempting after the 25-hour flight.

"Very nice," John said, trying the faucets of the shower which spluttered with instant reaction.

"It's no Waldorf Astoria, but we try our best for our VIP's," Tago said.

A regular *jongshik* course of rice, broiled beef and steamed fish was laid out for two in Tago's office. Sipping champagne, John unbelievingly fingered the chopsticks.

"You noticed," Tago said. "The tradition started from the first days of Saudi expeditions. The men, peaceable fellows ordinarily, were prone to losing their tempers over nothing at mealtime and flew at each other with anything that came to hand. Naturally sharp objects did the most damage. So it's been mandatory for all Korean contractors in the Middle East: No chopsticks or spoons. I guess it was from being cooped up for months on the compound, with no drink or women to relieve them. Did you know these Arabs don't permit prostitution? They have an interesting substitute, though. It's free, too. They have certain days of the month set aside to employ female prisoners for the purpose. On those long-looked-for days the male population of the region turns out in force at break of dawn and lines up for a turn. Unfortunately, foreigners are not allowed in the line. For them and for those improvident Arabs who don't get to have a turn at the prison, they have trained mares. For ten bucks one can have a go at the mares, either standing up or sitting on specially designed chairs."

"While somebody holds up the tail, I bet," John sneered.

"You think I am joking? My men swear . . . "

"Don't bother," John cut him short, having little taste for this Korean-Arabian strain of smut. "I believe you. I can believe anything in this country."

John and Tago went to Winthrop. His secretary made them wait in the anteroom while he pondered the serious breach of protocol—Tago turning up against his expectations with a bodyguard or something to crowd his peace. John was told to write out his credentials, so much irrelevant dross for getting accomplished the job at hand, before they were admitted into the Englishman's audience. Even with them in the office the pompous little man sat behind his huge desk poring over John's half-page scrawl through his thick glasses, scorn written on his pinched face. His highness was not at all impressed: anybody other than British and Cambridge was so much surplus weight to the already-burdened earth.

"Under no circumstances," he began enunciating with oracular gravity, "would I condone deviation from the specifications. Mixing or pouring concrete at 180 degrees in midday is out of the question. The concrete will not react chemically. Even at 4 a.m. the earth temperature here is around 120 degrees, still too high to give the concrete the specified strength."

"What do you suggest, then?" John asked.

"I don't know," Winthrop said blandly. "That's your problem. I can only say that the cement has to be mixed at the optimal temperature of 75 degrees, not a degree higher, or lower, for that matter. The specified 5,000 p.s.i. is essential in this earthquake-prone zone."

"You are no doubt acquainted with the recent articles in the *Journal of the American Concrete Institute* about mixing at excessive temperature using potassium compounds?" John put the question as tactfully as possible.

Winthrop stared at him, as if he had uttered some unspeakable obscenity.

"I don't hold with unorthodox American experiments," he said slowly. "The old and tried is the way to go, which incidentally accords with the specifications."

That left no room for further discussion. John rose and led his friend out of the room, leaving Winthrop to exult in his glory.

The interview had a devastating effect on Tago. John wondered how one could change so drastically in half an hour. The man seemed to have visibly shrunk, his clothes hanging loose around him, like a popped balloon.

"We'll give that son of a bitch his 75 degrees," John said. "A 20-ton capacity ice machine is what we need to chill the water with."

Tago showed no reaction and passively followed John, eyes not focusing, arms and legs moving mechanically. John took the Cadillac's wheel and drove back to the camp in silence, glancing now and then at the pathetic sight of his companion slumped in the corner. John had only himself to blame for the mess he was in. As if the consultantship had been an offer of the Nobel Prize or some singular honor, he had jumped and come running at the first call from Tago. To his chagrin, John had to admit, the real motive for his alacrity had been petty revenge. He had gloated that Seven Star was tottering, like so many upstart fortunes in post–War Korea, that Tycoon Tago, heir to Seven Star, would tumble and bite the dust, while he, John Bay, was the rising star. He had dropped everything and flown over not so much to help as to triumph over his old friend and rival in distress. Triumph over this overgrown child, wilting like some tender shoot at first breath of frost? John felt mortified at the complexes that still rankled, the grudges that still festered inside him against his fellow Koreans after seeing the continents and oceans, long after he thought he had put the accidents of his upbringing in their proper perspective.

Particularly galling was his vindictiveness toward Tago as successful romantic rival: it had no basis in fact. It was he himself who had brought Ayran to one of the fabulous New Year's Eve parties at the Byun residence in Seoul. A nice-looking girl from an impoverished aristocratic background in the country, like John's, she should not have been so cruelly exposed to the megaton radioactivity of wealth. Smitten with guilt for deflowering her and frustrated at not being able to marry her at once because of his uncertain prospects, he had secretly desired to be rid of her, to be freed from the burden. He still vividly remembered the startled look on her face when he introduced her to Tago as a distant cousin, hinting at her availability. Soon afterwards John was offered a full scholarship for his doctorate in engineering at the University of Hawaii and left Korea without even looking her up; paperwork for his passport and visa had indeed kept him on the run up to the very minute of his departure but he had been all too glad of the excuse to spare himself the embarrassing goodbye and empty promises. Almost immediately he was apprised of Ayran's marriage to Tago.

After Americanizing his name when he took the oath of allegiance for his naturalization, John had resolved, quite gratuitously and irrationally, never to have anything to do with his compatriots, consistently avoiding them in Honolulu and skipping newspaper articles with any reference to Korea. His former professor had to steer him to the ad in the *New York Times* about the contest for the design of the US-Korea Centennial Tower to commemorate the 100th anniversary of diplomatic relations between the two countries. The ad was in other major newspapers throughout the world, and the award money, jointly offered by the two governments, was a princely sum, far in excess of the usual architect's fee. By winning the contest John had attained instant fame and acclaim.

Polar Supply was the largest refrigeration supply company in Riyadh. Ted Bundy, an American, was the proprietor, in a strangely hobbled sense. The firm's ownership was 51 per cent Arab and 49 per cent American. No foreigner was allowed to do business in Saudi Arabia, unless he had an Arab partner with a majority vote. So the American had to find an Arab, who took no risk, put up no money, and did no work. Bundy told John that only Carrier built to order such giant-capacity ice machines at a cost of maybe a couple of million dollars. The transportation, another half million with insurance, would take seven months, as it had to come by ship. Only military transport planes had large enough freight bays.

"You have contacts at the Pentagon?" Bundy asked.

"Don't be absurd," John said.

"That's the only way to do business in this hellhole, my friend," Bundy said. "How do you think we survive at all without Uncle Sam's armed foot in visual range of these hooligans? Now and then he kicks them in the ass with it, hard, just to remind them."

A call to the Carrier office in Pittsburgh, Pa. confirmed the gloomiest projections. John took the bad news to Tago, who seemed to have gotten over his semicomatosity somewhat, though he still looked drained and crumpled.

"We have until the end of the year to finish," Tago said listlessly, like a chant. "Six months. After that, after New Year's Eve . . ."

Tago broke off, his eyes briefly meeting John's before they slid off to some distant object. Could he be thinking of the New Year's Eve parties at his ancestral mansion atop the headland parting the two branches of the Han—with their concert bands, dances, fireworks, food, resplendent guests? Could he be thinking of the particular New Year's Eve party to which John had brought Ayran? Neither of them had discussed Ayran or any other personal matter, however trivial, as if afraid that one might lead to another, and ultimately to the taboo: Ayran. After New Year's Eve, John knew, they would be slapped with a fine of one per cent per day. That was one million and a half. John shuddered at the barbarity of the stipulation.

"But surely they must understand unavoidable circumstances like war, earthquake, storm, or other calamities. Any court will."

Instantly, John reproached himself for the emptiness of his reassurances. He had had sufficient evidence that it was not *any* court that they had there; it was the worst jury-rigged affair in the world. The contract was written in Arabic. Translations in the Western languages might be attached, but in case of doubt or dispute one had to go by the original Arabic, which was notoriously lacking in precise technical terminology. One term for a bolt could serve for a hundred different things, ranging from nails to screws, bushings, nuts, and washers. So the intepretation was extremely flexible. Besides, who could read Arabic except the Arabs? And they were the types to give flexibility even to the most rigid mathematical symbols. No foreigner, especially those from the poorer countries like Korea, had a chance in an Arab court.

"We'll have to rig up a freezer big enough to handle the problem," John said.

Tago's eyes flashed with a glint of hope but quickly resumed their dull focuslessness.

"Can you do it?" Tago asked weakly.

"The engineering principle is simple enough," John went on. "I need a compressor, delivering at least a thousand horsepower, run by a V-belt on a diesel engine. Then I need some tanks, tubings of different sizes, ammonia. Maybe Ted Bundy has most of what we need. If not, we should be prepared to go shopping to Marseilles, London, wherever planes fly."

Tago nodded without enthusiasm.

"Don't you believe I can do it?" John said sharply, annoyed at his friend's progressive disintegration. "I need welders, iron-smiths, pipefitters."

"You can have everything here," Tago said absently.

John had never built a refrigeration system before, but there was no alternative. Cylinders of ammonia were bought at Al Madinah from a bankrupt Dutchman who had imported them for soap and toiletry manufacture, but had to close down because his Arab drone, a Bedouin, had disappeared into the trackless sand with his band of camel riders. The diesel-driven piston-type air compressor came from the harbor master at Az Zahran who was replacing it with an electric model. Made by General Motors in 1935, its valves were still good but had to be modified by new channels and ventricles for the suction and discharge of the refrigerant. The hairpin bends of the tubings for the condensing and evaporating coils were tricky, as they could easily kink and ruin the whole unit. Often a tubing of the required size couldn't be obtained and the next larger size had to be used, crimped the whole length.

Even after the tubing sizes and lengths seemed to be correctly proportioned according to the best calculations he could make, freezing did not occur. After a series of refittings and resizings with negative results, he had to start from scratch, doing away with the handbook-recommended ratios and computations, and going by gut feeling. A succession of elongations in the capillary showed a hint of frosting around the evaporator. More radical overhauls and readjustments had to be made throughout the system, checking against a table of dimensions to avoid repetitions, though under the circumstances the margin of error was so large that he felt like he was groping and fumbling in the dark.

Days went by with the whole compound anxiously watching his every move and expression for an encouraging sign. The pressure of such mass expectancy was unnerving. To them he was the great engineer from America come to deliver them from the impending peril. He simply couldn't disappoint them and worked feverishly night and day. One morning, exhausted, in desperation, John unthinkingly crimped one section of tubing with vandalistic abandon. The system coughed, kicked, and caught, quickly achieving an operational level of freezing.

Ice trays punched out of sheet metal with gallon size cups were shoved on shelves surrounding the cooling coils. No attempt was made to automate the emptying process. Men were detailed inside the freezing compartment to pull out the trays with an overhung hoist and tip them over to shake the chunks of ice into a collection bin which was carried out full by a forklift. At first the ice stuck to the metal and wouldn't shake loose, but a polyethylene coating solved the problem. The ice detail turned out to be the most popular duty among the men and had to be scheduled in short shifts to be fair to all. Everybody wanted to escape into the arctics, though in a few minutes they froze unless protected by heavy overalls, hoods, gloves, and boots.

Trucks brought water from an oasis forty miles away and filled a tank dug in the ground. The water in the tank was heated to near boiling by afternoon sun, then cooled slowly overnight. Even at 3 a.m. it was still above 120 degrees, and the ice dumped in it melted quickly away. The chilled water supplied a spray-nozzled hose mounted on a truck that circled the crater, dousing the installed rebars and adjacent ground. Hot steam shot up, filling the pit like a Turkish bath. Another pipeline fed the mixer. The hot cement and gravel hissed and crackled like wood on fire. The ready mix was pumped down a chute to where it was needed. The ice machine, motors, and pumps clanked on, working through the entire stock of cement, sand, and gravel, after finishing only half the foundation. New orders for cement and gravel had not arrived. Sand was no problem but gravel had to come from the quarries in the north, and cement from the port of Az Zahran.

John did not mind the hiatus, which he devoted to building the formwork for the superstructure, especially the globe. The initial plywood mold, held together by wires and beams, had been worked out by Tago's engineers but rejected by Winthrop for not reflecting the semicircular bulging caused by the rotating sun and for not allowing enough post-tension in the lower sections of the globe, where the thickness of the slab was over four feet. Winthrop's suggestion was to order a plastic form made by a West German firm, in which John found out Cagle and Manson had some stock interests. The estimated cost was $10 million.

According to John's analysis, the West German engineers were no miracle workers. After careful calculation of the bulging quotient and post-stress, the Germans used strong polystyrene instead of plywood. The plastic naturally gave the product a seamless finish, dispensing with post-cure sand-blasting, but it did not accomplish anything mechanically or structurally superior. John had to prepare a 300-page thesis, with detailed drawings and calculations, showing that the Korean workers could make the form with the given allowances for distortion using plywood.

From his office in the executive suite, where lately he was the sole occupant, John saw through the window the gravel trucks finally drive in one afternoon, most of them only half loaded.

"No unloading before you pay," said the Arab driver leading the convoy.

Haygoon Koo, the field manager who seemed to have taken over all the day-to-day decisions, offered to pay for ten yards per truck.

"It is twenty yards," the Arab said.

"How can it be? The maximum load is 15 yards. Look. The GVW, 20 yards, is factory stamped on the body of the truck. That's GVW. You have to deduct five yards tare for the vehicle weight and you get 10. And they're not even full."

"It is 20 yards. That's what my paper says."

"But . . ."

One of the Korean workers nudged at Koo's elbow and whispered, "Don't antagonize these guys. They'll never deliver another load and we need gravel."

Koo changed his tone, apologized for his error, and paid the Arab off. John thought he had seen everything, but this seemed to top them all. He felt he had to leave right away before he lost his sanity. Besides, there was another pressing reason for his departure. The Governor's office had called from Honolulu about the groundbreaking ceremony for the Centennial Tower in a week's time. Both countries, represented by cabinet-rank officials, would give John letters of appreciation for his award-winning design, as well as presenting him the check. The choice of Hawaii as the site for the tower was to honor its distinguished role in Korea's struggle for independence from Japan.

"Where is Tago?" John asked Koo, suddenly remembering that he had not seen him around for some time.

"He said he was flying to Morocco, sir," Koo said.

"Whatever for?"

"Seven Star is building the Marrakech airfield. It's been a big money loser."

Losing money seemed to be the theme of Seven Star. All those fat Arab sheiks must smell from miles away the Santa from Korea who kept cramming dollar bills into their already-brimming pockets.

"Why didn't he tell me?" John demanded.

"Perhaps he didn't want to disturb you in the middle of your work."

"I'm here to be disturbed and consulted," John thundered at Koo, who cringed submissively.

To leave him in the lurch like that! This latest stunt of Tago's was inexcusable. It was desertion in the face of fire, perfidy in the highest degree. But soon his anger gave way to pity for the rich kid destroyed in the wilds of real life. That he should have felt competitive, jealous, nay inferior, to such a babe in the woods! From another point of view, Tago's disappearance was opportune.

His own departure could now be hurried up. He'd leave this very minute. His conscience was clear. In fact, he had performed above and beyond what was called for in the consultantship. Besides, the rest of the work was more or less routine, just sticking to the plans and work schedule. The Abha towers would be a repetition of Buraydah and go without a hitch if the experience here were streamlined, though of course there was no such thing as replication in construction. Even the simplest job was new and original, with its space-time variables and unpredictables.

"Where are the cement trucks?" John asked.

"Swallowed up in the desert sand, sir," Koo said. "The Belgian customs broker at Az Zahran says the trucks left after being pressure-loaded at the silos on the docks a week ago, enough time for three round trips between here and there. But they are not here. We can't check their whereabouts. There is no highway patrol, no radio, no telephone."

John had just started packing when he heard a knock on his door. It was Koo, reporting the arrival of the cement trucks.

"What held them up?" John asked.

"They had a flat," Koo said.

"They all had a flat?"

"One flat or ten flats makes no difference to them. They all wait together."

"At least they could have sent half of the good trucks on, instead of all of them keeping company."

"Try to argue with the Arabs, sir," Koo said mournfully.

"You can start mixing now," John said, slamming down the lid of his suitcase.

"Sir, can you possibly reconsider waiting a few more days until the boss returns? Maybe we'll run into problems we can't handle . . ."

"You won't," John said, stepping out of the room. "I have a date in Honolulu that I must keep."

"Yes, we know. Of course you must be there. Congratulations, sir."

*

Staring into the clear Hawaiian sky, John lay in a half slumber on the veranda of his upper Manoa home built on stilts sprouting from the rock of the near-vertical slope. The tall ironwoods, sighing and swaying in the trade winds, ringed the railing like deferential courtiers. The setting sun hovered beyond Punahou Ridge, casting a veil of soft twilight over the valley. From their wooded perches birds sent up throaty even-songs. It was good to be back home. Nothing would induce him to leave it again, ever.

The telephone jangled, breaking the quiet of early dusk in the woods.

"Yes?" John said.

"Mr. John Bay?" queried the Korean-accented operator. "Long distance call from Seoul, Korea."

"I am he," John said, still trying to shake the cobwebs from his eyelids. He could hear the operator telling her client to go ahead in Korean.

"Hello," a woman's voice said, Ayran's. "I know you've just returned from Saudi Arabia but could you go back?"

"Well," John mumbled. "I've had a bellyful of Saudi Arabia and I have other engagements here. What's up anyway?"

"Tago is dead," she said hurriedly.

Strangely, the news did not surprise him, as if he had anticipated it all along.

"When did it happen?"

"They found his body two days ago."

"I thought he was in Morocco."

"That's what he told everybody. He had never left Saudi Arabia. His body was found in the sand near the Buraydah compound."

"It must have been an accident," John said, though he knew it to be otherwise.

"It doesn't matter," Ayran said curtly, as if disdaining his condolences. "There is no insurance or other complications to worry about."

"Is his funeral to be there?"

"No. His body has been flown home. I called to discuss something else. Seven Star needs somebody to tidy up its Middle East ventures, if it is not to be wiped out. He took on the Buraydah job to get the 20 per cent advance, $30 million, which he needed to service a government loan for the botched Morocco job. The next payment was due last week, which was to have been paid with another 20 per cent advance at the halfway point of the Buraydah tower. The payment never came. I guess the job didn't go too well."

"He never mentioned the interim payment or what it would be used for. We were just trying to beat the year-end deadline."

"The government has started foreclosure proceedings but there is still a chance of saving the situation, if payment is made soon. I've talked to the Minister of Commerce and Industry. Can you take charge, for *our* son's sake?"

"*Our* son?"

"Don't tell me you didn't know all this time. I sent you a photograph of him when he was six."

That must have been during the period when he threw away all mail from Korea unopened. It was some time before he digested the full import of the revelation.

"You mean you haven't suspected it?"

"Never. Why didn't you tell me then?"

"Would it have changed anything?"

"No," John replied. It was no time for dissembling or playing games. "Do you have any other children?"

"No."

"How old is he now?"

"Ten. And remarkably like you."

"Did Tago know?" John asked with a tremor in his voice.

"Only recently. The Seoul papers had a big write-up about you with your photographs in them. Yonday's framed birthday picture happened to be on the desk next to the newspaper photograph of yours. The resemblance suddenly penetrated Tago. He never asked me, but he knew. The realization must have been shattering. He had loved his son very much. You see, he didn't have to go to Saudi Arabia. His field managers would have done as good a job as he, or as bad. He just had to get away."

John called American Airlines and booked a passage to Riyadh leaving Honolulu in two hours.

WALTER K. LEW

The Korean *pyŏnsa* or "movieteller" was an orator who provided explanations, narration, and dialogue for silent films while seated off to one side of the projection screen. The most popular *pyŏnsa* also sang, injected political commentary (for example, turning the 1926 *Ben Hur* into a tale of anti-Japanese revolt), or carried on entertaining exchanges with the audience, and some of the films were actually "silenced" rather than silent—their volume turned down or off because moviegoers prefered live narration. Walter K. Lew's novella "The Movieteller" portrays a retired *pyŏnsa* who has moved to the United States and, in the midst of both recalling his turbulent past in Korea and encountering new heteroglot dramas in Los Angeles, gradually reawakens his skills to make sense of his increasingly cinematic and TV-like experience of the world. The excerpt presented here comprises the opening sections of "The Movieteller," which introduce two other main characters.

Born in 1955 in Baltimore, one year after his parents immigrated from war-devastated Korea, Walter K. Lew completed a B.A. in cognitive science at Hampshire College and M.A.s in English and Korean studies from Brown University (1981) and UCLA (1992) respectively. He has taught at Yale, Cornell, Columbia, and Brown

Universities, and edited *Crazy Melon and Chinese Apple: The Poems of Frances Chung* (2000), the acclaimed anthology of Asian American poetry *Premonitions* (1995), *Muae 1* (1995), and the "Reminiscences" section of *Quiet Fire, A Historical Anthology of Asian American Poetry,* edited by Juliana Chang (1996). He is the author of *Excerpts from: ∆IKTH DIKTE for* DICTEE *(1982)* (1992), a "critical collage" on the work of Theresa Hak Kyung Cha (see p. 244) and several forthcoming volumes of poetry. He is currently preparing translations with commentary of selected works by the Korean modernist author Yi Sang.

Lew began to create his own "movieteller" pieces in New York in 1982; these eventually developed into three-screen, multimedia performance works featuring live music, narration, and impersonation of films, some of which were made by Lewis Klahr, creator of *The Calendar Siamese, A Failed Cardigan Maneuver,* and other "tales of the forgotten future." Lew's work as a news and documentary producer has been broadcast on the PBS, CBS, NHK/Japan, and British ITV television networks. He has been awarded fellowships by the National Endowment for the Arts, New York State Council on the Arts, and the Korean Culture and Arts Foundation.

from *The Movieteller*

for EC

1993

I. DAVID

Grandpa and Grandma in a dingy ammo box of an apartment
near Hoover & Pico. They still say they live in K-town, but the
boundaries have changed. Koreans don't go to the Korean stores
here. They're more like outposts left by a tribe retreating, if not
north to Glendale, east to Riverside, southeast to Disneyland, or
all the way south to Garden Grove, then at least to the other side
of Wilshire near Western, where you can still order any hour of
the night a big tureen of haejang soup chock-full of tofu-like
cubes of ox blood to stave off tomorrow's hangover. A place to go
after you've blown all your money at clubs like Sixth Avenue or
The Morocco on a table charge, very expensive snacks ($15 for
grapes and a few slices of orange, apple and watermelon, or $25
for a handful of peanuts, dried cuttlefish and seaweed in cellophane) to go along with a $65 bottle of Passport to not seem
cheap as you check out and get snubbed by girls at other tables,
all wearing tight black won-pisu or white dresses with jackets
and stiletto heels, the same sweet tail of glossy hair dropping

down a smoothly exposed back. A place to make up for the wasted evening by arguing with scarlet-eyed, chain-smoking friends about "the Movement" or by teasing a waitress in worn-down slippers who'd rather read the Bible behind the counter than have to notice your dumb come-ons—though it always amazes you that there is an almost smiling light in her eyes that suddenly seems half-crazy as, for whatever-hundredth time that day, she pats fluorescent rice into rows of stainless steel bowls and covers them with dented lids half-heartedly etched with a vine pattern from some urn or tomb mural of eons ago, a SYMBOL OF OUR GLORIOUS PAST.

On the way to the men's room I pass the kitchen entrance and see a "Mekshigan" hunchbacked over a vat of sloshing broth he's lugging. A withered hand enters the frame, its wildly pointing gestures punctuated by a "globalized" tirade of Korean baby-talk, imitation Spanish, and You/Dis/Here/No, No! scraped together in a scratchy, dialect-looping grandma's voice. She jumps down from the shiny counter she was perched on and hits him around the shoulders with a big plastic scoop. Laughing, he cries out in mock pain, "Apayo! Apayo, Halmoni! Stop stop!"

"Si," she laughs back, "you pabo ya, dumb dumb Pranshis-co!"

I wonder what other words they know together. When I return from the w.c., a black & white GE is on, Francisco switching channels with pliers. He stops at a Spanish-language broadcast about the lambada that he tries to explain to her: "New dance! Ahh-ju hot. Caliente like kimchi, sexy like Halmoni! Ha, ha!" as he grabs her wrist and she screams, almost stepping into clumps of soybean sprouts floating in a huge red tub of water.

"Saekshi, saekshi?" she grins, repeating the Korean word for "young lady." "No, pabo—Nan saekshi anira, oldu grandma!"

I dally by the entrance, adrift in the polyglot like a happy otter when the waitress comes back and yells at them. She takes the pliers and twists the tuner over to the Korean station just in time for the nightly sermon.

"Hanunim talk," Francisco calls out.

"Yes, Pranshisco mori-ga cho-ah!" the grandmother says to the waitress, who just scowls, and then directly to him, translating by poking his temple and making a thumbs-up sign. The show cuts to a chorus singing hymns which they hum together, Francisco stirring over the stove. "Dok-dok hae smart boy!"

I wonder if the dok-dok han smart boy was paid more than $40 for a full night's work. That's all the men that rushed my car everytime I stopped at a corner asked for, thinking I was a factory or construction subcontractor looking for day workers. Now, after the riots, were they getting even that from Koreans with less, in a neighborhood that no one wants to visit anymore?

Haraboji and Halmoni at Hoover & Pico. The last place I expected to find a girlfriend. In fact, I usually go there only when I'm downtown late and too drunk or tired to drive all the way home. When this became a habit on weekend nights, they gave me a pair of keys and always left a quilt on the sofa with a pae-gae pillow—log-shaped, silk-embroidered. Both grateful and ashamed, I usually tried to leave before they got up in the morning.

They complain to my mother about how disrespectful I am, but how would we communicate even? They can't speak English and my Korean is little more than baby-talk. O.k. for joking around with friends, but humiliating before my grandfather, knowing how he scorns my stumbling, taking it as a sign of how I have no pride in my "blood," my pit-chulgi he keeps saying, pinching a vein in his forearm. Hey, I could be a genius and he'd never know because, in Korean, I can barely keep up with a five-year-old. The one time my mother told him it's not my fault, that you have to use American in America, he threw a fit, yelling that even when the schools forced everyone to change their names and speak Japanese, he ran away rather than abandon his mother tongue. On top of that, he was a Pyonsa! Mother absorbed his ourburst in silence, but on the way home, just the two of us in the car, she mimed in a sing-song voice, "Pyon-sa, Pyon-sa! What the Big Deal! What excuse for dropping out!"

She didn't explain what "Pyonsa" was, or what it had to do with dropping out. Who knows? Maybe I'm Pyonsa, too! My mind entertained exciting possibilities: street musician, gambler, wandering monk . . . I tried to imagine each one a dashing patriot outwitting police, leering at any fellow countryman who wiggled by in kimono, wooing and dropping the wives and daughters of Jap bureaucrats bored and lovelorn on the colonial frontier. But when I realized the only faces I could conjure were no different from the ones in Korean newspaper cartoons—brooding young men who looked like a forgotten gangster brother of Speed Racer, glowering with hatred at buffoons with horn-rimmed glasses and folding fans, their buck teeth protruding like a picket fence, I knew I was just wallowing in bigotry. Good enough for a cheap taekwon-do flick, but primitive in the court of my liberal values, especially when I thought of what the Japanese rounded up here had lost during much of the same period—tough, kind people like the old Issei I'd met in places like Gardena or gift shops and nurseries along Sawtelle.

Besides, it was getting difficult to imagine Haraboji doing anything heroic. Maybe it reveals a lack of sympathy on my part —What did I know about the Korea of 50 years ago?—but, except when he wanted to dis me, he never (through Mom) told me any stories of the past and just seemed to be slowly slipping away. A sure indication was the times I sneaked into the apartment at 2 or 3 in the morning and found him sitting in front of a TV in the kitchen, the sound off, and talking in a weird, high-pitched whinny, while occasionally pointing a finger or making other gestures at the muffled characters, whether info-mercials, B-movies, or a rebroadcast of the news.

One night I stood for a half-hour on the other side of the door, hoping to lift a string of meaningful phrases out of his galloping gibberish. Suddenly the normal sound came on—a local anchor dimly intoning yet another rehash of last year's verdict and riots. I thought the English might give me a clue to what Haraboji would say next, but he fell silent. I peeked in and saw he was just sitting there, completely still, rheumy-eyed in front of the hazy flickers—more proof he was falling into his own dark past.

"You no unnerstan anysing!" That was Florence's favorite line whenever I got too weird on her. The first time we met I was tiptoeing out of my grandparents' apartment as usual on a Sunday morning. No, actually, I was coming down the ladder from a trapdoor to the roof. I'd just spent 20 minutes trying to clear out my head with yoga and morning smog: four complete "Welcoming the Sun" asanas to the east, then meditation and deep breathing, trying to blow down or up the blank H=O=L=L=Y=W=O=O=D letters propped listless along the Hills to the north. But the glare, its heat held by the tar and asphalt roof, came up so quickly I began to sweat through my shirt and socks, already musty from last night's clubbing. I decided to leave the rest of the sequence for next weekend.

As I eased down into the shadowy hall, I concentrated so much on not missing a step that I was only a few rungs above the landing before I saw the saekshi standing there, flat-footed in flip-flops. She was wearing cut-off jeans, a white running shirt, and little, if any make-up. Her slender hands formed pale fists around the last rung—I wanted to step on them—and there was a very stern expression on her face, her dark eyebrows hunching into each other. "WHat You do-ING?" she asked in a jerky intonation I recognized as Kyongsang-do dialect.

"My Haraboji lives here," I answered.

"I aX whY you up theRe, not whO live here," she shot back.

"Uhh, I visit my grandparents every weekend . . . to, uh, take them shopping. I was up on the roof to check the weather for them . . ."

"Ai ch'am, hyoja inneh!" (Such a filial boy!)

I tried to act bashful.

She said, "I NEVer been go up there. So diRdy." Shiny forearms folded across her ribs now, eyebrows eased back into a smile,
she pretended to look up through the trapdoor I had pulled shut,
leaning this way and that for a better angle.

"Kugyong-ul kashigo shipu-shimnikka?" I inquired in heavily
decorous grammar ("Would it respectfully please you to do some
honorable sightseeing?"). She said o.k., but only if there were no
gangsters hiding on the roof, and also I had to promise I wouldn't
leave her up there.

I turned around and began to climb back up. When I pushed
open the trapdoor dust and paint chips fell out of the blank sky's
glare, into our upturned faces. Silly, but I wondered if the down-
draft carried the smell of my unchanged underwear into her
elegant nose so directly beneath my butt. No matter, she kept
climbing up behind me. It occured to me that she must have been
following me a while anyway, since we were several flights up in
the about-to-be condemned rear part of the building.

From the roof we surveyed each direction, shading our eyes.
The busiest area was just a block away: a large lot with makeshift
booths, card tables, and spread-out blankets strewn with cheap
sundry goods. There were already many vendors and browsers, including a Korean here and there, sometimes in a security uniform
and cap, mixing among Mexicans at the macadam flea market.
Some were grinning, patting people on the back, while others
phlegmatically ordered them around, probably in a language they
couldn't su habla. I shook my head over the fact that, even after
the riots, Koreans were still proud or dense enough to condescend
to other non-Whites. Or maybe they didn't see it that way. A lot
of training had gone into making even the most downtrodden
Korean man believe it was his reponsibilty to be righteous and
paternal (mildly or arrogantly) toward any person beneath him in
social status, which included sons, girls, employees, shoeshine
and delivery boys, Chinese immigrants, people with dark skin or
curly hair, and various combinations of the above. It was, in turn,
the role of the paternalized to be hyoja—or hyonyo (fem.)—even
if, now and then, they used their own righteous rage to rebel. De-

stroyed the businesses that had underpaid them. Looted the stores whose cheap garments and other sweatshop items had made pseudonymous entrepreneurs across the sky so rich. Cycles of exploitation and retribution. From the fatalistic Korean viewpoint, it seemed an almost natural history: maybe one could get out quickly in an up-phase. "What hurt most," said the creamy-faced manager of a home appliances store, "they did not take things but threw them around, burned the hell place down. No way I can keep them out, so I tell them, 'Here, come get the TVs, all the stereo, enjoy them!' It was a shame they were crazy and the good things destroyed. That's my big regret."

Or if you were me, drank yourself shit-faced every weekend night to forget the fighting at home, while lusting with yet more ardor and credit cards after every moon-faced girl in a club, since she seemed the only product of Korean culture or DNA that was of any delight. For fools like me, pride in my race had been reduced to the invention of ironclad warships and moveable-type press, the world's most rational alphabet, and, above all, some poor saekshi's comeliness and manners, the flower of eons of peninsular cultivation. Perhaps all I strove for was really just a date: a sweet meeting over tea and rice cakes . . . in some lakeside pavilion . . . in the mists of . . .

Florence was sleek, not sedentary and moon-faced, very narrow in the cheeks, with brown eyes that showed a hint of October sky and forest in them. Like many Koreans, there were streaks of ochre in her hair registering some long-ago commingling with Mongols or Slavs during the many exiles and migrations a catastrophic history had forced. She was gullible, game, I thought, and already impressed with me!

I began to brag about my family.

About an hour later, my grandparents were certainly surprised when I drove them to the Korea Plaza shopping center in a BMW, Florence in the front seat constantly turning around to listen to my Halmoni—who maybe had someone to talk to finally—to flatter them both, and praise their hyoja grandson! I kept peeking in the rearview mirror to see what Haraboji was thinking as, muttering beneath his breath, he watched the blocks jerk past him on the other side of the tinted glass.

II. HARABOJI

On the warm bright sidewalk, they meet again. Again, she's wearing cutoffs and a white sweatshirt. Sweat, shirt, no lipstick and flip-flops. Flips, flops just like an American girl. A girl he dares to ask, "Is that your baby?" and expects her to say something mean, but she doesn't. "Not, my neighbor baby," followed quickly by something in Kyongsang dialect that he doesn't understand. They nod as if he understood. She smiles as if she thinks he's cute. No, he doesn't understand, and she certainly couldn't think he's handsome. But already she's acting as if Davey's the one for her. What's going on? How come she has a BMer and luxury rooms in this dilapidated building? How is she getting money? Maybe she's in hiding, a scandalized starlet flown here for an abortion or the L.A. Lady of a Pusan tycoon who limos through Hanin-town once in a while. Crazy that she's already spoiling Davey—like he were Ondal the village moron and she the Princess come to save him. If he only knew Korean, I would tell him that story!

III. FLORENCE

"Yah! YAH!" I stick one sparkling foot—I scrub it with pumice every morning—into his idiot mouth. When he bites the toes, I scream in delight because it feels like I have a kochu, too—five of them! Then he pulls them out, wipes my foot along his butt hair and stands above me singing:

> *Baby, Baby, Please don't weep!*
> *Sweet girls, Get your beauty sleep!*
> *Uncle, Eat and drink your fill!*
> *Grandma, Trip and roll downhill!*

"What?!"

"I made it up! Can't translate your dumb song—don't rhyme and the beat's not right."

"That's o.k. Nan chot'a. THE END!!!" and I jump on him and grind him with my ankles clasped around him and my back to the mirror while rubbing his head like *it's* going to come out so he can look over my shoulders and see how sleek I am. Make up for the fact that there's nothing on me to grab. Like I told him, my big brother once said my chest was like "kosok t'oro-e ggom": chewing gum on the highway. Of course, afterwards when in the evening falling outside my big picture window he points affectionately at each nub and says, "ggom" and expects me to laugh along, I don't and just say, "More than enough for you" or "Bigger than your kochu," as if I'd been insulted and didn't know how on earth he could make such a crass comparison.

> *Agasheeeeee, mani yeppo-chuseyo!*
> *Halmoneeeeee, orae saseyo!*
> *Ajosheeeeee, balli nomo chuseyo!*

Why couldn't he translate that? Just a kid's song—he must be stupid, kuro-chi?

That's o.k. Finally found what I came here for. Me a student? That's only what I told my mother I had to leave the country for. I even registered at Otis Parsons School of Design, but I'm 32 years old. Majored in the best dance department in Seoul, but always got too nervous onstage. You're an "Old Miss" if not married by 26. But I'm a free woman like Isadora Duncan and won't settle down until I've had a fun romance in every famous city in the world. I'm really pretty! I can do it!

Davey keeps scolding me for not studying—*kong-bu, kong-bu* —but little does he know what a steal I am! I'll suck him inside out like Kol-la up a straw. Then I'll help him make a million dollars. Nope, first I'll disguise myself a little longer. I'm a lady, after all, from a rich & powerful family . . . yah! some dignity—I'm beginning to think like a LA-LA girl or some slut from Fukuoka. *Noran takushii!* Oh, if I could only make a drama out of this, a play about me!

WILLYCE KIM

Willyce Kim, who was born in 1946 in Honolulu, studied English literature at Lone Mountain College for Women in San Francisco, close to the Haight, where she graduated in 1968. She has written three books of poetry: *Curtains of Light* (1971), illustrated by her sister Carmel; *Eating Artichokes* (1972); and *Under the Rolling Sky* (1973). Her two novels, *Dancer Dawkins and the California Kid* (1985) and its sequel *Dead Heat* (1988), were published over a decade later. Kim's short stories and poems have appeared in numerous anthologies of gay and lesbian literature and she is currently completing a third novel while working in the main library of the University of California, Berkeley.

Kim thinks of herself as first and foremost a poet "devoted to the journey rather than the destination." So it is no surprise that the writers that she names as having deeply influenced her work are Adrienne Rich, Olga Broumas, Diane Di Prima, Judy Grahn, and Pat Parker. "Much can be said about the textures of women's lives, the culture of the lesbian nation, and they have said it best," she has commented. The first openly lesbian Asian American poet, Kim joined the Women's Press Collective, co-founded by Grahn and others, carrying the manuscript that became *Eating Artichokes*, during the early years of the women's press movement of the late 1960s and early 1970s. A frequent goer to the women's dances and poetry readings of the time, Kim deliberately broke with the stereotype that "Asians are the last out of the closet."

Kim's ties to poetry may partially explain why she is an especially quick and prankish stylist of comic prose who can dart the way Dancer Dawkins runs back kickoffs near the beginning of *Dancer Dawkins and the California Kid*. The poetic mode of metaphor-driven writing persists in her novels' swiftly culminated scenes and careening subtitles, similes, and puns. Such leaps help to propel the overall subversiveness of her narratives; *Dancer Dawkins,* for instance, concludes with the total defoliation of Bohemian Grove in Sonoma County, California, just before the annual all-male convocation there of corporate and political heads. The following excerpt from the novel, comprising its second through ninth sections, introduces three of its main characters.

from *Dancer Dawkins and the California Kid*

Dancer's Name

The first time Dancer Dawkins saw a football was on a June day when the temperature cracked 100 degrees. Sweat beading along the rim of her glasses, bare feet skimming blades of swooning bluegrass, Dancer was flying, was a blur, was a hot mirage of action as her hands plucked the piece of leather from the sky. "I think I have a problem," she said, when she saw the two defenders in front of her. "I think they're going to make a ham sandwich out of me," she said again, when she saw them part down the middle leaving her a pathway that even a pencil wouldn't poke through. Dancer slipped the football under her armpit and veered right.

The two defenders shifted with her.

She swiveled her hips left. The defender closest to her went with the rhythm of her body.

Dancer laughed. For an instant her body hung left. For an instant the two defenders were caught up in that motion.

Three leaning towers.

With one sweeping bladelike move Dancer cut right and was gone.

In those days after a touchdown no one spiked footballs. So

Dancer just spit on the ground, wiped off her face, cleaned her glasses and said: "Gimme a cream soda." She felt magnificent. Now she knew why her parents named her Dancer.

The Dream

Once many years ago Dancer had this dream. She was walking along the beach carrying her fishing pole. The sky met the ocean in a splash of blue. There was no sound. No lapping of waves. No birds diving in and out of each other's cries. Nothing. Dancer found a cluster of rocks on which to stand and cast her line out. An hour. Two hours passed. Dancer was nodding off when she felt a hand on her shoulder. Mumbling something under her breath, Dancer slowly turned around. Three women stood in front of her without a stitch of clothing on. Dancer closed her eyes and opened them again. They were still there. One of them took her hand and led her away from the beach. The other two followed closely behind. As they walked, Dancer's clothes started to drop off and disappear. Dancer looked down and saw her right nipple harden. Oh shit, she mouthed. But it was already too late for that.

Dancer remembered her dream in the morning. In fact, she never forgot *that* dream. Every time she recalled certain details Dancer noticed a change in her breathing. Short driving spurts of air would emerge from her lungs, and her heart would be dipsy-doodling somewhere in her chest.

Wowie-Zowie

While Dancer Dawkins was busy juking down a football field, Little Willy Gutherie was trying to stuff her sixth piece of Rubbles Dubble bubble gum into the already bulging corner pocket of her left cheek. Two months ago Willy had tried chewing tobacco. The tobacco made it. Willy didn't. Some friends had found Willy leaning over one of Whitehall Amusement Park's railings looking very green and very limp. A tiny stream of brown juice dribbled down Willy's chin. Before anyone could say wowie-zowie Little Willy Gutherie flashed the five knuckles of her right fist. No one ever mentioned chewing tobacco to Willy Gutherie again.

The California Kid

For as long as there were full hot yellow moons and buckets of stars dotting up summer skies, for as long as the berries on Pine Hill had resembled thick ruby nuggets, maybe even longer than all that, she was always Little Willy Gutherie.

Never Gutherie. Sometimes Willy Gutherie. But most of the time, "Little Willy Gutherie" rolled off tongues faster than cascading sparks from a dangling tailpipe.

The truth of the matter was Willy Gutherie was not little. She was not big either. Willy Gutherie likened herself to one of those electric blue dragonflies that were always buzzing over her favorite swimming holes.

One night Little Willy Gutherie caught the last half of a grade-B western. Someone was dying:

"Well, pardner, I guess I'm not going to make it."

"Nope. Guess we'll have to make it for you."

"Say, Arizona, how come if you never been to Arizona you got a name like that? . . ."

"Well, pardner—*gasp*—I always wanted to go there."

Clunk.

Little Willy Gutherie walked out of the room and crammed four pieces of Rubbles Dubble into her mouth. It took her two hours to pack her duffel bag and one minute to change her name to the California Kid.

Where was she going? To California, naturally.

Scribbles

Dancer Dawkins was born accidentally . . . a genuine miscalculated rhythm-method child . . . on November 5 somewhere outside of Los Angeles. When she was twelve she lost her cherry while riding a horse named Tinker.

The California Kid was born and raised in Bangor, Maine. It

has been rumored that her first words were "bow-wow." Unlike Dancer Dawkins, the Kid had never even put her butt in a western saddle until she was sixteen.

Dancer Dawkins, a double Scorpio, was heading up the California coastline via Highway One.

The California Kid, having crossed the Rocky Mountains, was lickety-splitting it for the land of giant artichokes and golden sunshine.

Their collision course was set.

Absent

Dancer spelled relief r-o-l-l-i-n-g. And that's exactly what she was doing. While clipping along at a comfortable sixty miles an hour Dancer was busily manufacturing a joint with her right hand. This was not an easy task. Perfection was achieved through practice. Many hundreds of hours and many thousands of sheets of wheat straws did not go up in smoke. They went straight down the toilet . . . until Dancer's nimble fingers could coax and caress and roll right and left the finest of sun-cured flower tops.

A long lick, a fleeting look, and a quick light left Dancer tingling. The first toke exploded in a profusion of sage, scrub, and pulsating Humboldt County fields; hundreds of sun-kissed resins rat-a-tat-tatted across Dancer's tastebuds, parade right, they closed ranks and goose-stepped through her pearly gates. Upstairs. No one was home.

Gloriously cooked, Dancer's mind meandered right.

The highway faded left.

Just past San Luis Obispo her pulse quickened, and her heart flip-flopped one hundred times.

Jessica.

Lolo

Jessica Nahale Riggins. Product of a back-seat quickie in a '49 Ford, raised near the Kona Coast on the Big Island of Hawaii, migrated eastward to experience the Atlantic Ocean. Her parents wrote her off as "lolo," crazy. Nevertheless, whenever the good fortune of work had occasion to visit her, Jessica always wired money home. She was a good responsible girl; she was, and this is when Dancer's heart flip-flopped, green-eyed and tawny; a splash of sloe gin settling on the rocks; she was Dancer's "Nahale," her forest, two months gone to San Francisco and up to her tits in . . . what? Salvation?

Dancer's smile melted off into the sunset. Her foot floored the accelerator as last night's phone conversation rattled around in her memory bank.

Dancer grimaced. Jessica's parents were as right as rain. Jessica is "lolo." Which makes me "lolo" because I'm "lolo" over her.

Salvation

Dancer had just finished a superb meal of spaghetti squash stuffed with mushrooms, green peppers, and onions, smothered by a thick tomato sauce laced with cheddar, when the phone rang. She crossed her fingers hoping it wasn't Bucky; she owed Bucky money and wasn't in the mood to make excuses for her delinquency.

The familiar buzz of long distance welled in her ear as a voice murmured, "Sweetie?" Dancer walked the phone into the kitchen. Dessert had arrived, just in the nick of time.

"Hey honey," Dancer purred, "I was just thinking of dropping you a line. How's it going up north?"

"Fine. Just fine," replied Jessica as she prostrated herself on the living room floor. "Dancer."

"I'm right here."

"I've found salvation."

Dancer stifled a laugh. "Is this a cousin of Sal Mineo or a relative of salmonella?"

Jessica groaned. "Be serious, Dancer, and please listen to me. I've been shown the way to salvation."

Dancer got up from the kitchen table. She was hysterical with laughter and almost dropped the phone. "Jessie," she gasped, "did you drop acid today?"

Jessica shifted around on the floor. This was not proving to be a fruitful conversation. "Dancer, maybe I should write you a letter. We don't seem to be connecting, and this is important."

"OK. OK. I'll be serious. You be serious, too," sighed Dancer, who felt as if she were sitting in a dentist's chair wavering somewhere between dread and tranquility.

"Well," said Jessica, "I now know what I would like to do for the rest of my life. I'm committed to being an emissary for Violia Vincente and her Venerable Brigade."

Far away in the recessed cavity of her upper molar Dancer heard the menacing sound of a dentist's drill. "What is that, some kind of drum and bugle corps?" she snapped. "Two months. You leave L. A. You leave me. Is this a job, or what? You're not being very clear."

"And you're not even listening to me. I'm sooo happy."

"For godsake, Jess, you sound like you had a handful of reds for dinner."

"That's it. *Finis. Pau-hana.* The end," sputtered the self-annointed emissary. "I'll write you a letter."

"No letters," growled Dancer. "I'm coming up."

"I don't know if you can. The Reverend Mother runs a tight ship, and he's in the process of readying himself for some Bohemian festival, so security is tighter than usual."

"The who?"

"The Reverend Mother. Fatin Satin Aspen, our leader. We call him that behind his back," the exasperated Jessica replied.

"Jesus H," Dancer swore, "you've been brainwashed."

"Good-bye Dancer," Jessica replied, severing the connection.

Dancer slammed the receiver down and hurled the phone against the wall. It was the third set in six months; she was three for six at the plate.

Jessica remained lying on the living room floor. She felt as if she had just been pulled through a knothole backwards; her neck muscles were in spasm. "Oh cripes," she swore, and pulled out her Lebanese hash pipe.

NORA OKJA KELLER

In 1968, at age three, Nora Okja Keller moved from Seoul, where she was born, to Hawai'i. She subsequently lived in several places on the U.S. mainland, returning to Korea each summer. Although she and her family have resided in Hawai'i since 1971, in a place where people of mixed race are hardly unique, she has explored the complex themes defining Korean American identity formation in very particular and profound ways. These are themes, she says, that she "struggles with in waking life," themes that make writing, for her, "a site in which to explore the paradoxes of mixed-race identity." She is particularly aware of the irony of "being drawn to the Korean culture and yet not knowing how to speak the language."

In *Comfort Woman* (1997), from which we take this excerpt, Keller grapples with one of the most searing aspects of recent Korean history—the sexual enslavement of Korean women by the Japanese military; and perhaps the most resonant and deeply rooted of Korea's cultural traditions—woman-centered shamanism. The novel alternates between two narrators: Akiko, whose Japanese name is forced upon her by her captors after she is conscripted as a comfort woman (a euphemism for a military sex slave) and Beccah, her daughter by the American missionary who tries to save Akiko through marriage when she finally escapes from the "recreation camp" in Manchuria at the end of the war. Though it was published at a time when the issue of comfort women was a highly visible topic in the news, it is full of the kind of unexpected specificity that makes for gripping reading.

Akiko, who is symbolically linked to river and water imagery throughout the novel, becomes Beccah's literal connection to the "motherland" of Korea. Conscious and unconscious symbolic associations carry much of the resonance of *Comfort Woman,* mirroring precisely the kind of associative logic that governs shamanic ritual. In fact, the novel itself ultimately takes on the ceremonial qualities of an initiation ritual as Beccah, by the end, inherits the spirit that has inhabited her mother and perpetuates the shamanic lineage. Akiko is caught between the worlds of the living and the dead and Beccah is caught between her Korean and American selves. *Comfort Woman* deals with the profound and intricate threads of pain and love that connect mothers and daughters. Simultaneously, it elegantly dramatizes the problem of liminality, that unmoored state of being constantly "betwixt and between," a theme particularly relevant to those of mixed race.

Keller is careful to mediate her audience's tendency to read *Comfort Woman* as autobiography. She admits that it does, indeed, draw on her relationship with her mother, but she is also careful to point out that the meaning of reality-based depictions can change profoundly in their fictional context. She also does not hesitate to point out that the novel was inspired by the story of Hwang Kum-ju, a survivor of the Japanese military sex camps who gave testimony at the 1993 symposium on human rights held at the University of Hawai'i. *Comfort Woman* won an American Book Award in 1998.

from *Comfort Woman*

Beccah

When I entered the world, bottom first, arrows impacted my body with such force that it took twelve years for them to work their way back to the surface of my skin. My mother said she tried to protect me from the barbs the doctors who delivered me let loose into the air with their male eyes and breath, but they tied her hands and put her to sleep. By the time my mother saw me, two days later, she said she knew the *sal* had embedded themselves deep into my body by the way my yellow eyes turned away from her breast. My mother spent two weeks in the hospital waiting, she said, to see how the arrows would harm me: so swift and deadly that she would never have time to fight their power, or slow detonating, festering for years, until I formed either an immunity or an addiction to its poison.

Years later, when the evil-energy arrows began to work their way from my body, I often wished the *sal* had killed me outright so that I would not have had to endure my mother's protection.

At the start of each Korean New Year, my mother would throw grains of rice and handfuls of brass coins onto a meal tray to see my luck for the coming year. In the year of the fire snake, I turned twelve, and my mother missed the divination tray completely.

"Mistake! Mistake!" my mother yelled toward our ceiling as she scooted on her hands and knees to pluck coins and rice from the carpet. As soon as she collected enough to fill both fists, she held her hands above the tray, closed her eyes, and chanted, calling down the Birth Grandmother to reveal my yearly fortune. When my mother cast for the second time, she poured the riches from her hands rather than threw them, hoping to fill the tray with a better reading.

When she opened her eyes and saw that she had again missed the tray, she cried. She wrapped her arms around her body and rocked. "*Aigu, aigu,*" she moaned. My mother chanted and swayed until she fell into a trance. Then she got up and, eyes sealed, danced through the apartment: on the sofa bed, around the black-lacquered coffee table, over dining room chairs, around me. And as she danced, my mother touched our possessions, feeling—she later explained—for the red. My mother held her hands in front of her, and like divining rods, they swung toward the color of blood. She ripped red-bordered good luck talismans from our walls and furniture, where they fluttered like price tags. She knocked over our altars, sending the towers of fruit and sticky rice crashing to the floor, and rummaged for the apples and plums. Clawing through the bedroom closets and drawers, she collected everything red, from T-shirts and running shorts to a library copy of *The Catcher in the Rye* to the bag of Red Hots I bought with my own money and stashed in my sock drawer.

When she was through piling the red things into a mountain in our living room, my mother said, "We need to burn the red from your life. Everything."

At first, I didn't understand what she meant to do; sometimes she said such things to her clients, then just waved a lit incense stick or a moxa ball over their heads. But when my mother took an armload of clothes to the kitchen sink and lit a match, I scrambled to the floor and rooted through my possessions, trying to save something.

When the material in the sink caught fire, my mother came and took the one thing of mine I had managed to find: the tie-dye T-shirt I had made with rubber bands, melted crayon, and Rit dye in Arts and Crafts the year before. "Beccah," she told me, "*Honyaek,* the cloud of Red Disaster, is all around you. I am trying to weaken it so it won't trigger your *sal* and make you sick."

Red Disaster, the way my mother explained it, was like the bacteria we had learned about in health class: invisible and everywhere in the air around us, *honyaek* was contagious and sometimes deadly. Burning the red from our apartment was my mother's version of washing my hands.

The fire in the sink kept sputtering out, held in check by flame-resistant clothing, until my mother added her talismans and money envelopes and a dash of lighter fluid. When she held a match to this kindling, the fire licked, hesitant at first, and then devoured what was offered. Flames shot up amidst coils of thick smoke that blackened our kitchen walls and ceiling. When this first batch had almost burned down, the smoke alarm sputtered to life with grunts and whines and a final full-strength shriek before my mother whacked it with a broom. After she cracked open a window, my mother continued to burn our possessions, even the Red Hots, which melted like drops of blood-red wax, filling the apartment with the stench of burning cinnamon.

Since I was particularly susceptible to Red Disaster that year, my mother did not want me wandering about in unknown places, picking up foreign *honyaek* germs. I was not allowed to ride the bus without her or to swim at all. Consequently I was not supposed to attend school field trips. When my classmates went to Bishop Museum and to Foster Botanical Gardens and to Dole pineapple cannery, where they sampled fresh juice and fruit slices, I stayed behind in the school library, reading and helping Mrs. Okimoto shelve books according to the Dewey decimal system.

But when my sixth-grade social science teacher arranged a snorkeling expedition at Hanauma Bay, I signed my own permission slip after practicing my mother's signature for so long that even now I cannot write her name without my letters cramping into her small, painfully precise script. I remember my hands shook when I turned in this first forgery on the day of the excursion, but Miss Ching just shuffled the form and the fare I had stolen from the Wishing Bowl into her carryall folder. Pushing me into line with the rest of the class, she counted our heads and led us like ducklings onto the bus.

Since my mother had burned my red-heart bathing suit, I wore an olive-green leotard—not the sparkling Danskin kind with spaghetti straps, which might have passed, but one that was cap-sleeved and frayed in the butt. I knew I would catch stares and snickers from the Toots Entourage (led now by Tiffi Sugimoto, since Toots spent all field trips in detention hall), but I also knew that this trip would be worth it. And even though I had to pair up with Miss Ching in the walk down the winding trail from parking lot to beach, and even though I sucked in water each time I tried to breathe through the snorkel, and my mask fogged no matter how many times I washed it with spit, the trip was worth the teasing and the lies. Because when I trudged across the network of coral reef to dive into pockets of water as deep and clear as God's blue eyeball, I felt perfect, seamless, and as whole as the water that closed over me.

Only afterward, on the hike back to the parking lot, did I begin to feel the sting of Red Disaster. With each step, I felt a prick against my heel. By the time we reached the top, what had started out as an irritation had turned into bolts of fire shooting jagged through my leg.

In the middle of that night, my mother said she woke up in a suffocating heat, the sheets clinging to her body, a damp second skin. She fought to take each breath, her throat and lungs burning, and worked her way toward the bedroom, where the waves of heat originated.

"I thought there was a fire in there, that you were burning to death," my mother told me when I woke the next morning, my feet bandaged in strips of bedsheet.

"I swam through heat so heavy the room rippled before my

eyes, and when I touched the bedroom door—*aigu!* Red hot!" My mother flung her hands into the air, showing off the raised welts on the palms of her hands. "I had to take my pajama, hold like this, then open."

The night of the terrible heat, sure that I was surrounded by a ring of fire, my mother wrapped the bottom of her nightgown around the doorknob and, waist bared, burst into the bedroom to rescue me. She was knocked immediately to the ground from the heat and enveloped in smoke that was not black but red. She pulled the collar of her nightgown over her nose and mouth to filter out the worst of the heat and the red smoke. "Just like a dust storm," she said. "Or like that plague curse in *The Ten Commandments* that killed off all the children—only red, not black.

"Red Death filled the room, thickening every breath I took, clouding my eyes so that I could barely see you—a motionless lump—on the bed. I called on the Birth Grandmother to help me beat a path through the *honyaek* to the windows. I tried to push some of the poison out, but the wind blew in even more *honyaek*."

My mother, who could not swim in water, would always pantomime the breast stroke when she told this part of the story. "I dove into red thick as blood pudding, fighting the tentacles of *honyaek* that tried to pull me under, and found you sweating and shivering under the blankets. I reached out to feel your forehead, but you burned so hot I could not touch you with my bare hands. I tucked the blankets underneath your body and carried you just like you were a baby again. But I could barely lift you; the Red Death sucked my energy, fed on my fear for you, so that I felt weak and unsure. I could barely force my legs forward as the fog of *honyaek* swirled around us, trying to trip my feet into missteps. I knew one wrong turn would lead us into the land of homeless hobo ghosts, *yongson,* where we could wander for ten thousand years without even one person knowing we were gone.

"I closed my eyes and told the Birth Grandmother to guide my feet, and when I opened them, she had led us to the bathroom. I placed you in the bathtub and turned on the water. At first the water evaporated as soon as it left the faucet, turning into red steam when it hit your body. I turned the cold on full blast, and finally enough trickled out to dampen the blankets and cool you off."

When I was out of immediate danger of "burning to ash," my mother said she needed to leave me in order to prepare her weapons. She opened the hallway closet, shook out our extra bedsheet, and, after studying it briefly, tore it into seven long strips. Then, with a felt marker, over and over again, she wrote my name, birth date, and genealogy—what she referred to as my "spiritual address." When I first looked at my feet in the morning, I thought they were bound in black-and-white striped material, so densely written were my mother's words.

"You needed to be tied into your body," she told me when I asked her about the linen around my feet. "And in case you slipped out, these words would have led you back." She pointed to one of the lines. "Look here—this character means you. This is me, this is the Birth Grandmother, this is each of her sisters. I linked us all together, a chain to fight the Red Death."

My mother said she forced the Birth Grandmother to call upon her sisters, the Seven Stars—each of them named Soon-something, which my mother said meant "pure"—to come protect me. "I didn't want to be rude," she said, "but really, if your spirit guardian can't protect you on her own, she should call for help, don't you think? I mean, I'm your mother, but I still ask her to help me watch you." My mother huffed as if disgusted and insulted by her spirit guardian's overbearing pride and lack of common sense. "Finally I had to get rough with her.

"'Induk,' I said, using her personal name to show how upset I was, 'this Red Death is too much for an old lady spirit like you!'

"When the Birth Grandmother did not answer, I knew I had been too blunt, but I could not waste time massaging the ego of a fickle spirit. 'Call on the Seven Stars, or I will find a new Birth Grandmother and you will be just another lost ghost,' I told her. 'My daughter is dying.'"

When I choked, my mother interrupted her story to scold me. "Pay attention." She scowled. "I told you this was serious."

The Birth Grandmother, responding to either her threats or her plea, must have listened to my mother, because a path of white light cracked the red cloud. My mother walked through— "Floated," she said. "I didn't even have to move my feet"—and found herself transported to my side in the bathtub.

She peeled the blankets from my body, stripping me naked. When I shivered, she placed each of the seven strips of bedsheet— one for each of the Star Sisters—on my body. Starting from my head, she smoothed the linen against my contours, asking for blessings from the protective spirits. She ran her hands down my face, throat, arms, torso, legs, and when she touched my feet, her hands vibrated.

"The Sisters were telling me where the *honyaek* entered your body. This," my mother said as she tapped at my feet, which I could barely feel under their wrap, "is your weak point. Didn't I always say you got them from your father?"

"They were balloons—so swollen, red, and tender," she said, "they melted into pus when I touched them. I took a razor from the medicine cabinet and—zhaa! zhaa! just like gutting fish— opened your feet to let the sickness out." My mother brandished imaginary knives, slicing the air with sure, quick strokes, reliving her battle. "Red Death shot from your feet, fouling the air with its stench of rotting meat and rat feces. I cut deeper, catching and killing the poison with the bandages blessed by the spirits. At first, as soon as I placed the cloth by your feet, the whole thing turned red, becoming slick and saturated with Red Death. I was like a demon myself, possessed, pushing clean cloths against your feet with one hand, pulling away the ones drenched in Red Death with the other hand. And all the while, I could see the battle between the Sisters and the *honyaek* on the strips of cloth, as the good spirits fought to turn the bandages back to pure white.

"Finally, toward the morning, when all the Red Death had been sucked from the room through the balls of your feet, when all the bandages were white again—even the one against your feet, which by then wept only clear water—the arrowhead, the *sal* triggered by the *honyaek,* popped out. Wait, I'll show you." My mother scuttled off the bed and rushed into the kitchen. I could hear her rummaging through the glass cupboard, and when she returned, she held above her head like a small trophy a Smucker's jelly jar.

She shook the jar in my face, and what looked like bits of bone jumped and rattled around the bottom. "*Sal,*" she announced. "This is the shattered arrowhead working its way out, making all kinds of trouble. We've got to watch for more of these."

I took the jar from her, interested in something I could touch from the spirit world, something tangible from the place where my mother lived half her life. I looked into the jar, then shook the contents onto my palm.

"Don't make that face," my mother said as I stared at the *sal*. "Wrinkles will freeze in your forehead." When I didn't say anything, she knelt beside me and wailed, "It's not my fault! In Korea, everything is safe for the mother and baby—you're not even supposed to leave the bed for two weeks after you give birth! Here, anybody, any man, can come right into the delivery room and cut you, so how could I protect you when you first came into this world? At first I thought since you were half American you would be immune. But now I see that in your second life transition, the arrows are coming home."

I cupped my mother's chin in my hand, forcing her to look at me, worried that she was losing the present and drifting away from me. "Mom? What are you talking about? Where are you?"

She slapped my hand down. "Sometimes you ask stupid questions," she said. "I am explaining to you how the *sal* got in your body and what we can do about it. This is the critical year, the year you become a woman and vulnerable—just like when a snake first sheds his skin—so we got to purge the clouds of Red Disaster from the home—done—and then this building and then the school. Then we got to purify your mind. You got to—"

"Stop, Mommy, stop!" I held my palm toward her, displaying the white flecks. "This isn't *sal* or an arrow or whatever; it's coral."

"Coral?" My mother picked up a small piece and rolled it in her fingers.

"Yeah," I said, carefully dropping the rest of the rocks back into the jar so I wouldn't have to look at her. "You know, like stones from the sea."

"Yes," my mother said, her words measured, as if she were talking to someone mentally slow. "*Sal* is like stones from the sea."

"No, I mean coral is stones from the sea." I took a deep breath and exhaled in a rush. "I rode a bus and went swimming on a field trip. I lied to you before. I'm sorry. No need to watch me anymore."

My mother lifted the jar from my hands and swirled it until the coral skimmed across the bottom in an even hum. "I know you went swimming," she said. "The office called to tell me your bus would be getting back to school late."

"So you lied!" I yelled. "You know it's not *sal*."

My mother slammed the glass down on the night table. Bits of coral flew across the bed and onto the floor at her feet. "It is *sal*," she screamed back at me. "That's what made you lie in the first place. It's what made your feet swell up and stink. And I can see you still have more *sal* in your mouth, making it mean and stupid. Now—" Here my mother suddenly quieted and dropped down to kiss me on the forehead. "You are not well. Just rest. I'm going to keep you safe. I will watch for *sal* and pluck them out when you show the signs."

My mother pounced on the signs of *sal* with quick efficiency, spotting the evidence of my decay in every shortcoming. Whenever I snapped at her, or overslept, or forgot something as simple as leaving an offering for the Seven Stars on the seventh day of the seventh month, she'd wave a lit incense stick about my head and yell, "*Sal!*"

Where earlier I had cherished the moments my mother paid attention to me, recognizing me as her flesh-and-blood daughter, I now began to cringe whenever she studied me, targeting a single part of my anatomy for any length of time. Because I knew that if I did not move out of her scope, she would hit me with another barb. Once, when I was about to kiss my mother goodbye before leaving for school, she grabbed my face, pressing my cheeks into my lips for a fish pucker. She held me that way for a blink or two, then announced, "Stink-breath. *Sal* from your father."

Sal seeped from the pores of my skin—proclaiming itself in feet that smelled like stale popcorn and armpits that smelled like fermenting potatoes—and pushed my body beyond its known topography. Knees and elbows erupted into sharp and dangerous angles. Zits bubbled onto my forehead and chin. Hair sprouted in damp, unexplored crevices. Knots of flesh fisted behind my nipples, punching up small hills.

And my mother's eyes and hands darted in to pinch and pull, poke and worry over each development.

I learned to study my body carefully in order to find and eliminate the signs of *sal* before my mother saw them. I sucked on breath mints, rubbed deodorant under my arms and on my feet. When my hands started to sweat, I swiped a layer of Secret across them too. And each night in the bath, I'd lie back and wait for strands of downy hair to float away from my body in exploratory tendrils, then pluck them out with eyebrow tweezers. The removal of each hair brought a flash of tears to my eyes, the sting of a tiny arrow.

I wore large, oversize T-shirts, which I pulled toward my knees to flatten my breasts. The kids called me a "mini-moke," because I slunk around campus rolling my hands into the front of my shirts and slouched over my desk like one of the big, tough boys who smoked dope at the bus stop before school started. All of my shirts looked misshapen and distorted that year, even after Miss Ching announced during health education that "Some girls, who shall remain nameless, are ruining their clothes when they really, in the name of decency, should just go out and buy a bra." She looked right at me, and though I could feel my face burning red, I looked right back, sending a *sal* to strike her eyes. And her mouth.

My mother prayed for me. Alternately wailing over my out-of-control body and cursing my father, who passed on his *sal* to me, she berated the spirits and begged them for advice on how to save me. "Beccah," she told me after a long conference with Induk the Birth Grandmother. "No matter how much we cleanse the Red Disaster away from you, it comes back, because the *sal* keeps getting stronger." She sniffed at my skin, and under the mint and the "rain-fresh" scent of Secret, she detected another genetically embedded arrow, more evidence of impurity left by my haole father: the odor of cheese and milk and meat—animal waste. "You have to stop feeding the sickness in your body, and starve the *sal* out of you."

To cleanse the impurities from my system, I ate food blessed by the spirits. For breakfast and dinner, my mother set blocks of white rice cake, bowls of water, oranges, and mixed vegetable *namul* onto our altar, offering the Birth Grandmother and her sisters first helpings. After rubbing her hands in prayerful supplication, she'd bow stiffly from the waist. "Please share with us our food and your blessings," she'd say. "Please make this house peaceful. Please make the child turn out well." Then we would both kneel, waiting for the spirits to finish their meal. When the rice no longer sent spirals of steam into the air, we knew that the spirits were finished and that it was our turn to eat.

I tried cheating, eating the hot lunch at school. Pizza and Tater Tots, or loco-mocos—over-easy egg over gravy over beef patty over rice—cost twenty-five cents, so if I took only one money envelope from the Wishing Bowl, I could eat whatever I wanted for several weeks.

But my body always betrayed me. My mother listened to my stomach's noises, looked into my eyes, smelled my feet, and knew that I had eaten dirty food. "Rotten cow's milk, pigs guts, and red-hot fat," she would comment, and that night I would have to drink endless bowls of blessed water while my mother chanted and sprinkled the ashes of burnt incense stick on my stinking parts. Sometimes this would go on through the night, so that when I woke in the early-morning hours to use the bathroom, I created landslides from ashes piled on the pillow near my mouth, on the sheets near my hands, on my stomach and crotch and feet.

When I stopped fighting and ate only what was acceptable to my guardian spirits, I wondered why I had fought in the first place. Eating food that had been blessed, I began to feel the spirits fill my body, making me stronger, smarter, purer than my normal self. Each bite of the food tasted and tested by the Birth Grandmother and the Seven Stars seemed to ripen and bloom in my mouth, so that even one grain of rice, one section of orange, one strand of bean sprout, filled me to fullness.

I became so full that I consumed only what the spirits themselves ate, feasting on the steam evaporating from freshly made rice, on the scent of oranges and pears. I saw food take flight from its physical manifestation, turning into light that shot through my body. And I saw the light flow through me, swirling like blood under skin turned translucent as the shade of a lamp, until it eddied in the tips of my fingers.

My mother saw the light in my hands as well. "Your hands are so pale," she murmured once, "I can see the blue *hyolgwan* burning under its skin."

And when I massaged her back, my fingers migrated toward the *sal* hidden in her muscles, alongside her bones. "Saa, saa, saaa," my mother would groan with pain and pleasure. "Kill the *sal*." And I would press my fingers into the knotted muscles until I felt them loosen and dissolve under my heat. With the light, I could dip into her body to pull out the walnuts of pain lodged in her back, sucking like leeches against her spine or between her shoulder blades. Sometimes when I massaged my mother, I felt my arms disappear up to the elbows, my body reabsorbed by hers.

In those moments, I knew I was truly my mother's daughter, that I nursed her with my light.

I aimed the light into myself, feeling for the poisoned arrowheads implanted in my body in order to kill my own pain. I fed the light with more spirit food, until it grew larger than myself. The bigger the light within me became, the smaller my body got, until I seemed to shrink into myself, becoming as elemental as the food offered to and consumed by the gods.

My body reabsorbed my hips, my breasts, the small belly that sloped between my pelvic bones. My hair fell out, leaving tufts of dry lifeless strands tangled in hairbrushes or in the shower drain. I knew that except for the down—like the woolly lanugo coating the fetus in the womb—developing on my arms and legs, I would soon become hairless as a newborn. I continued to devour the steam of rice, waiting until I would be tiny enough to slip completely into the world my mother lived in.

But no matter how clean, how small I became, the *sal*—too deep within me to uproot—remained, a seed burrowed low in my belly, to kill the light.

To ensure my safe passage through the critical year of the fire snake, my mother decided to meet me after school one day in order to purify the campus. Taking the same route as the morning bus, my mother walked and chanted her way from The Shacks to Ala Wai Elementary. Every few yards, she dipped into her shoulder bag and threw out handfuls of barley and rice—scrap offerings to lure the wandering dead and noxious influences away from the path I took to and from home every day. By the time she reached the campus, she had collected a gang of kids. "Eh, bag lady! Eh, crazy lady," they called out as they circled her. "Watchu doing? Feeding the birds?"

When my mother continued to chant and toss out grain, ignoring them, they must have grown bolder, pressing in on her with outstretched hands. "I like. I like," some teased. "Gimme some." And others, with their hands outstretched, came to slap at her bag or maybe her hands before scurrying back to the safety of the group.

Seeing that these devil children refused to be tempted by the meager handfuls of rice, my mother probably stepped up the exorcism. She had come prepared with lucky talismans that attracted luck, incense sticks that purified the air and flushed out hidden pockets of Red Disaster, and lumps of moxa and red pepper to scare away troublesome imps. After first trying to bribe the children to go away by offering them her prized goodluck packets, my mother took out a handful of moxa and red pepper balls. One by one, she lit the pellets with her Bic and threw them at the children.

"Shame on you! Your mothers must be so sad to have given birth to monsters," she scolded, flinging the smoldering lumps into the growing crowd.

"Hey, you crazy!" one or two of the kids yelled when a ball of moxa or pepper hit its mark, leaving a small ash-gray circle on a piece of clothing or a body part. The rest of the children edged in closer, hooting with laughter at each word my mother spoke.

"Shame-u, shame-u!" they mimicked in singsong voices. "You maddahs mustu be so sad-u!"

When I first saw the frail, wild-haired lady in pajamas throwing handfuls of pebbles into the crowd, I did not realize she was my mother. Only when she raised her arms into the air and pivoted toward me for a moment, only when I caught the faint cry of "Induk," did I recognize her. I wanted to scream, to tell the kids to shut their mouths and go to hell. I wanted to pound their laughing heads into their necks. But I couldn't; looking at the only part of myself that I thought contained power, I saw my hands as the others around me must have seen them: feeble, scrawny, ineffectual. And I knew them then for what they were: the skeleton hands of death; and the light for what it was: Saja laughing just under my skin.

I wanted to help my mother, shield her from the children's

sharp-toothed barbs, and take her home. And yet I didn't want to. Because for the first time, as I watched and listened to the children taunting my mother, using their tongues to mangle what she said into what they heard, I saw and heard what they did. And I was ashamed.

"Shame-u shame-u, sad-u sad-u!" my schoolmates chanted, unintimidated by the moxa balls or my mother promising vengeance from Induk, until they were interrupted by the vice principal and several burly teachers.

"What the hell is going on?" Vice Principal Pili demanded once the crowd had quieted. When no one spoke up, he looked around for familiar faces, children he recognized from detention hall. "You, Angelo Villanueva. You, Primo Beaton, You, Toots Tutivena. You causing trouble again?"

"No, Mr. Pili! Wasn't us. Was that crazy lady," said Angelo.

"Yeah, was her t'rowing fire at us," agreed Primo, who rubbed at a black mark on his forehead.

And Toots Tutivena, whom I dubbed my eternal archnemesis in that moment, said: "Was that crazy lady who I know for a fact is Beccah Bradley's maddah."

Vice principal Pili scowled at them. "Okay, all of yous. Get out. I don't wanna see your faces hangin' around here after school no more unless it's in detention." After the three he singled out worked their way to the edge of the crowd, where they remained, reluctant to leave before the action died and the bag lady went home, he swung his face toward my mother. "Can I help you?" He frowned, his question almost mocking.

Recognizing authority, my mother straightened the strap of her shoulder bag and smoothed the front of her pajamas with fingers that left black streaks. "Yes, sir," she said. "I looking for daughteh. Name is Roh-beccah Blad-u-ley."

"Rebeccah Bradley?" Pili asked. "Is that right?"

When my mother nodded, he yelled out, "Rebeccah Bradley! Is Rebeccah Bradley here? Does anyone know Rebeccah Bradley?"

Before Toots Tutivena could finger me in the crowd I had joined, merely curious, when they started chanting, "Shame-u shame-u, sad-u sad-u," I slipped away. At the moment I was called upon to claim my mother, I couldn't. Instead I ran away, and the farther I ran from my mother, the smaller I seemed to shrink, until I was smaller and flimsier than the cheap moxa balls my mother burned to ward off the *sal* of malevolent beings.

THERESA HAK KYUNG CHA

Born in 1951 in Pusan, South Korea, Theresa Hak Kyung Cha emigrated with her family at the age of eleven—first to Hawai'i and then to San Francisco, where she attended a Catholic high school. At the University of California, Berkeley, Cha earned two B.A. degrees, in comparative literature (1973) and art (1975), as well as both an M.A. and M.F.A. in art (1977, 1978); she also spent a year studying film theory at the Centre d'Études Américaines du Cinéma à Paris. Cha's early work included performance art pieces, and she went on to create several well-received films and videos, including the three-monitor installation *Passages Paysages* and *Exilée*. Cha also innovatively edited *Apparatus* (1981), a collection of writings on film that includes work by such theorists as Roland Barthes, Maya Deren, and Dziga Vertov and Cha's own "Commentaire." At the time of her death at the age of thirty-one in New York, Cha was working on several artistic and scholarly projects.

Cha's artist's book *DICTEE* (1982) made startling contributions in several areas of recurring philosophical and spiritual concern to the most serious of Korean American authors. These include integration of East Asian and Western poetics and metaphysics, elucidation of the dependence of lived experience on the depth of one's engagement in historical change, and entry to the realms of the miraculous and salvational. Cha was deeply influenced by, on the one hand, Chinese Taoism and Korean shamanism and, on the other, alchemy and Roman Catholicism. She was also a student of semiotic theory, experimental film, and European avant-garde and postmodernist authors such as Samuel Beckett and Monique Wittig. Profoundly aware of nearly vanquished narratives of Korea and female heroism, Cha eschewed the euphony of typically "poetic" language as something that concealed historical disaster and deeply repressed experiences of the relation between self and cosmos, memory and time, consciousness and matter.

It is in *DICTEE,* published during the last year of Cha's brief life, that a multi-generational, Korean diasporic sense of constant linguistic displacement, communal loss, and nostalgic recuperation explicitly comes to the foreground. It incorporates material from eclectic sources, including French language-learning exercises, a photograph of Korean independence fighters being executed by Japanese colonial troops, stills from Carl Theodor Dreyer's classic silent film *The Passion of Joan of Arc,* a chart of the articulatory organs involved in speech, an account of the martyrdom of Yu Guan Soon (Yu Kwansun) during the Korean March First Independence Movement, and excerpts from the autobiography of St. Thérèse de Lisieux. The following selection, which we present in facsimile to preserve the visual integrity of the original, is the eighth of *DIC-TEE*'s nine inner chapters, each of which is named after a different muse. Placed between "Thalia Comedy" and "Polymnia Sacred Poetry," "Terpsichore Choral Dance" gives a harrowing account of spiritual and bodily metamorphosis as the initiate/poet passes through or near death in order to more purely mediate language that is now newly capable of consummate echoing. Its alternately ecstatic and eschatological interfusion with other realms through stunning mastery of bits of dislocated language and cascading levels of perception make up an appropriate final *kŏri* of the present anthology's own more loosely coordinated dance.

from *DICTEE*

TERPSICHORE   CHORAL DANCE

極儀才象行合星卦子連圍 環

太兩三四五六七八九重

1. 2. 3. 4. 5. 6. 7. 8. 9. 10.

*You remain dismembered with the belief that
magnolia blooms white even on seemingly dead
branches and you wait. You remain apart from
the congregation.*

You wait when you think it is conceiving you wait it
to seed you think you can see through the dark earth
the beginning of a root, the air entering with the
water being poured dark earth harbouring dark taken
for granted the silence and the dark the conception
seedling. Chaste the silence and the dark the conception seedling. Chaste you wait you are supposed to
you are to wait for the silence to break you wait for
the implanting of some dark silence same constant as
a field distant and close at the same time all around
sound far and near at the same time you shiver some
place in between one of the dandelion seedling vague
air shivering just before the entire flower to burst and
scatter without designated time, even before its own
realization of the act, no premonition not preparation. All of a sudden. All of a sudden without
warning. No holding back, no retreat, no second
thought forward. Backward. There and not there.
Remass and disperse. Convene and scatter.

Does not move. Not a sound. None. No sound.
Do not move.

Inside the atmosphere. No access is given to sight. Invisible and hueless. Even. Still. The thickness of the
air weighs. Weight upon weight. Still. Heavy, inert is
duration without the knowledge of its enduring.

Does not wait. No wait. It has not the knowl-
edge of wait. Knows not how. How to.

Affords no penetration. Hence no depth, No disrup-
tion. Hence, no time. No wait. Hence, no distance.

Full.   Utter most full. Can contain no longer. Fore
shadows the fullness. Still. Silence. Within moments
of. The eclipse. Inside the eclipse. Both. Fulmination
and concealment of light. Imminent crossing, face to
face, moon before the sun pronounces. All. This.
Time. To pronounce without prescribing purpose. It
prescribes nothing. The time thought to have fixed,
dead, reveals the very rate of the very movement.
Velocity. Lentitude. Of its own larger time.

Withholds brilliance as the evanescent light of a dark
pearl. Shone internally. As the light of the eclipse,
both disparition. Both radiance. Mercurial light,
nacrous. No matter, not the cloister of the shell.
Luminous all the same. Waits the hour. To break.
Then break.

For now, nothing enters. Still. No addition to the
fullness. Grows, without accumulation. Augments,
without increase. Abundance, Plenitude, Without
gain.

Further, Further inside. Further than. To middle.
Deeper. Without measure. Deeper than. Without
means of measure. To core. In another tongue. Same
word. Slight mutation of the same. Undefinable.
Shift. Shift slightly. Into a different sound. The difference. How it discloses the air. Slight. Another
word. Same. Parts of the same atmosphere. Deeper.
Center. Without distance. No particular distance
from center to periphery. Points of measure effaced.
To begin there. There. In Media Res.

Do not move.
Not a sound. None. No sound.

Carrier, you hold in the palm of your hand the silver white spirit the lustre mass quiver and fall away from the center

one by one.
Sound.
Give up the sound.
Replace the sound.
With voice.

At a time. Stops. Returns to rest, again, in the center of your palm. You turn the seasons by the directions
South
North
West
East
Your palm a silver pool of liquid then as the seasons choose affix as stone in blue metal ice.

At times, starts again. Noise. Semblance of
noise. Speech perhaps. Broken. One by one. At
a time. Broken tongue. Pidgeon tongue. Sem-
blance of speech.

You seek the night that you may render the air pure. Distillation extending breath to its utmost pure. Its first exhale at dawn to be collected. In the recesses of the leaves is an inlet of dew, clearest tears. You stow them before their fall by their own weight. You stand a column of white lustre, atoned with tears, restored in breath.

Maimed. Accident. Stutters. Almost a name.
Half a name. Almost a place. Starts. About to.
Then stops. Exhale swallowed to a sudden
arrest. Pauses. How vast this page. Stillness, the
page. Without. Can do without rests. Pause.
Without them. All. Stop start.

Earth is dark. Darker. Earth is a blue-black stone
upon which moisture settles evenly, flawlessly. Dust
the stone with a fine powder. Earth is dark, a blue-
black substance, moisture and dust rise in a mist. Veil
of dust smoke between sky and earth's boundaries. In
black darkness, pale, luminant band of haze. You induce the stone by offering exchange of your own.
Own flesh. Cry supplication wail resound song to the
god to barter you, your sight. For the lenience. Make
lenient, the immobility of sediment. Entreat with
prayer to the god his eloquence. To conduct to stone.
Thawing of the knotted flesh. Your speech as
ransom. You crumple and sift by each handful the
last enduring particle. Hands buried to earth dis-
solved to same dust. And you wait. Still. Having
bartered away your form, now you are formless.
Blind. Mute. Given to stillness to whiteness only too
still. Waiting. Scribe. Diving. In whiteness beyond
matter. Sight. Speech.

Cling. Cling more. At the sight of.
At last in sight at last. Cleared for the sighting.
So clear cling so fast cling fast at the site.
Clear and clearer.

Hours day sheet by sheet
one pile. Next pile. Then the next
from one pile to the next pile. One sheet below
the crack of closed door
slide piled up on the other side
no overlapping. One at a time. One sheet.
End in sight. With accumulation. Without prosper.

Earth is made porous. Earth heeds. Inward. Inception
in darkness. In the blue-black body commences lu-
ment. Like firefly, a slow rhythmic relume to yet
another and another opening.

The name. Half a name.
Past. Half passed.
Forgotten word leaving out a word
Letter. Letter by letter to the letter.

Open to the view. Come forth. Witness bound to no
length no width no depth. Witness sees that which
contains the witness in its view. Pale light cast inside
the thin smoke, blowing. Then all around. No matter
how sparse the emission, each subtle ascent is bared
before the surrounding black screen. Then extinguish.
Emerge. Look forth. The succession of colors.
Filtered beforehand to utmost. Pure. True. Stark.
Foreboding. Red as never been. Bled to crimson.
Trembling with its entire, the knowledge, of the
given time. Given the mark of bloom, its duration.
Abiding. Not more. Not less. The color that already
was always was before its exhibition into sight.

Being broken. Speaking broken. Saying broken.
Talk broken. Say broken. Broken speech. Pidg-
on tongue. Broken word. Before speak. As being
said. As spoken. To be said. To say. Then speak

Immaterial now, and formless, having surrendered
to dissolution limb by limb, all parts that compose a
body. Liquid and marrow once swelled the muscle
and bone, blood made freely the passages through in-
numerable entries, all give willingly to exile. From
the introit, preparation is made for communion when
the inhabitation should occur, of this body, by the
other body, the larger body.

Stands now, an empty column of artery, of vein,
fixed in stone. Void of wing. Void of hands, feet. It
continues. This way. It should, with nothing to alter
or break the fullness, nothing exterior to impose
upon the plenitude of this void. It remains thus. For a
time. Then without a visible mark of transition, it
takes the identity of a duration. It stays. All chronol-
ogy lost, indecipherable, the passage of time, until it
is forgotten. Forgotten how it stays, how it endures.

A new sign of moisture appears in the barren
column that had congealed to stone. Floods the stone
from within, collects water as to a mere, layering first
the very bottom.

From stone, A single stone. Column. Carved on
one stone, the labor of figures. The labor of
tongues. Inscribed to stone. The labor of voices.

Water inhabits the stone, conducts absorption of implantation from the exterior. In tones, the inscriptions resonate the atmosphere of the column, repeating over the same sounds, distinct words. Other melodies, whole, suspended between song and speech in still the silence.

Water on the surface of the stone captures the light in motion and appeals for entry. All is entreat to stir inside the mass weight of the stone.

Render voices to meet the weight of stone with weight of voices.

Muted colors appear from the transparency of the white and wash the stone's periphery, staining the hue-less stone.
wall.
For the next phase. Next to last. Before the last. Before completing. Draw from stains the pigment as it spills from within, with in each repetition, extract even darker, the stain, until it falls in a single stroke of color, crimson, red, as a flame caught in air for its sustenance.

Stone to pigment. Stone. Wall.
Page.
To stone, water, teinture, blood.

All rise. At once. One by one. Voices absorbed into the bowl of sound. Rise voices shifting upwards circling the bowl's hollow. In deep metal voice spiraling up wards to pools   no visible light lighter   no audible higher quicken shiver the air in pool's waves to raise all else where all memory all echo

SUGGESTED READINGS

PRIMARY SOURCES

Ahn, Me-K. "Living in Half Tones" (excerpt). In *Seeds from a Silent Tree, An Anthology by Korean Adoptees,* edited by Tonya Bishoff and Jo Rankin. San Luis Capistrano, CA: Pandal Press, 1997.

Ando, Me-K [Me-K. Ahn]. "Living in Half Tones" (excerpt). In *The Adoption Reader: Birth Mothers, Adoptive Mothers and Adoptive Daughters Tell Their Stories,* edited by Susan Wadia-Ells. Seattle: Seal Press, 1995.

Bishoff, Tonya, and Jo Rankin, eds. *Seeds from a Silent Tree, An Anthology by Korean Adoptees.* San Luis Capistrano, CA: Pandal Press, 1997.

Cha, Theresa Hak Kyung, ed. *Apparatus. Cinematographic Apparatus: Selected Writings.* New York: Tanam Press, 1981.

———. "Commentaire." In Cha, ed., *Apparatus.*

———. "Exilée," In *Hotel.* New York: Tanam Press, 1980.

———. "Temps Morts." In *Hotel.*

———. *DICTEE.* New York: Tanam Press, 1982.

Theresa Hak Kyung Cha Archive. Berkeley Art Museum/Pacific Film Archive. University of California, Berkeley <www.bampfa.berkeley.edu/collections/findingaids/bampfa-cha.ead.html>.

Chang, Leonard. *The Fruit 'N Food.* Seattle: Black Heron Press, 1996.

———. *Dispatches from the Cold.* Seattle: Black Heron Press, 1998.

———. *Over the Shoulder.* New York: Ecco Press/HarperCollins, 2001.

Choi, Sook Nyul. *Year of Impossible Goodbyes.* Boston: Houghton Mifflin, 1991.

Choi, Susan. *The Foreign Student.* New York: HarperCollins, 1998.

Clement, Thomas Park. *The Unforgotten War: Dust of the Streets.* Bloomfield, IN: Truepeny Press, 1998.

Fenkl, Heinz Insu. *Memories of My Ghost Brother.* New York: Dutton, 1996.

Hyun, Peter. *Man Sei! The Making of a Korean American.* Honolulu: University of Hawai'i Press, 1986.

Kang, K. Connie. *Home Was the Land of the Morning Calm.* New York: Addison-Wesley, 1995.

Kang, Hyun Yi, ed. *Writing Away Here: A Korean/American Anthology.* Oakland, CA: Korean American Arts Festival, 1994.

Kang, Younghill. *The Grass Roof.* 1931. Reprint, Chicago: Follett, 1966.

———. *The Happy Grove.* Illustrated by Leroy Baldridge. New York: Charles Scribner's Sons, 1933.

———. *East Goes West: The Making of An Oriental Yankee.* New York: Charles Scribner's Sons, 1937.

———. "How It Feels to be a Korean . . . in Korea." *U.N. World* 2, no. 4 (May 1948): 18–21.

Keller, Nora Okja. *Comfort Woman.* New York: Viking, 1997.

Kim, Helen. *The Long Season of Rain.* New York: Henry Holt, 1996.

Kim, Patti. *A Cab Called Reliable.* New York: St. Martin's Press, 1997.

Kim, Richard E. *The Martyred.* New York: George Braziller, 1964.

———. *The Innocent.* Boston: Houghton Mifflin, 1968.

———. *Lost Names: Scenes from a Korean Boyhood.* 1970. Reprint, Berkeley: University of California Press, 1998.

Kim, Ronyoung. *Clay Walls.* Sag Harbor, NY: The Permanent Press, 1996.

Kim, Willyce. *Dancer Dawkins and the California Kid.* Boston: Alyson Press, 1985.

———. *Dead Heat.* Boston: Alyson Press, 1988.

———. "Homecoming." In *Premonitions,* edited by Walter K. Lew. New York: Kaya Production, 1995.

———. "In this Heat." In Lew, ed. *Premonitions.*

Kim, Yong Ik. *The Diving Gourd.* New York: Alfred A. Knopf, 1962.

———. *The Shoes from Yang San Valley.* Garden City: Doubleday, 1970.

Lee, Chang-rae. *Native Speaker.* New York: Riverhead Books, 1995.

———. *A Gesture Life.* New York: Riverhead Books, 1999.

Lee, Marie G. *Finding My Voice.* Boston: Houghton Mifflin, 1994.

———. *If It Hadn't Been for Yoon Jun.* Avon Books, 1995.

———. *Necessary Roughness.* New York: HarperCollins, 1996.

Lee, Mary Paik. *Quiet Odyssey: A Pioneer Korean Woman in America.* Seattle: University of Washington Press, 1990.

Lew, Walter K. *Excerpts from: ΔIKTH DIKTE, for DICTEE (1982).* Seoul: Yeul

Eum Sa, 1992. <www2.hawaii.edu/~spahr/dikte/>. Reprint, in-press, Tuscon: Chax Press.

————. "1982" (excerpts). *BOMB* 46 (Winter 1994): 72–74.

————. "The Movieteller" (excerpt). *Chain* 3, no. 2 (Fall 1996): 90–97.

Pahk, Induk. *September Monkey.* New York: Harper & Brothers, 1954.

Pai, Margaret K. *The Dreams of Two Yi-min.* Honolulu: University of Hawai'i Press, 1989.

Pak, Gary. *The Watcher of Waipuna and Other Stories.* Honolulu: Bamboo Ridge Press, 1992.

————. *A Ricepaper Airplane.* Honolulu: University of Hawai'i Press, 1998.

Pak, Ty. *Guilt Payment.* Honolulu: Bamboo Ridge Press, 1983.

————. *Cry Korea Cry.* New York: Woodhouse, 1999.

————. *Moonbay.* New York: Woodhouse, 1999.

Park, No-Yong. *Chinaman's Chance.* 3d ed. Boston: Meador Publishing Company, 1948.

Ryu, Sukhee. "Wishes." *Yisei* 10, no. 1 (Winter 1996–97). <www.hcs.harvard.edu/~yisei/backissues/winter_96/wishing.html>.

Yun, Mia. *House of the Winds.* New York: Interlink Publishing Group, 1998.

Poetry

Grosjean, Ok-Koo Kang. *A Hummingbird's Dance.* Berkeley: Parallax Press, 1994.

Kim, Chungmi. *Chungmi (Selected Poems).* Anaheim: Korean Pioneer Press, 1982.

Kim, Myung Mi. *Under Flag.* Berkeley: Kelsey St. Press, 1991.

————. *The Bounty.* Minneapolis: Chax Press, 1996.

Kim, Willyce. *Eating Artichokes.* Oakland, CA: Women's Press Collective, 1972.

————. *Under the Rolling Sky.* Oakland, CA: Maud Gonne Press, 1973.

Ko Won [Ko Sung-Won]. *The Turn of Zero.* Merrick, NY: Cross-Cultural Communications, 1974.

————. *With Birds of Paradise.* Los Angeles: Azalea Press, 1984.

Song, Cathy. *Picture Bride.* New Haven: Yale University Press, 1983.

————. *Frameless Windows, Squares of Light.* New York: W. W. Norton, 1988.

————. *School Figures.* Pittsburgh: University of Pittsburgh Press, 1995.

Stefans, Brian Kim. *Free Space Comix.* New York: Roof, 1998.

————. *Gulf.* New York: Object Editions, poetscoop, 1998.

SECONDARY SOURCES

Abelmann, Nancy, and John Lie. *Blue Dreams: Korean Americans and the 1992 L. A. Riots.* Cambridge: Harvard University Press, 1995.

Altstein, Howard, and Rita J. Simon, eds. *Intercountry Adoption: A Multinational Perspective.* New York: Praeger, 1991.

Cumings, Bruce. *Korea's Place in the Sun: A Modern History.* New York: W. W. Norton: 1997.

Eckert, Carter J., et al. *Korea Old and New: A History.* Seoul: Ilchogak, 1990.

Fenkl, Heinz Insu. "Mu: A Reflection on Shamanism and Synthesis" (and other essays on folklore and mythology). *The Endicott Studio Forum* <www.endi cott-studio.com/forum.html>.

Fujikane, Candace. "Between Nationalisms: Hawai'i's Local Nation and Its Troubled Paradise." *Critical Mass: A Journal of Asian American Cultural Criticism* 1, no. 2 (Spring/Summer 1994): 23–57.

Harvey, Youngsook Kim. *Six Korean Women: The Socialization of Shamans.* St. Paul: West Publishing, 1979.

Howard, Keith, ed. *True Stories of the Korean Comfort Women.* London: Cassell, 1995.

Kendall, Laurel. *Shamans, Housewives, and Other Restless Spirits: Women in Korean Ritual Life.* Honolulu: University of Hawai'i Press, 1985.

Kim, Bok-Lim. "Asian Wives of U. S. Servicemen: Women in Shadows." *Amerasia Journal* 4 (1977): 91–115.

Kim, Elaine H. "Korean American Literature." In *An Interethnic Companion to Asian American Literature,* edited by King-Kok Cheung. New York: Cambridge University Press, 1997.

Kim, Elaine H., and Eui-Young Yi, eds. *East to America: Korean American Life Stories.* New York: New Press, 1996.

Kim, Kwang Chung, ed. *Koreans in the Hood: Conflict with African Americans.* Baltimore: Johns Hopkins University Press, 1999.

Kim, Willyce. "Willyce Kim, Reluctant Pioneer." Interview with Kate Brandt, 7 September 1991. In Kate Brandt, *Happy Endings: Lesbian Writers Talk About Their Lives and Work.* Tallahassee, FL: The Naiad Press, 1993, 217–26.

Kister, Daniel A. *Korean Shamanist Ritual: Symbols and Dramas of Transformation.* Bibliotheca Shamanistica, 5. Budapest, Hungary: Akadémiai Kiadó, 1997.

Kwon, Brenda Lee. *Beyond Ke'eaumoku: Koreans, Nationalism, and Local Culture in Hawai'i.* New York: Garland Publishing, 1999.

Lee, James Kyung-Jin. "Best-Selling Korean American: Revisiting Richard E. Kim." In Buswell, Robert, ed. *Korean Culture,* 19, no. 1 (Spring 1998): 30–39.

Lee, Jung Young. *Korean Shamanistic Rituals.* The Hague: Mouton, 1981.

Lew, Walter K. "Grafts, Transplants, Translation: The Americanizing of Younghill Kang." In *Modernism, Inc: Body, Memory, Capital,* edited by Jani Scandura and Michael Thurston. New York: New York University Press, 2001.

————. "Making Silent Movies Speak: Shin Ch'ul's Narration of 'The Prosecutor and the Lady Teacher.'" *Korean Culture* 21, no. 4 (Winter 2000): 4–8.

Lyu, Kingsley K. "Korean Nationalist Activities in Hawaii and the Continental United States, 1900–1945. Part I: 1900–1919." *Amerasia Journal* 4, no. 1 (1977): 23–90.

————. "Korean Nationalist Activities in Hawaii and the Continental United States, 1900–1945. Part II: 1919–45." *Amerasia Journal* 4, no. 2 (1977): 53–100.

Min, Eun Kyung. "Reading the Figure of Dictation in Theresa Hak Kyung Cha's *DICTEE*." In *Other Sisterhoods: Literary Theory and U.S. Women of Color,* edited by Sandra K. Stanley. Urbana: University of Illinois Press, 1998.

Park, Kyeyoung. *The Korean American Dream: Immigrants and Small Business in New York City.* Ithaca: Cornell University Press, 1997.

Patterson, Wayne. *The Ilse: First-Generation Korean Immigrants in Hawai'i, 1903–1973.* Honolulu: University of Hawai'i Press, 2000.

Scharper, Alice M. "The Golden Thread: Younghill Kang and the Origins of Korean American Literature." Ph.D. diss., University of California, Davis. 1997.

Triseliotis, John. "Inter-country Adoption: In Whose Best Interest?" In *Inter-country Adoption: Practical Experiences,* edited by Michael and Heather Humphrey. New York: Routledge, 1993.

ACKNOWLEDGMENTS

We would like to thank the following individuals for their advice, expertise, and patient support throughout the planning and preparation of this volume: Helene Atwan, Christopher Vyce, and David Coen of Beacon Press, Wu Shengqing, Kyeyoung Park, King-Kok Cheung, Anne B. Dalton, and Isabella Myŏng-wŏl.